Oscar Fingal O'Flahertie Wills Wilde (16 October 1854 – 30 November 1900) was an Irish poet and playwright. After writing in different forms throughout the 1880s, he became one of London's most popular playwrights in the early 1890s. He is best remembered for his epigrams and plays, his novel The Picture of Dorian Gray, and the circumstances of his criminal conviction for homosexuality, imprisonment, and early death at age 46. Wilde's parents were successful Anglo-Irish intellectuals in Dublin. Their son became fluent in French and German early in life. At university, Wilde read Greats; he proved himself to be an outstanding classicist, first at Trinity College Dublin, then at Oxford. He became known for his involvement in the rising philosophy of aestheticism, led by two of his tutors, Walter Pater and John Ruskin. After university, Wilde moved to London into fashionable cultural and social circles. (Source: Wikipedia)

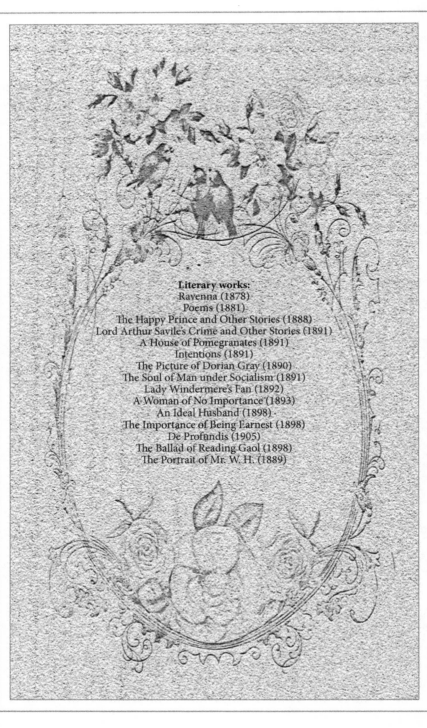

Literary works:
Ravenna (1878)
Poems (1881)
The Happy Prince and Other Stories (1888)
Lord Arthur Savile's Crime and Other Stories (1891)
A House of Pomegranates (1891)
Intentions (1891)
The Picture of Dorian Gray (1890)
The Soul of Man under Socialism (1891)
Lady Windermere's Fan (1892)
A Woman of No Importance (1893)
An Ideal Husband (1898)
The Importance of Being Earnest (1898)
De Profundis (1905)
The Ballad of Reading Gaol (1898)
The Portrait of Mr. W. H. (1889)

POEMS
&
SALOMÉ
A TRAGEDY IN ONE ACT
Oscar Wilde

PRINCE CLASSICS

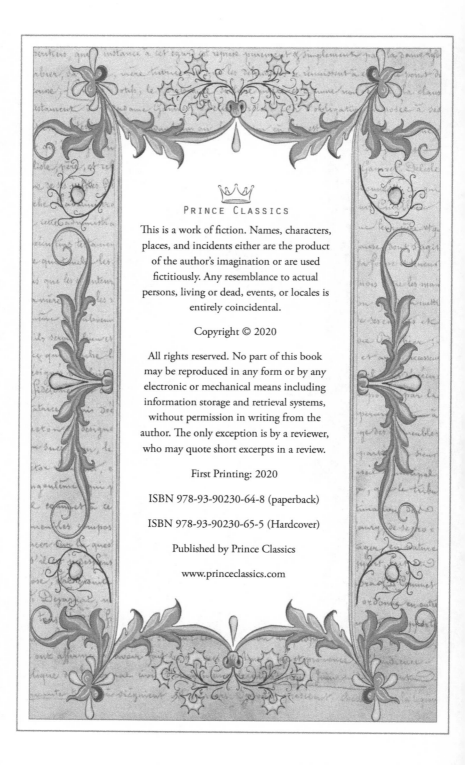

PRINCE CLASSICS

Copyright © 2020

First Printing: 2020

ISBN 978-93-90230-64-8 (paperback)

ISBN 978-93-90230-65-5 (Hardcover)

Published by Prince Classics

www.princeclassics.com

Contents

POEMS
&
SALOMÉ
A TRAGEDY IN ONE ACT

POEMS

NOTE

This collection of Wilde's Poems contains the volume of 1881 in its entirety, 'The Sphinx', 'The Ballad of Reading Gaol,' and 'Ravenna.' Of the Uncollected Poems published in the Uniform Edition of 1908, a few, including the Translations from the Greek and the Polish, are omitted. Two new poems, 'Désespoir' and 'Pan,' which I have recently discovered in manuscript, are now printed for the first time. Particulars as to the original publication of each poem will be found in 'A Bibliography of the Poems of Oscar Wilde,' by Stuart Mason, London 1907.

ROBERT ROSS.

HÉLAS!

To drift with every passion till my soul

Is a stringed lute on which all winds can play,

Is it for this that I have given away

Mine ancient wisdom, and austere control?

Methinks my life is a twice-written scroll

Scrawled over on some boyish holiday

With idle songs for pipe and virelay,

Which do but mar the secret of the whole.

Surely there was a time I might have trod

The sunlit heights, and from life's dissonance

Struck one clear chord to reach the ears of God:

Is that time dead? lo! with a little rod

I did but touch the honey of romance—

And must I lose a soul's inheritance?

ELEUTHERIA

SONNET TO LIBERTY

Not that I love thy children, whose dull eyes

See nothing save their own unlovely woe,

Whose minds know nothing, nothing care to know,—

But that the roar of thy Democracies,

Thy reigns of Terror, thy great Anarchies,

Mirror my wildest passions like the sea

And give my rage a brother—! Liberty!

For this sake only do thy dissonant cries

Delight my discreet soul, else might all kings

By bloody knout or treacherous cannonades

Rob nations of their rights inviolate

And I remain unmoved—and yet, and yet,

These Christs that die upon the barricades,

God knows it I am with them, in some things.

AVE IMPERATRIX

Set in this stormy Northern sea,

   Queen of these restless fields of tide,

England! what shall men say of thee,

Before whose feet the worlds divide?

The earth, a brittle globe of glass,
  Lies in the hollow of thy hand,
And through its heart of crystal pass,
  Like shadows through a twilight land,

The spears of crimson-suited war,
  The long white-crested waves of fight,
And all the deadly fires which are
  The torches of the lords of Night.

The yellow leopards, strained and lean,
  The treacherous Russian knows so well,
With gaping blackened jaws are seen
  Leap through the hail of screaming shell.

The strong sea-lion of England's wars
  Hath left his sapphire cave of sea,
To battle with the storm that mars
  The stars of England's chivalry.

The brazen-throated clarion blows

Across the Pathan's reedy fen,

And the high steeps of Indian snows

Shake to the tread of armèd men.

And many an Afghan chief, who lies

Beneath his cool pomegranate-trees,

Clutches his sword in fierce surmise

When on the mountain-side he sees

The fleet-foot Marri scout, who comes

To tell how he hath heard afar

The measured roll of English drums

Beat at the gates of Kandahar.

For southern wind and east wind meet

Where, girt and crowned by sword and fire,

England with bare and bloody feet

Climbs the steep road of wide empire.

O lonely Himalayan height,

Grey pillar of the Indian sky,

Where saw'st thou last in clanging flight

Our wingèd dogs of Victory?

The almond-groves of Samarcand,

  Bokhara, where red lilies blow,

And Oxus, by whose yellow sand

  The grave white-turbaned merchants go:

And on from thence to Ispahan,

  The gilded garden of the sun,

Whence the long dusty caravan

  Brings cedar wood and vermilion;

And that dread city of Cabool

  Set at the mountain's scarpèd feet,

Whose marble tanks are ever full

  With water for the noonday heat:

Where through the narrow straight Bazaar

  A little maid Circassian

Is led, a present from the Czar

  Unto some old and bearded khan,—

Here have our wild war-eagles flown,

  And flapped wide wings in fiery fight;

But the sad dove, that sits alone

  In England—she hath no delight.

In vain the laughing girl will lean

  To greet her love with love-lit eyes:

Down in some treacherous black ravine,

  Clutching his flag, the dead boy lies.

And many a moon and sun will see

  The lingering wistful children wait

To climb upon their father's knee;

  And in each house made desolate

Pale women who have lost their lord

  Will kiss the relics of the slain—

Some tarnished epaulette—some sword—

  Poor toys to soothe such anguished pain.

For not in quiet English fields

  Are these, our brothers, lain to rest,

Where we might deck their broken shields

  With all the flowers the dead love best.

me are by the Delhi walls,

And many in the Afghan land,

And many where the Ganges falls

   Through seven mouths of shifting sand.

And some in Russian waters lie,

   And others in the seas which are

The portals to the East, or by

   The wind-swept heights of Trafalgar.

O wandering graves! O restless sleep!

   O silence of the sunless day!

O still ravine! O stormy deep!

   Give up your prey! Give up your prey!

And thou whose wounds are never healed,

   Whose weary race is never won,

O Cromwell's England! must thou yield

   For every inch of ground a son?

Go! crown with thorns thy gold-crowned head,

   Change thy glad song to song of pain;

Wind and wild wave have got thy dead,

   And will not yield them back again.

Wave and wild wind and foreign shore

Possess the flower of English land—

Lips that thy lips shall kiss no more,

Hands that shall never clasp thy hand.

What profit now that we have bound

The whole round world with nets of gold,

If hidden in our heart is found

The care that groweth never old?

What profit that our galleys ride,

Pine-forest-like, on every main?

Ruin and wreck are at our side,

Grim warders of the House of Pain.

Where are the brave, the strong, the fleet?

Where is our English chivalry?

Wild grasses are their burial-sheet,

And sobbing waves their threnody.

ved ones lying far away,

vord of love can dead lips send!

O wasted dust! O senseless clay!

   Is this the end! is this the end!

Peace, peace! we wrong the noble dead

   To vex their solemn slumber so;

Though childless, and with thorn-crowned head,

   Up the steep road must England go,

Yet when this fiery web is spun,

   Her watchmen shall descry from far

The young Republic like a sun

   Rise from these crimson seas of war.

TO MILTON

Milton! I think thy spirit hath passed away

From these white cliffs and high-embattled towers;

   This gorgeous fiery-coloured world of ours

Seems fallen into ashes dull and grey,

And the age changed unto a mimic play

   Wherein we waste our else too-crowded hours:

   For all our pomp and pageantry and powers

We are but fit to delve the common clay,

Seeing this little isle on which we stand,

   This England, this sea-lion of the sea,

By ignorant demagogues is held in fee,

Who love her not: Dear God! is this the land

Which bare a triple empire in her hand

When Cromwell spake the word Democracy!

LOUIS NAPOLEON

Eagle of Austerlitz! where were thy wings

When far away upon a barbarous strand,

In fight unequal, by an obscure hand,

Fell the last scion of thy brood of Kings!

Poor boy! thou shalt not flaunt thy cloak of red,

Or ride in state through Paris in the van

Of thy returning legions, but instead

Thy mother France, free and republican,

Shall on thy dead and crownless forehead place

The better laurels of a soldier's crown,

That not dishonoured should thy soul go down

To tell the mighty Sire of thy race

That France hath kissed the mouth of Liberty,

And found it sweeter than his honied bees,

And that the giant wave Democracy

Breaks on the shores where Kings lay couched at ease.

SONNET ON THE MASSACRE OF THE CHRISTIANS IN BULGARIA

Christ, dost Thou live indeed? or are Thy bones

Still straitened in their rock-hewn sepulchre?

And was Thy Rising only dreamed by her

Whose love of Thee for all her sin atones?

For here the air is horrid with men's groans,

The priests who call upon Thy name are slain,

Dost Thou not hear the bitter wail of pain

From those whose children lie upon the stones?

Come down, O Son of God! incestuous gloom

Curtains the land, and through the starless night

Over Thy Cross a Crescent moon I see!

If Thou in very truth didst burst the tomb

Come down, O Son of Man! and show Thy might

Lest Mahomet be crowned instead of Thee!

QUANTUM MUTATA

There was a time in Europe long ago

When no man died for freedom anywhere,

But England's lion leaping from its lair

Laid hands on the oppressor! it was so

27

While England could a great Republic show.

Witness the men of Piedmont, chiefest care

Of Cromwell, when with impotent despair

The Pontiff in his painted portico

Trembled before our stern ambassadors.

How comes it then that from such high estate

We have thus fallen, save that Luxury

With barren merchandise piles up the gate

Where noble thoughts and deeds should enter by:

Else might we still be Milton's heritors.

LIBERTATIS SACRA FAMES

Albeit nurtured in democracy,

And liking best that state republican

Where every man is Kinglike and no man

Is crowned above his fellows, yet I see,

Spite of this modern fret for Liberty,

Better the rule of One, whom all obey,

Than to let clamorous demagogues betray

Our freedom with the kiss of anarchy.

Wherefore I love them not whose hands profane

Plant the red flag upon the piled-up street

For no right cause, beneath whose ignorant reign

Arts, Culture, Reverence, Honour, all things fade,

Save Treason and the dagger of her trade,

Or Murder with his silent bloody feet.

THEORETIKOS

This mighty empire hath but feet of clay:

Of all its ancient chivalry and might

Our little island is forsaken quite:

Some enemy hath stolen its crown of bay,

And from its hills that voice hath passed away

Which spake of Freedom: O come out of it,

Come out of it, my Soul, thou art not fit

For this vile traffic-house, where day by day

Wisdom and reverence are sold at mart,

And the rude people rage with ignorant cries

Against an heritage of centuries.

It mars my calm: wherefore in dreams of Art

And loftiest culture I would stand apart,

Neither for God, nor for his enemies.

THE GARDEN OF EROS

It is full summer now, the heart of June;

   Not yet the sunburnt reapers are astir

Upon the upland meadow where too soon

   Rich autumn time, the season's usurer,

Will lend his hoarded gold to all the trees,

And see his treasure scattered by the wild and spendthrift breeze.

Too soon indeed! yet here the daffodil,

   That love-child of the Spring, has lingered on

To vex the rose with jealousy, and still

   The harebell spreads her azure pavilion,

And like a strayed and wandering reveller

Abandoned of its brothers, whom long since June's messenger

The missel-thrush has frighted from the glade,

   One pale narcissus loiters fearfully

Close to a shadowy nook, where half afraid

   Of their own loveliness some violets lie

That will not look the gold sun in the face

For fear of too much splendour,—ah! methinks it is a place

Which should be trodden by Persephone

   When wearied of the flowerless fields of Dis!

Or danced on by the lads of Arcady!

   The hidden secret of eternal bliss

Known to the Grecian here a man might find,

Ah! you and I may find it now if Love and Sleep be kind.

There are the flowers which mourning Herakles

   Strewed on the tomb of Hylas, columbine,

Its white doves all a-flutter where the breeze

   Kissed them too harshly, the small celandine,

That yellow-kirtled chorister of eve,

And lilac lady's-smock,—but let them bloom alone, and leave

Yon spirèd hollyhock red-crocketed

   To sway its silent chimes, else must the bee,

Its little bellringer, go seek instead

   Some other pleasaunce; the anemone

That weeps at daybreak, like a silly girl

Before her love, and hardly lets the butterflies unfurl

Their painted wings beside it,—bid it pine

In pale virginity; the winter snow

Will suit it better than those lips of thine

   Whose fires would but scorch it, rather go

And pluck that amorous flower which blooms alone,

Fed by the pander wind with dust of kisses not its own.

The trumpet-mouths of red convolvulus

   So dear to maidens, creamy meadow-sweet

Whiter than Juno's throat and odorous

   As all Arabia, hyacinths the feet

Of Huntress Dian would be loth to mar

For any dappled fawn,—pluck these, and those fond flowers which are

Fairer than what Queen Venus trod upon

   Beneath the pines of Ida, eucharis,

That morning star which does not dread the sun,

   And budding marjoram which but to kiss

Would sweeten Cytheræa's lips and make

Adonis jealous,—these for thy head,—and for thy girdle take

Yon curving spray of purple clematis

   Whose gorgeous dye outflames the Tyrian King,

And foxgloves with their nodding chalices,

But that one narciss which the startled Spring

Let from her kirtle fall when first she heard

In her own woods the wild tempestuous song of summer's bird,

Ah! leave it for a subtle memory

   Of those sweet tremulous days of rain and sun,

When April laughed between her tears to see

   The early primrose with shy footsteps run

From the gnarled oak-tree roots till all the wold,

   Spite of its brown and trampled leaves, grew bright with shimmering gold.

Nay, pluck it too, it is not half so sweet

   As thou thyself, my soul's idolatry!

And when thou art a-wearied at thy feet

   Shall oxlips weave their brightest tapestry,

For thee the woodbine shall forget its pride

And veil its tangled whorls, and thou shalt walk on daisies pied.

And I will cut a reed by yonder spring

   And make the wood-gods jealous, and old Pan

Wonder what young intruder dares to sing

   In these still haunts, where never foot of man

Should tread at evening, lest he chance to spy

The marble limbs of Artemis and all her company.

And I will tell thee why the jacinth wears

   Such dread embroidery of dolorous moan,

And why the hapless nightingale forbears

   To sing her song at noon, but weeps alone

When the fleet swallow sleeps, and rich men feast,

And why the laurel trembles when she sees the lightening east.

And I will sing how sad Proserpina

   Unto a grave and gloomy Lord was wed,

And lure the silver-breasted Helena

   Back from the lotus meadows of the dead,

So shalt thou see that awful loveliness

For which two mighty Hosts met fearfully in war's abyss!

And then I'll pipe to thee that Grecian tale

   How Cynthia loves the lad Endymion,

And hidden in a grey and misty veil

   Hies to the cliffs of Latmos once the Sun

Leaps from his ocean bed in fruitless chase

Of those pale flying feet which fade away in his embrace.

And if my flute can breathe sweet melody,

We may behold Her face who long ago

Dwelt among men by the Ægean sea,

   And whose sad house with pillaged portico

And friezeless wall and columns toppled down

Looms o'er the ruins of that fair and violet cinctured town.

Spirit of Beauty! tarry still awhile,

   They are not dead, thine ancient votaries;

Some few there are to whom thy radiant smile

   Is better than a thousand victories,

Though all the nobly slain of Waterloo

Rise up in wrath against them! tarry still, there are a few

Who for thy sake would give their manlihood

   And consecrate their being; I at least

Have done so, made thy lips my daily food,

   And in thy temples found a goodlier feast

Than this starved age can give me, spite of all

Its new-found creeds so sceptical and so dogmatical.

Here not Cephissos, not Ilissos flows,

   The woods of white Colonos are not here,

On our bleak hills the olive never blows,

No simple priest conducts his lowing steer

Up the steep marble way, nor through the town

Do laughing maidens bear to thee the crocus-flowered gown.

Yet tarry! for the boy who loved thee best,

   Whose very name should be a memory

To make thee linger, sleeps in silent rest

   Beneath the Roman walls, and melody

Still mourns her sweetest lyre; none can play

The lute of Adonais: with his lips Song passed away.

Nay, when Keats died the Muses still had left

   One silver voice to sing his threnody,

But ah! too soon of it we were bereft

   When on that riven night and stormy sea

Panthea claimed her singer as her own,

And slew the mouth that praised her; since which time we walk alone,

Save for that fiery heart, that morning star

   Of re-arisen England, whose clear eye

Saw from our tottering throne and waste of war

   The grand Greek limbs of young Democracy

Rise mightily like Hesperus and bring

The great Republic! him at least thy love hath taught to sing,

And he hath been with thee at Thessaly,
  And seen white Atalanta fleet of foot
In passionless and fierce virginity
  Hunting the tuskèd boar, his honied lute
Hath pierced the cavern of the hollow hill,
And Venus laughs to know one knee will bow before her still.

And he hath kissed the lips of Proserpine,
  And sung the Galilæan's requiem,
That wounded forehead dashed with blood and wine
  He hath discrowned, the Ancient Gods in him
Have found their last, most ardent worshipper,
And the new Sign grows grey and dim before its conqueror.

Spirit of Beauty! tarry with us still,
  It is not quenched the torch of poesy,
The star that shook above the Eastern hill
  Holds unassailed its argent armoury
From all the gathering gloom and fretful fight—
O tarry with us still! for through the long and common night,

Morris, our sweet and simple Chaucer's child,

Dear heritor of Spenser's tuneful reed,

With soft and sylvan pipe has oft beguiled

   The weary soul of man in troublous need,

And from the far and flowerless fields of ice

Has brought fair flowers to make an earthly paradise.

We know them all, Gudrun the strong men's bride,

   Aslaug and Olafson we know them all,

How giant Grettir fought and Sigurd died,

   And what enchantment held the king in thrall

When lonely Brynhild wrestled with the powers

That war against all passion, ah! how oft through summer hours,

Long listless summer hours when the noon

   Being enamoured of a damask rose

Forgets to journey westward, till the moon

   The pale usurper of its tribute grows

From a thin sickle to a silver shield

And chides its loitering car—how oft, in some cool grassy field

Far from the cricket-ground and noisy eight,

   At Bagley, where the rustling bluebells come

Almost before the blackbird finds a mate

And overstay the swallow, and the hum

Of many murmuring bees flits through the leaves,

Have I lain poring on the dreamy tales his fancy weaves,

And through their unreal woes and mimic pain

   Wept for myself, and so was purified,

And in their simple mirth grew glad again;

   For as I sailed upon that pictured tide

The strength and splendour of the storm was mine

Without the storm's red ruin, for the singer is divine;

The little laugh of water falling down

   Is not so musical, the clammy gold

Close hoarded in the tiny waxen town

   Has less of sweetness in it, and the old

Half-withered reeds that waved in Arcady

Touched by his lips break forth again to fresher harmony.

Spirit of Beauty, tarry yet awhile!

   Although the cheating merchants of the mart

With iron roads profane our lovely isle,

   And break on whirling wheels the limbs of Art,

Ay! though the crowded factories beget

The blindworm Ignorance that slays the soul, O tarry yet!

For One at least there is,—He bears his name
   From Dante and the seraph Gabriel,—
Whose double laurels burn with deathless flame
   To light thine altar; He too loves thee well,
Who saw old Merlin lured in Vivien's snare,
And the white feet of angels coming down the golden stair,

Loves thee so well, that all the World for him
   A gorgeous-coloured vestiture must wear,
And Sorrow take a purple diadem,
   Or else be no more Sorrow, and Despair
Gild its own thorns, and Pain, like Adon, be
Even in anguish beautiful;—such is the empery

Which Painters hold, and such the heritage
   This gentle solemn Spirit doth possess,
Being a better mirror of his age
   In all his pity, love, and weariness,
Than those who can but copy common things,
And leave the Soul unpainted with its mighty questionings.

But they are few, and all romance has flown,

And men can prophesy about the sun,

And lecture on his arrows—how, alone,

　Through a waste void the soulless atoms run,

How from each tree its weeping nymph has fled,

And that no more 'mid English reeds a Naiad shows her head.

Methinks these new Actæons boast too soon

　That they have spied on beauty; what if we

Have analysed the rainbow, robbed the moon

　Of her most ancient, chastest mystery,

Shall I, the last Endymion, lose all hope

Because rude eyes peer at my mistress through a telescope!

What profit if this scientific age

　Burst through our gates with all its retinue

Of modern miracles! Can it assuage

　One lover's breaking heart? what can it do

To make one life more beautiful, one day

More godlike in its period? but now the Age of Clay

Returns in horrid cycle, and the earth

　Hath borne again a noisy progeny

Of ignorant Titans, whose ungodly birth

Hurls them against the august hierarchy

Which sat upon Olympus; to the Dust

They have appealed, and to that barren arbiter they must

Repair for judgment; let them, if they can,

From Natural Warfare and insensate Chance,

Create the new Ideal rule for man!

Methinks that was not my inheritance;

For I was nurtured otherwise, my soul

Passes from higher heights of life to a more supreme goal.

Lo! while we spake the earth did turn away

Her visage from the God, and Hecate's boat

Rose silver-laden, till the jealous day

Blew all its torches out: I did not note

The waning hours, to young Endymions

Time's palsied fingers count in vain his rosary of suns!

Mark how the yellow iris wearily

Leans back its throat, as though it would be kissed

By its false chamberer, the dragon-fly,

Who, like a blue vein on a girl's white wrist,

Sleeps on that snowy primrose of the night,

Which 'gins to flush with crimson shame, and die beneath the light.

Come let us go, against the pallid shield
   Of the wan sky the almond blossoms gleam,
The corncrake nested in the unmown field
   Answers its mate, across the misty stream
On fitful wing the startled curlews fly,
And in his sedgy bed the lark, for joy that Day is nigh,

Scatters the pearlèd dew from off the grass,
   In tremulous ecstasy to greet the sun,
Who soon in gilded panoply will pass
   Forth from yon orange-curtained pavilion
Hung in the burning east: see, the red rim
O'ertops the expectant hills! it is the God! for love of him

Already the shrill lark is out of sight,
   Flooding with waves of song this silent dell,—
Ah! there is something more in that bird's flight
   Than could be tested in a crucible!—
But the air freshens, let us go, why soon
The woodmen will be here; how we have lived this night of June!

ROSA MYSTICA

REQUIESCAT

Tread lightly, she is near
   Under the snow,
Speak gently, she can hear
   The daisies grow.

All her bright golden hair
   Tarnished with rust,
She that was young and fair
   Fallen to dust.

Lily-like, white as snow,
   She hardly knew
She was a woman, so
   Sweetly she grew.

Coffin-board, heavy stone,
   Lie on her breast,
I vex my heart alone,

She is at rest.

Peace, Peace, she cannot hear

  Lyre or sonnet,

All my life's buried here,

  Heap earth upon it.

AVIGNON.

SONNET ON APPROACHING ITALY

I reached the Alps: the soul within me burned,

  Italia, my Italia, at thy name:

  And when from out the mountain's heart I came

And saw the land for which my life had yearned,

I laughed as one who some great prize had earned:

  And musing on the marvel of thy fame

  I watched the day, till marked with wounds of flame

The turquoise sky to burnished gold was turned.

The pine-trees waved as waves a woman's hair,

  And in the orchards every twining spray

  Was breaking into flakes of blossoming foam:

But when I knew that far away at Rome

  In evil bonds a second Peter lay,

I wept to see the land so very fair.

Turin.

SAN MINIATO

See, I have climbed the mountain side

Up to this holy house of God,

Where once that Angel-Painter trod

Who saw the heavens opened wide,

And throned upon the crescent moon

The Virginal white Queen of Grace,—

Mary! could I but see thy face

Death could not come at all too soon.

O crowned by God with thorns and pain!

Mother of Christ! O mystic wife!

My heart is weary of this life

And over-sad to sing again.

O crowned by God with love and flame!

O crowned by Christ the Holy One!

O listen ere the searching sun

Show to the world my sin and shame.

AVE MARIA GRATIA PLENA

Was this His coming! I had hoped to see

    A scene of wondrous glory, as was told

    Of some great God who in a rain of gold

Broke open bars and fell on Danae:

Or a dread vision as when Semele

    Sickening for love and unappeased desire

    Prayed to see God's clear body, and the fire

Caught her brown limbs and slew her utterly:

With such glad dreams I sought this holy place,

    And now with wondering eyes and heart I stand

    Before this supreme mystery of Love:

Some kneeling girl with passionless pale face,

    An angel with a lily in his hand,

    And over both the white wings of a Dove.

FLORENCE.

ITALIA

Italia! thou art fallen, though with sheen

    Of battle-spears thy clamorous armies stride

    From the north Alps to the Sicilian tide!

Ay! fallen, though the nations hail thee Queen

Because rich gold in every town is seen,

    And on thy sapphire-lake in tossing pride

    Of wind-filled vans thy myriad galleys ride

Beneath one flag of red and white and green.

O Fair and Strong! O Strong and Fair in vain!

    Look southward where Rome's desecrated town

    Lies mourning for her God-anointed King!

Look heaven-ward! shall God allow this thing?

    Nay! but some flame-girt Raphael shall come down,

    And smite the Spoiler with the sword of pain.

Venice.

SONNET WRITTEN IN HOLY WEEK AT GENOA

I wandered through Scoglietto's far retreat,

    The oranges on each o'erhanging spray

    Burned as bright lamps of gold to shame the day;

Some startled bird with fluttering wings and fleet

Made snow of all the blossoms; at my feet

    Like silver moons the pale narcissi lay:

    And the curved waves that streaked the great green bay

Laughed i' the sun, and life seemed very sweet.

Outside the young boy-priest passed singing clear,

'Jesus the son of Mary has been slain,

O come and fill His sepulchre with flowers.'

Ah, God! Ah, God! those dear Hellenic hours

Had drowned all memory of Thy bitter pain,

The Cross, the Crown, the Soldiers and the Spear.

ROME UNVISITED

I.

The corn has turned from grey to red,

Since first my spirit wandered forth

From the drear cities of the north,

And to Italia's mountains fled.

And here I set my face towards home,

For all my pilgrimage is done,

Although, methinks, yon blood-red sun

Marshals the way to Holy Rome.

O Blessed Lady, who dost hold

Upon the seven hills thy reign!

O Mother without blot or stain,

Crowned with bright crowns of triple gold!

49

O Roma, Roma, at thy feet

   I lay this barren gift of song!

   For, ah! the way is steep and long

That leads unto thy sacred street.

II.

And yet what joy it were for me

   To turn my feet unto the south,

   And journeying towards the Tiber mouth

To kneel again at Fiesole!

And wandering through the tangled pines

   That break the gold of Arno's stream,

   To see the purple mist and gleam

Of morning on the Apennines

By many a vineyard-hidden home,

   Orchard and olive-garden grey,

   Till from the drear Campagna's way

The seven hills bear up the dome!

III.

A pilgrim from the northern seas—
    What joy for me to seek alone
    The wondrous temple and the throne
Of him who holds the awful keys!

When, bright with purple and with gold
    Come priest and holy cardinal,
    And borne above the heads of all
The gentle Shepherd of the Fold.

O joy to see before I die
    The only God-anointed king,
    And hear the silver trumpets ring
A triumph as he passes by!

Or at the brazen-pillared shrine
    Holds high the mystic sacrifice,
    And shows his God to human eyes
Beneath the veil of bread and wine.

IV.

For lo, what changes time can bring!

The cycles of revolving years

  May free my heart from all its fears,

And teach my lips a song to sing.

Before yon field of trembling gold

  Is garnered into dusty sheaves,

  Or ere the autumn's scarlet leaves

Flutter as birds adown the wold,

I may have run the glorious race,

  And caught the torch while yet aflame,

  And called upon the holy name

Of Him who now doth hide His face.

ARONA.

URBS SACRA ÆTERNA

Rome! what a scroll of History thine has been;

  In the first days thy sword republican

  Ruled the whole world for many an age's span:

Then of the peoples wert thou royal Queen,

Till in thy streets the bearded Goth was seen;

  And now upon thy walls the breezes fan

  (Ah, city crowned by God, discrowned by man!)

The hated flag of red and white and green.

When was thy glory! when in search for power

   Thine eagles flew to greet the double sun,

   And the wild nations shuddered at thy rod?

Nay, but thy glory tarried for this hour,

   When pilgrims kneel before the Holy One,

   The prisoned shepherd of the Church of God.

MONTRE MARIO.

SONNET ON HEARING THE DIES IRÆ SUNG IN THE SISTINE CHAPEL

Nay, Lord, not thus! white lilies in the spring,

Sad olive-groves, or silver-breasted dove,

   Teach me more clearly of Thy life and love

Than terrors of red flame and thundering.

The hillside vines dear memories of Thee bring:

   A bird at evening flying to its nest

   Tells me of One who had no place of rest:

I think it is of Thee the sparrows sing.

Come rather on some autumn afternoon,

   When red and brown are burnished on the leaves,

   And the fields echo to the gleaner's song,

Come when the splendid fulness of the moon

Looks down upon the rows of golden sheaves,

And reap Thy harvest: we have waited long.

EASTER DAY

The silver trumpets rang across the Dome:

The people knelt upon the ground with awe:

And borne upon the necks of men I saw,

Like some great God, the Holy Lord of Rome.

Priest-like, he wore a robe more white than foam,

And, king-like, swathed himself in royal red,

Three crowns of gold rose high upon his head:

In splendour and in light the Pope passed home.

My heart stole back across wide wastes of years

To One who wandered by a lonely sea,

And sought in vain for any place of rest:

'Foxes have holes, and every bird its nest.

I, only I, must wander wearily,

And bruise my feet, and drink wine salt with tears.'

E TENEBRIS

Come down, O Christ, and help me! reach Thy hand,

For I am drowning in a stormier sea

Than Simon on Thy lake of Galilee:

The wine of life is spilt upon the sand,

My heart is as some famine-murdered land

    Whence all good things have perished utterly,

    And well I know my soul in Hell must lie

If I this night before God's throne should stand.

'He sleeps perchance, or rideth to the chase,

    Like Baal, when his prophets howled that name

    From morn to noon on Carmel's smitten height.'

Nay, peace, I shall behold, before the night,

    The feet of brass, the robe more white than flame,

    The wounded hands, the weary human face.

VITA NUOVA

I stood by the unvintageable sea

    Till the wet waves drenched face and hair with spray;

    The long red fires of the dying day

Burned in the west; the wind piped drearily;

And to the land the clamorous gulls did flee:

    'Alas!' I cried, 'my life is full of pain,

    And who can garner fruit or golden grain

From these waste fields which travail ceaselessly!'

My nets gaped wide with many a break and flaw,

    Nathless I threw them as my final cast

    Into the sea, and waited for the end.

When lo! a sudden glory! and I saw

From the black waters of my tortured past

The argent splendour of white limbs ascend!

MADONNA MIA

A lily-girl, not made for this world's pain,

With brown, soft hair close braided by her ears,

And longing eyes half veiled by slumberous tears

Like bluest water seen through mists of rain:

Pale cheeks whereon no love hath left its stain,

Red underlip drawn in for fear of love,

And white throat, whiter than the silvered dove,

Through whose wan marble creeps one purple vein.

Yet, though my lips shall praise her without cease,

Even to kiss her feet I am not bold,

Being o'ershadowed by the wings of awe,

Like Dante, when he stood with Beatrice

Beneath the flaming Lion's breast, and saw

The seventh Crystal, and the Stair of Gold.

THE NEW HELEN

Where hast thou been since round the walls of Troy

The sons of God fought in that great emprise?

Why dost thou walk our common earth again?

Hast thou forgotten that impassioned boy,

His purple galley and his Tyrian men

And treacherous Aphrodite's mocking eyes?

For surely it was thou, who, like a star

Hung in the silver silence of the night,

Didst lure the Old World's chivalry and might

Into the clamorous crimson waves of war!

Or didst thou rule the fire-laden moon?

In amorous Sidon was thy temple built

Over the light and laughter of the sea

Where, behind lattice scarlet-wrought and gilt,

Some brown-limbed girl did weave thee tapestry,

All through the waste and wearied hours of noon;

Till her wan cheek with flame of passion burned,

And she rose up the sea-washed lips to kiss

Of some glad Cyprian sailor, safe returned

From Calpé and the cliffs of Herakles!

No! thou art Helen, and none other one!

It was for thee that young Sarpedôn died,

And Memnôn's manhood was untimely spent;

It was for thee gold-crested Hector tried

With Thetis' child that evil race to run,

In the last year of thy beleaguerment;

Ay! even now the glory of thy fame

Burns in those fields of trampled asphodel,

Where the high lords whom Ilion knew so well

Clash ghostly shields, and call upon thy name.

Where hast thou been? in that enchanted land

Whose slumbering vales forlorn Calypso knew,

Where never mower rose at break of day

But all unswathed the trammelling grasses grew,

And the sad shepherd saw the tall corn stand

Till summer's red had changed to withered grey?

Didst thou lie there by some Lethæan stream

Deep brooding on thine ancient memory,

The crash of broken spears, the fiery gleam

From shivered helm, the Grecian battle-cry?

Nay, thou wert hidden in that hollow hill

With one who is forgotten utterly,

That discrowned Queen men call the Erycine;

Hidden away that never mightst thou see

The face of Her, before whose mouldering shrine

To-day at Rome the silent nations kneel;

Who gat from Love no joyous gladdening,

But only Love's intolerable pain,

Only a sword to pierce her heart in twain,

Only the bitterness of child-bearing.

The lotus-leaves which heal the wounds of Death

Lie in thy hand; O, be thou kind to me,

While yet I know the summer of my days;

For hardly can my tremulous lips draw breath

To fill the silver trumpet with thy praise,

So bowed am I before thy mystery;

So bowed and broken on Love's terrible wheel,

That I have lost all hope and heart to sing,

Yet care I not what ruin time may bring

If in thy temple thou wilt let me kneel.

Alas, alas, thou wilt not tarry here,

But, like that bird, the servant of the sun,

Who flies before the north wind and the night,

So wilt thou fly our evil land and drear,

Back to the tower of thine old delight,

And the red lips of young Euphorion;

Nor shall I ever see thy face again,

But in this poisonous garden-close must stay,

Crowning my brows with the thorn-crown of pain,

Till all my loveless life shall pass away.

O Helen! Helen! Helen! yet a while,

Yet for a little while, O, tarry here,

Till the dawn cometh and the shadows flee!

For in the gladsome sunlight of thy smile

Of heaven or hell I have no thought or fear,

Seeing I know no other god but thee:

No other god save him, before whose feet

In nets of gold the tired planets move,

The incarnate spirit of spiritual love

Who in thy body holds his joyous seat.

Thou wert not born as common women are!

But, girt with silver splendour of the foam,

Didst from the depths of sapphire seas arise!

And at thy coming some immortal star,

Bearded with flame, blazed in the Eastern skies,

And waked the shepherds on thine island-home.

Thou shalt not die: no asps of Egypt creep

Close at thy heels to taint the delicate air;

No sullen-blooming poppies stain thy hair,

Those scarlet heralds of eternal sleep.

Lily of love, pure and inviolate!

Tower of ivory! red rose of fire!

Thou hast come down our darkness to illume:

For we, close-caught in the wide nets of Fate,

Wearied with waiting for the World's Desire,

Aimlessly wandered in the House of gloom,

Aimlessly sought some slumberous anodyne

For wasted lives, for lingering wretchedness,

Till we beheld thy re-arisen shrine,

And the white glory of thy loveliness.

THE BURDEN OF ITYS

This English Thames is holier far than Rome,

    Those harebells like a sudden flush of sea

Breaking across the woodland, with the foam

    Of meadow-sweet and white anemone

To fleck their blue waves,—God is likelier there

Than hidden in that crystal-hearted star the pale monks bear!

Those violet-gleaming butterflies that take

    Yon creamy lily for their pavilion

Are monsignores, and where the rushes shake

    A lazy pike lies basking in the sun,

His eyes half shut,—he is some mitred old

Bishop in partibus! look at those gaudy scales all green and gold.

The wind the restless prisoner of the trees

    Does well for Palæstrina, one would say

The mighty master's hands were on the keys

    Of the Maria organ, which they play

When early on some sapphire Easter morn

In a high litter red as blood or sin the Pope is borne

From his dark House out to the Balcony

    Above the bronze gates and the crowded square,

Whose very fountains seem for ecstasy

    To toss their silver lances in the air,

And stretching out weak hands to East and West

In vain sends peace to peaceless lands, to restless nations rest.

Is not yon lingering orange after-glow

    That stays to vex the moon more fair than all

Rome's lordliest pageants! strange, a year ago

    I knelt before some crimson Cardinal

Who bare the Host across the Esquiline,

And now—those common poppies in the wheat seem twice as fine.

The blue-green beanfields yonder, tremulous

    With the last shower, sweeter perfume bring

Through this cool evening than the odorous

    Flame-jewelled censers the young deacons swing,

When the grey priest unlocks the curtained shrine,

And makes God's body from the common fruit of corn and vine.

Poor Fra Giovanni bawling at the mass

Were out of tune now, for a small brown bird

Sings overhead, and through the long cool grass

I see that throbbing throat which once I heard

On starlit hills of flower-starred Arcady,

Once where the white and crescent sand of Salamis meets sea.

Sweet is the swallow twittering on the eaves

At daybreak, when the mower whets his scythe,

And stock-doves murmur, and the milkmaid leaves

Her little lonely bed, and carols blithe

To see the heavy-lowing cattle wait

Stretching their huge and dripping mouths across the farmyard gate.

And sweet the hops upon the Kentish leas,

And sweet the wind that lifts the new-mown hay,

And sweet the fretful swarms of grumbling bees

That round and round the linden blossoms play;

And sweet the heifer breathing in the stall,

And the green bursting figs that hang upon the red-brick wall,

And sweet to hear the cuckoo mock the spring

While the last violet loiters by the well,

And sweet to hear the shepherd Daphnis sing

The song of Linus through a sunny dell

Of warm Arcadia where the corn is gold

And the slight lithe-limbed reapers dance about the wattled fold.

And sweet with young Lycoris to recline

In some Illyrian valley far away,

Where canopied on herbs amaracine

We too might waste the summer-trancèd day

Matching our reeds in sportive rivalry,

While far beneath us frets the troubled purple of the sea.

But sweeter far if silver-sandalled foot

Of some long-hidden God should ever tread

The Nuneham meadows, if with reeded flute

Pressed to his lips some Faun might raise his head

By the green water-flags, ah! sweet indeed

To see the heavenly herdsman call his white-fleeced flock to feed.

Then sing to me thou tuneful chorister,

Though what thou sing'st be thine own requiem!

Tell me thy tale thou hapless chronicler

Of thine own tragedies! do not contemn

These unfamiliar haunts, this English field,

For many a lovely coronal our northern isle can yield

Which Grecian meadows know not, many a rose
   Which all day long in vales Æolian
A lad might seek in vain for over-grows
   Our hedges like a wanton courtesan
Unthrifty of its beauty; lilies too
Ilissos never mirrored star our streams, and cockles blue

Dot the green wheat which, though they are the signs
   For swallows going south, would never spread
Their azure tents between the Attic vines;
   Even that little weed of ragged red,
Which bids the robin pipe, in Arcady
Would be a trespasser, and many an unsung elegy

Sleeps in the reeds that fringe our winding Thames
   Which to awake were sweeter ravishment
Than ever Syrinx wept for; diadems
   Of brown bee-studded orchids which were meant
For Cytheræa's brows are hidden here
Unknown to Cytheræa, and by yonder pasturing steer

There is a tiny yellow daffodil,

The butterfly can see it from afar,

Although one summer evening's dew could fill

  Its little cup twice over ere the star

Had called the lazy shepherd to his fold

And be no prodigal; each leaf is flecked with spotted gold

As if Jove's gorgeous leman Danae

  Hot from his gilded arms had stooped to kiss

The trembling petals, or young Mercury

  Low-flying to the dusky ford of Dis

Had with one feather of his pinions

Just brushed them! the slight stem which bears the burden of its suns

Is hardly thicker than the gossamer,

  Or poor Arachne's silver tapestry,—

Men say it bloomed upon the sepulchre

  Of One I sometime worshipped, but to me

It seems to bring diviner memories

Of faun-loved Heliconian glades and blue nymph-haunted seas,

Of an untrodden vale at Tempe where

  On the clear river's marge Narcissus lies,

The tangle of the forest in his hair,

The silence of the woodland in his eyes,

Wooing that drifting imagery which is

No sooner kissed than broken; memories of Salmacis

Who is not boy nor girl and yet is both,

   Fed by two fires and unsatisfied

Through their excess, each passion being loth

   For love's own sake to leave the other's side

Yet killing love by staying; memories

Of Oreads peeping through the leaves of silent moonlit trees,

Of lonely Ariadne on the wharf

   At Naxos, when she saw the treacherous crew

Far out at sea, and waved her crimson scarf

   And called false Theseus back again nor knew

That Dionysos on an amber pard

Was close behind her; memories of what Mæonia's bard

With sightless eyes beheld, the wall of Troy,

   Queen Helen lying in the ivory room,

And at her side an amorous red-lipped boy

   Trimming with dainty hand his helmet's plume,

And far away the moil, the shout, the groan,

As Hector shielded off the spear and Ajax hurled the stone;

Of wingèd Perseus with his flawless sword
   Cleaving the snaky tresses of the witch,
And all those tales imperishably stored
   In little Grecian urns, freightage more rich
Than any gaudy galleon of Spain
Bare from the Indies ever! these at least bring back again,

For well I know they are not dead at all,
   The ancient Gods of Grecian poesy:
They are asleep, and when they hear thee call
   Will wake and think 't is very Thessaly,
This Thames the Daulian waters, this cool glade
The yellow-irised mead where once young Itys laughed and played.

If it was thou dear jasmine-cradled bird
   Who from the leafy stillness of thy throne
Sang to the wondrous boy, until he heard
   The horn of Atalanta faintly blown
Across the Cumnor hills, and wandering
Through Bagley wood at evening found the Attic poets' spring,—

Ah! tiny sober-suited advocate

That pleadest for the moon against the day!

If thou didst make the shepherd seek his mate

  On that sweet questing, when Proserpina

Forgot it was not Sicily and leant

Across the mossy Sandford stile in ravished wonderment,—

Light-winged and bright-eyed miracle of the wood!

  If ever thou didst soothe with melody

One of that little clan, that brotherhood

  Which loved the morning-star of Tuscany

More than the perfect sun of Raphael

And is immortal, sing to me! for I too love thee well.

Sing on! sing on! let the dull world grow young,

  Let elemental things take form again,

And the old shapes of Beauty walk among

  The simple garths and open crofts, as when

The son of Leto bare the willow rod,

And the soft sheep and shaggy goats followed the boyish God.

Sing on! sing on! and Bacchus will be here

  Astride upon his gorgeous Indian throne,

And over whimpering tigers shake the spear

With yellow ivy crowned and gummy cone,

While at his side the wanton Bassarid

Will throw the lion by the mane and catch the mountain kid!

Sing on! and I will wear the leopard skin,

And steal the moonèd wings of Ashtaroth,

Upon whose icy chariot we could win

Cithæron in an hour ere the froth

Has over-brimmed the wine-vat or the Faun

Ceased from the treading! ay, before the flickering lamp of dawn

Has scared the hooting owlet to its nest,

And warned the bat to close its filmy vans,

Some Mænad girl with vine-leaves on her breast

Will filch their beech-nuts from the sleeping Pans

So softly that the little nested thrush

Will never wake, and then with shrilly laugh and leap will rush

Down the green valley where the fallen dew

Lies thick beneath the elm and count her store,

Till the brown Satyrs in a jolly crew

Trample the loosestrife down along the shore,

And where their hornèd master sits in state

Bring strawberries and bloomy plums upon a wicker crate!

Sing on! and soon with passion-wearied face
  Through the cool leaves Apollo's lad will come,
The Tyrian prince his bristled boar will chase
  Adown the chestnut-copses all a-bloom,
And ivory-limbed, grey-eyed, with look of pride,
After yon velvet-coated deer the virgin maid will ride.

Sing on! and I the dying boy will see
  Stain with his purple blood the waxen bell
That overweighs the jacinth, and to me
  The wretched Cyprian her woe will tell,
And I will kiss her mouth and streaming eyes,
And lead her to the myrtle-hidden grove where Adon lies!

Cry out aloud on Itys! memory
  That foster-brother of remorse and pain
Drops poison in mine ear,—O to be free,
  To burn one's old ships! and to launch again
Into the white-plumed battle of the waves
And fight old Proteus for the spoil of coral-flowered caves!

O for Medea with her poppied spell!

O for the secret of the Colchian shrine!

O for one leaf of that pale asphodel

　Which binds the tired brows of Proserpine,

And sheds such wondrous dews at eve that she

Dreams of the fields of Enna, by the far Sicilian sea,

Where oft the golden-girdled bee she chased

　From lily to lily on the level mead,

Ere yet her sombre Lord had bid her taste

　The deadly fruit of that pomegranate seed,

Ere the black steeds had harried her away

Down to the faint and flowerless land, the sick and sunless day.

O for one midnight and as paramour

　The Venus of the little Melian farm!

O that some antique statue for one hour

　Might wake to passion, and that I could charm

The Dawn at Florence from its dumb despair,

Mix with those mighty limbs and make that giant breast my lair!

Sing on! sing on! I would be drunk with life,

　Drunk with the trampled vintage of my youth,

I would forget the wearying wasted strife,

The riven veil, the Gorgon eyes of Truth,

The prayerless vigil and the cry for prayer,

The barren gifts, the lifted arms, the dull insensate air!

Sing on! sing on! O feathered Niobe,

   Thou canst make sorrow beautiful, and steal

From joy its sweetest music, not as we

   Who by dead voiceless silence strive to heal

Our too untented wounds, and do but keep

Pain barricadoed in our hearts, and murder pillowed sleep.

Sing louder yet, why must I still behold

   The wan white face of that deserted Christ,

Whose bleeding hands my hands did once enfold,

   Whose smitten lips my lips so oft have kissed,

And now in mute and marble misery

Sits in his lone dishonoured House and weeps, perchance for me?

O Memory cast down thy wreathèd shell!

   Break thy hoarse lute O sad Melpomene!

O Sorrow, Sorrow keep thy cloistered cell

   Nor dim with tears this limpid Castaly!

Cease, Philomel, thou dost the forest wrong

To vex its sylvan quiet with such wild impassioned song!

Cease, cease, or if 't is anguish to be dumb
   Take from the pastoral thrush her simpler air,
Whose jocund carelessness doth more become
   This English woodland than thy keen despair,
Ah! cease and let the north wind bear thy lay
Back to the rocky hills of Thrace, the stormy Daulian bay.

A moment more, the startled leaves had stirred,
   Endymion would have passed across the mead
Moonstruck with love, and this still Thames had heard
   Pan plash and paddle groping for some reed
To lure from her blue cave that Naiad maid
Who for such piping listens half in joy and half afraid.

A moment more, the waking dove had cooed,
   The silver daughter of the silver sea
With the fond gyves of clinging hands had wooed
   Her wanton from the chase, and Dryope
Had thrust aside the branches of her oak
To see the lusty gold-haired lad rein in his snorting yoke.

A moment more, the trees had stooped to kiss

Pale Daphne just awakening from the swoon

Of tremulous laurels, lonely Salmacis

   Had bared his barren beauty to the moon,

And through the vale with sad voluptuous smile

Antinous had wandered, the red lotus of the Nile

Down leaning from his black and clustering hair,

   To shade those slumberous eyelids' caverned bliss,

Or else on yonder grassy slope with bare

   High-tuniced limbs unravished Artemis

Had bade her hounds give tongue, and roused the deer

From his green ambuscade with shrill halloo and pricking spear.

Lie still, lie still, O passionate heart, lie still!

   O Melancholy, fold thy raven wing!

O sobbing Dryad, from thy hollow hill

   Come not with such despondent answering!

No more thou wingèd Marsyas complain,

Apollo loveth not to hear such troubled songs of pain!

It was a dream, the glade is tenantless,

   No soft Ionian laughter moves the air,

The Thames creeps on in sluggish leadenness,

And from the copse left desolate and bare

Fled is young Bacchus with his revelry,

Yet still from Nuneham wood there comes that thrilling melody

So sad, that one might think a human heart

Brake in each separate note, a quality

Which music sometimes has, being the Art

Which is most nigh to tears and memory;

Poor mourning Philomel, what dost thou fear?

Thy sister doth not haunt these fields, Pandion is not here,

Here is no cruel Lord with murderous blade,

No woven web of bloody heraldries,

But mossy dells for roving comrades made,

Warm valleys where the tired student lies

With half-shut book, and many a winding walk

Where rustic lovers stray at eve in happy simple talk.

The harmless rabbit gambols with its young

Across the trampled towing-path, where late

A troop of laughing boys in jostling throng

Cheered with their noisy cries the racing eight;

The gossamer, with ravelled silver threads,

Works at its little loom, and from the dusky red-eaved sheds

Of the lone Farm a flickering light shines out
　Where the swinked shepherd drives his bleating flock
Back to their wattled sheep-cotes, a faint shout
　Comes from some Oxford boat at Sandford lock,
And starts the moor-hen from the sedgy rill,
And the dim lengthening shadows flit like swallows up the hill.

The heron passes homeward to the mere,
　The blue mist creeps among the shivering trees,
Gold world by world the silent stars appear,
　And like a blossom blown before the breeze
A white moon drifts across the shimmering sky,
Mute arbitress of all thy sad, thy rapturous threnody.

She does not heed thee, wherefore should she heed,
　She knows Endymion is not far away;
'Tis I, 'tis I, whose soul is as the reed
　Which has no message of its own to play,
So pipes another's bidding, it is I,
Drifting with every wind on the wide sea of misery.

Ah! the brown bird has ceased: one exquisite trill

About the sombre woodland seems to cling

Dying in music, else the air is still,

So still that one might hear the bat's small wing

Wander and wheel above the pines, or tell

Each tiny dew-drop dripping from the bluebell's brimming cell.

And far away across the lengthening wold,

Across the willowy flats and thickets brown,

Magdalen's tall tower tipped with tremulous gold

Marks the long High Street of the little town,

And warns me to return; I must not wait,

Hark! 't is the curfew booming from the bell at Christ Church gate.

WIND FLOWERS

IMPRESSION DU MATIN

The Thames nocturne of blue and gold
    Changed to a Harmony in grey:
    A barge with ochre-coloured hay
Dropt from the wharf: and chill and cold

The yellow fog came creeping down
    The bridges, till the houses' walls
    Seemed changed to shadows and St. Paul's
Loomed like a bubble o'er the town.

Then suddenly arose the clang
    Of waking life; the streets were stirred
    With country waggons: and a bird
Flew to the glistening roofs and sang.

But one pale woman all alone,
    The daylight kissing her wan hair,
    Loitered beneath the gas lamps' flare,
With lips of flame and heart of stone.

MAGDALEN WALKS

The little white clouds are racing over the sky,

    And the fields are strewn with the gold of the flower of March,

    The daffodil breaks under foot, and the tasselled larch

Sways and swings as the thrush goes hurrying by.

A delicate odour is borne on the wings of the morning breeze,

    The odour of deep wet grass, and of brown new-furrowed earth,

    The birds are singing for joy of the Spring's glad birth,

Hopping from branch to branch on the rocking trees.

And all the woods are alive with the murmur and sound of Spring,

    And the rose-bud breaks into pink on the climbing briar,

    And the crocus-bed is a quivering moon of fire

Girdled round with the belt of an amethyst ring.

And the plane to the pine-tree is whispering some tale of love

    Till it rustles with laughter and tosses its mantle of green,

    And the gloom of the wych-elm's hollow is lit with the iris sheen

Of the burnished rainbow throat and the silver breast of a dove.

See! the lark starts up from his bed in the meadow there,

    Breaking the gossamer threads and the nets of dew,

81

And flashing adown the river, a flame of blue!

The kingfisher flies like an arrow, and wounds the air.

ATHANASIA

To that gaunt House of Art which lacks for naught

   Of all the great things men have saved from Time,

The withered body of a girl was brought

   Dead ere the world's glad youth had touched its prime,

And seen by lonely Arabs lying hid

In the dim womb of some black pyramid.

But when they had unloosed the linen band

   Which swathed the Egyptian's body,—lo! was found

Closed in the wasted hollow of her hand

   A little seed, which sown in English ground

Did wondrous snow of starry blossoms bear

And spread rich odours through our spring-tide air.

With such strange arts this flower did allure

   That all forgotten was the asphodel,

And the brown bee, the lily's paramour,

   Forsook the cup where he was wont to dwell,

For not a thing of earth it seemed to be,

But stolen from some heavenly Arcady.

In vain the sad narcissus, wan and white

   At its own beauty, hung across the stream,

The purple dragon-fly had no delight

   With its gold dust to make his wings a-gleam,

Ah! no delight the jasmine-bloom to kiss,

Or brush the rain-pearls from the eucharis.

For love of it the passionate nightingale

   Forgot the hills of Thrace, the cruel king,

And the pale dove no longer cared to sail

   Through the wet woods at time of blossoming,

But round this flower of Egypt sought to float,

With silvered wing and amethystine throat.

While the hot sun blazed in his tower of blue

   A cooling wind crept from the land of snows,

And the warm south with tender tears of dew

   Drenched its white leaves when Hesperos up-rose

Amid those sea-green meadows of the sky

On which the scarlet bars of sunset lie.

But when o'er wastes of lily-haunted field

The tired birds had stayed their amorous tune,

And broad and glittering like an argent shield

   High in the sapphire heavens hung the moon,

Did no strange dream or evil memory make

Each tremulous petal of its blossoms shake?

Ah no! to this bright flower a thousand years

   Seemed but the lingering of a summer's day,

It never knew the tide of cankering fears

   Which turn a boy's gold hair to withered grey,

The dread desire of death it never knew,

Or how all folk that they were born must rue.

For we to death with pipe and dancing go,

   Nor would we pass the ivory gate again,

As some sad river wearied of its flow

   Through the dull plains, the haunts of common men,

Leaps lover-like into the terrible sea!

And counts it gain to die so gloriously.

We mar our lordly strength in barren strife

   With the world's legions led by clamorous care,

It never feels decay but gathers life

84

From the pure sunlight and the supreme air,

We live beneath Time's wasting sovereignty,

It is the child of all eternity.

SERENADE

(FOR MUSIC)

The western wind is blowing fair

   Across the dark Ægean sea,

And at the secret marble stair

   My Tyrian galley waits for thee.

Come down! the purple sail is spread,

   The watchman sleeps within the town,

O leave thy lily-flowered bed,

   O Lady mine come down, come down!

She will not come, I know her well,

   Of lover's vows she hath no care,

And little good a man can tell

   Of one so cruel and so fair.

True love is but a woman's toy,

   They never know the lover's pain,

And I who loved as loves a boy

   Must love in vain, must love in vain.

O noble pilot, tell me true,

    Is that the sheen of golden hair?

Or is it but the tangled dew

    That binds the passion-flowers there?

Good sailor come and tell me now

    Is that my Lady's lily hand?

Or is it but the gleaming prow,

    Or is it but the silver sand?

No! no! 'tis not the tangled dew,

    'Tis not the silver-fretted sand,

It is my own dear Lady true

    With golden hair and lily hand!

O noble pilot, steer for Troy,

    Good sailor, ply the labouring oar,

This is the Queen of life and joy

    Whom we must bear from Grecian shore!

The waning sky grows faint and blue,

    It wants an hour still of day,

Aboard! aboard! my gallant crew,

    O Lady mine, away! away!

O noble pilot, steer for Troy,

  Good sailor, ply the labouring oar,

O loved as only loves a boy!

  O loved for ever evermore!

ENDYMION

(FOR MUSIC)

The apple trees are hung with gold,

  And birds are loud in Arcady,

The sheep lie bleating in the fold,

The wild goat runs across the wold,

But yesterday his love he told,

  I know he will come back to me.

O rising moon! O Lady moon!

  Be you my lover's sentinel,

  You cannot choose but know him well,

For he is shod with purple shoon,

You cannot choose but know my love,

  For he a shepherd's crook doth bear,

And he is soft as any dove,

  And brown and curly is his hair.

The turtle now has ceased to call

Upon her crimson-footed groom,

The grey wolf prowls about the stall,

The lily's singing seneschal

Sleeps in the lily-bell, and all

   The violet hills are lost in gloom.

O risen moon! O holy moon!

   Stand on the top of Helice,

   And if my own true love you see,

Ah! if you see the purple shoon,

The hazel crook, the lad's brown hair,

   The goat-skin wrapped about his arm,

Tell him that I am waiting where

   The rushlight glimmers in the Farm.

The falling dew is cold and chill,

   And no bird sings in Arcady,

The little fauns have left the hill,

Even the tired daffodil

Has closed its gilded doors, and still

   My lover comes not back to me.

False moon! False moon! O waning moon!

   Where is my own true lover gone,

   Where are the lips vermilion,

The shepherd's crook, the purple shoon?

Why spread that silver pavilion,

   Why wear that veil of drifting mist?

Ah! thou hast young Endymion,

   Thou hast the lips that should be kissed!

LA BELLA DONNA DELLA MIA MENTE

My limbs are wasted with a flame,

   My feet are sore with travelling,

For, calling on my Lady's name,

   My lips have now forgot to sing.

O Linnet in the wild-rose brake

   Strain for my Love thy melody,

O Lark sing louder for love's sake,

   My gentle Lady passeth by.

She is too fair for any man

   To see or hold his heart's delight,

Fairer than Queen or courtesan

   Or moonlit water in the night.

Her hair is bound with myrtle leaves,

   (Green leaves upon her golden hair!)

Green grasses through the yellow sheaves

   Of autumn corn are not more fair.

Her little lips, more made to kiss

   Than to cry bitterly for pain,

Are tremulous as brook-water is,

   Or roses after evening rain.

Her neck is like white melilote

   Flushing for pleasure of the sun,

The throbbing of the linnet's throat

   Is not so sweet to look upon.

As a pomegranate, cut in twain,

   White-seeded, is her crimson mouth,

Her cheeks are as the fading stain

   Where the peach reddens to the south.

O twining hands! O delicate

   White body made for love and pain!

O House of love! O desolate

   Pale flower beaten by the rain!

CHANSON

A ring of gold and a milk-white dove

   Are goodly gifts for thee,

And a hempen rope for your own love

   To hang upon a tree.

For you a House of Ivory,

   (Roses are white in the rose-bower)!

A narrow bed for me to lie,

   (White, O white, is the hemlock flower)!

Myrtle and jessamine for you,

   (O the red rose is fair to see)!

For me the cypress and the rue,

   (Finest of all is rosemary)!

For you three lovers of your hand,

   (Green grass where a man lies dead)!

For me three paces on the sand,

   (Plant lilies at my head)!

CHARMIDES

I.

He was a Grecian lad, who coming home

   With pulpy figs and wine from Sicily

Stood at his galley's prow, and let the foam

   Blow through his crisp brown curls unconsciously,

And holding wave and wind in boy's despite

Peered from his dripping seat across the wet and stormy night.

Till with the dawn he saw a burnished spear

   Like a thin thread of gold against the sky,

And hoisted sail, and strained the creaking gear,

   And bade the pilot head her lustily

Against the nor'west gale, and all day long

Held on his way, and marked the rowers' time with measured song.

And when the faint Corinthian hills were red

   Dropped anchor in a little sandy bay,

And with fresh boughs of olive crowned his head,

   And brushed from cheek and throat the hoary spray,

And washed his limbs with oil, and from the hold

Brought out his linen tunic and his sandals brazen-soled,

And a rich robe stained with the fishers' juice
   Which of some swarthy trader he had bought
Upon the sunny quay at Syracuse,
   And was with Tyrian broideries inwrought,
And by the questioning merchants made his way
Up through the soft and silver woods, and when the labouring day

Had spun its tangled web of crimson cloud,
   Clomb the high hill, and with swift silent feet
Crept to the fane unnoticed by the crowd
   Of busy priests, and from some dark retreat
Watched the young swains his frolic playmates bring
The firstling of their little flock, and the shy shepherd fling

The crackling salt upon the flame, or hang
   His studded crook against the temple wall
To Her who keeps away the ravenous fang
   Of the base wolf from homestead and from stall;
And then the clear-voiced maidens 'gan to sing,
And to the altar each man brought some goodly offering,

A beechen cup brimming with milky foam,

A fair cloth wrought with cunning imagery

Of hounds in chase, a waxen honey-comb

   Dripping with oozy gold which scarce the bee

Had ceased from building, a black skin of oil

Meet for the wrestlers, a great boar the fierce and white-tusked spoil

Stolen from Artemis that jealous maid

   To please Athena, and the dappled hide

Of a tall stag who in some mountain glade

   Had met the shaft; and then the herald cried,

And from the pillared precinct one by one

Went the glad Greeks well pleased that they their simple vows had done.

And the old priest put out the waning fires

   Save that one lamp whose restless ruby glowed

For ever in the cell, and the shrill lyres

   Came fainter on the wind, as down the road

In joyous dance these country folk did pass,

And with stout hands the warder closed the gates of polished brass.

Long time he lay and hardly dared to breathe,

   And heard the cadenced drip of spilt-out wine,

And the rose-petals falling from the wreath

As the night breezes wandered through the shrine,

And seemed to be in some entrancèd swoon

Till through the open roof above the full and brimming moon

Flooded with sheeny waves the marble floor,

  When from his nook up leapt the venturous lad,

And flinging wide the cedar-carven door

  Beheld an awful image saffron-clad

And armed for battle! the gaunt Griffin glared

From the huge helm, and the long lance of wreck and ruin flared

Like a red rod of flame, stony and steeled

  The Gorgon's head its leaden eyeballs rolled,

And writhed its snaky horrors through the shield,

  And gaped aghast with bloodless lips and cold

In passion impotent, while with blind gaze

The blinking owl between the feet hooted in shrill amaze.

The lonely fisher as he trimmed his lamp

  Far out at sea off Sunium, or cast

The net for tunnies, heard a brazen tramp

  Of horses smite the waves, and a wild blast

Divide the folded curtains of the night,

And knelt upon the little poop, and prayed in holy fright.

And guilty lovers in their venery

   Forgat a little while their stolen sweets,

Deeming they heard dread Dian's bitter cry;

   And the grim watchmen on their lofty seats

Ran to their shields in haste precipitate,

Or strained black-bearded throats across the dusky parapet.

For round the temple rolled the clang of arms,

   And the twelve Gods leapt up in marble fear,

And the air quaked with dissonant alarums

   Till huge Poseidon shook his mighty spear,

And on the frieze the prancing horses neighed,

And the low tread of hurrying feet rang from the cavalcade.

Ready for death with parted lips he stood,

   And well content at such a price to see

That calm wide brow, that terrible maidenhood,

   The marvel of that pitiless chastity,

Ah! well content indeed, for never wight

Since Troy's young shepherd prince had seen so wonderful a sight.

Ready for death he stood, but lo! the air

Grew silent, and the horses ceased to neigh,

And off his brow he tossed the clustering hair,

And from his limbs he throw the cloak away;

For whom would not such love make desperate?

And nigher came, and touched her throat, and with hands violate

Undid the cuirass, and the crocus gown,

And bared the breasts of polished ivory,

Till from the waist the peplos falling down

Left visible the secret mystery

Which to no lover will Athena show,

The grand cool flanks, the crescent thighs, the bossy hills of snow.

Those who have never known a lover's sin

Let them not read my ditty, it will be

To their dull ears so musicless and thin

That they will have no joy of it, but ye

To whose wan cheeks now creeps the lingering smile,

Ye who have learned who Eros is,—O listen yet awhile.

A little space he let his greedy eyes

Rest on the burnished image, till mere sight

Half swooned for surfeit of such luxuries,

And then his lips in hungering delight

Fed on her lips, and round the towered neck

He flung his arms, nor cared at all his passion's will to check.

Never I ween did lover hold such tryst,

   For all night long he murmured honeyed word,

And saw her sweet unravished limbs, and kissed

   Her pale and argent body undisturbed,

And paddled with the polished throat, and pressed

His hot and beating heart upon her chill and icy breast.

It was as if Numidian javelins

   Pierced through and through his wild and whirling brain,

And his nerves thrilled like throbbing violins

   In exquisite pulsation, and the pain

Was such sweet anguish that he never drew

His lips from hers till overhead the lark of warning flew.

They who have never seen the daylight peer

   Into a darkened room, and drawn the curtain,

And with dull eyes and wearied from some dear

   And worshipped body risen, they for certain

Will never know of what I try to sing,

How long the last kiss was, how fond and late his lingering.

The moon was girdled with a crystal rim,
  The sign which shipmen say is ominous
Of wrath in heaven, the wan stars were dim,
  And the low lightening east was tremulous
With the faint fluttering wings of flying dawn,
Ere from the silent sombre shrine his lover had withdrawn.

Down the steep rock with hurried feet and fast
  Clomb the brave lad, and reached the cave of Pan,
And heard the goat-foot snoring as he passed,
  And leapt upon a grassy knoll and ran
Like a young fawn unto an olive wood
Which in a shady valley by the well-built city stood;

And sought a little stream, which well he knew,
  For oftentimes with boyish careless shout
The green and crested grebe he would pursue,
  Or snare in woven net the silver trout,
And down amid the startled reeds he lay
Panting in breathless sweet affright, and waited for the day.

On the green bank he lay, and let one hand

Dip in the cool dark eddies listlessly,

And soon the breath of morning came and fanned

His hot flushed cheeks, or lifted wantonly

The tangled curls from off his forehead, while

He on the running water gazed with strange and secret smile.

And soon the shepherd in rough woollen cloak

With his long crook undid the wattled cotes,

And from the stack a thin blue wreath of smoke

Curled through the air across the ripening oats,

And on the hill the yellow house-dog bayed

As through the crisp and rustling fern the heavy cattle strayed.

And when the light-foot mower went afield

Across the meadows laced with threaded dew,

And the sheep bleated on the misty weald,

And from its nest the waking corncrake flew,

Some woodmen saw him lying by the stream

And marvelled much that any lad so beautiful could seem,

Nor deemed him born of mortals, and one said,

'It is young Hylas, that false runaway

Who with a Naiad now would make his bed

Forgetting Herakles,' but others, 'Nay,

It is Narcissus, his own paramour,

Those are the fond and crimson lips no woman can allure.'

And when they nearer came a third one cried,

  'It is young Dionysos who has hid

His spear and fawnskin by the river side

  Weary of hunting with the Bassarid,

And wise indeed were we away to fly:

They live not long who on the gods immortal come to spy.'

So turned they back, and feared to look behind,

  And told the timid swain how they had seen

Amid the reeds some woodland god reclined,

  And no man dared to cross the open green,

And on that day no olive-tree was slain,

Nor rushes cut, but all deserted was the fair domain,

Save when the neat-herd's lad, his empty pail

  Well slung upon his back, with leap and bound

Raced on the other side, and stopped to hail,

  Hoping that he some comrade new had found,

And gat no answer, and then half afraid

Passed on his simple way, or down the still and silent glade

A little girl ran laughing from the farm,
    Not thinking of love's secret mysteries,
And when she saw the white and gleaming arm
    And all his manlihood, with longing eyes
Whose passion mocked her sweet virginity
Watched him awhile, and then stole back sadly and wearily.

Far off he heard the city's hum and noise,
    And now and then the shriller laughter where
The passionate purity of brown-limbed boys
    Wrestled or raced in the clear healthful air,
And now and then a little tinkling bell
As the shorn wether led the sheep down to the mossy well.

Through the grey willows danced the fretful gnat,
    The grasshopper chirped idly from the tree,
In sleek and oily coat the water-rat
    Breasting the little ripples manfully
Made for the wild-duck's nest, from bough to bough
Hopped the shy finch, and the huge tortoise crept across the slough.

On the faint wind floated the silky seeds

As the bright scythe swept through the waving grass,

The ouzel-cock splashed circles in the reeds

And flecked with silver whorls the forest's glass,

Which scarce had caught again its imagery

Ere from its bed the dusky tench leapt at the dragon-fly.

But little care had he for any thing

Though up and down the beech the squirrel played,

And from the copse the linnet 'gan to sing

To its brown mate its sweetest serenade;

Ah! little care indeed, for he had seen

The breasts of Pallas and the naked wonder of the Queen.

But when the herdsman called his straggling goats

With whistling pipe across the rocky road,

And the shard-beetle with its trumpet-notes

Boomed through the darkening woods, and seemed to bode

Of coming storm, and the belated crane

Passed homeward like a shadow, and the dull big drops of rain

Fell on the pattering fig-leaves, up he rose,

And from the gloomy forest went his way

Past sombre homestead and wet orchard-close,

And came at last unto a little quay,

And called his mates aboard, and took his seat

On the high poop, and pushed from land, and loosed the dripping sheet,

And steered across the bay, and when nine suns

  Passed down the long and laddered way of gold,

And nine pale moons had breathed their orisons

  To the chaste stars their confessors, or told

Their dearest secret to the downy moth

That will not fly at noonday, through the foam and surging froth

Came a great owl with yellow sulphurous eyes

  And lit upon the ship, whose timbers creaked

As though the lading of three argosies

  Were in the hold, and flapped its wings and shrieked,

And darkness straightway stole across the deep,

Sheathed was Orion's sword, dread Mars himself fled down the steep,

And the moon hid behind a tawny mask

  Of drifting cloud, and from the ocean's marge

Rose the red plume, the huge and hornèd casque,

  The seven-cubit spear, the brazen targe!

And clad in bright and burnished panoply

Athena strode across the stretch of sick and shivering sea!

To the dull sailors' sight her loosened looks
  Seemed like the jagged storm-rack, and her feet
Only the spume that floats on hidden rocks,
  And, marking how the rising waters beat
Against the rolling ship, the pilot cried
To the young helmsman at the stern to luff to windward side

But he, the overbold adulterer,
  A dear profaner of great mysteries,
An ardent amorous idolater,
  When he beheld those grand relentless eyes
Laughed loud for joy, and crying out 'I come'
Leapt from the lofty poop into the chill and churning foam.

Then fell from the high heaven one bright star,
  One dancer left the circling galaxy,
And back to Athens on her clattering car
  In all the pride of venged divinity
Pale Pallas swept with shrill and steely clank,
And a few gurgling bubbles rose where her boy lover sank.

And the mast shuddered as the gaunt owl flew

105

With mocking hoots after the wrathful Queen,

And the old pilot bade the trembling crew

Hoist the big sail, and told how he had seen

Close to the stern a dim and giant form,

And like a dipping swallow the stout ship dashed through the storm.

And no man dared to speak of Charmides

Deeming that he some evil thing had wrought,

And when they reached the strait Symplegades

They beached their galley on the shore, and sought

The toll-gate of the city hastily,

And in the market showed their brown and pictured pottery.

II.

But some good Triton-god had ruth, and bare

The boy's drowned body back to Grecian land,

And mermaids combed his dank and dripping hair

And smoothed his brow, and loosed his clenching hand;

Some brought sweet spices from far Araby,

And others bade the halcyon sing her softest lullaby.

And when he neared his old Athenian home,

A mighty billow rose up suddenly

Upon whose oily back the clotted foam

   Lay diapered in some strange fantasy,

And clasping him unto its glassy breast

Swept landward, like a white-maned steed upon a venturous quest!

Now where Colonos leans unto the sea

   There lies a long and level stretch of lawn;

The rabbit knows it, and the mountain bee

   For it deserts Hymettus, and the Faun

Is not afraid, for never through the day

Comes a cry ruder than the shout of shepherd lads at play.

But often from the thorny labyrinth

   And tangled branches of the circling wood

The stealthy hunter sees young Hyacinth

   Hurling the polished disk, and draws his hood

Over his guilty gaze, and creeps away,

Nor dares to wind his horn, or—else at the first break of day

The Dryads come and throw the leathern ball

   Along the reedy shore, and circumvent

Some goat-eared Pan to be their seneschal

   For fear of bold Poseidon's ravishment,

And loose their girdles, with shy timorous eyes,

Lest from the surf his azure arms and purple beard should rise.

On this side and on that a rocky cave,

   Hung with the yellow-belled laburnum, stands

Smooth is the beach, save where some ebbing wave

   Leaves its faint outline etched upon the sands,

As though it feared to be too soon forgot

By the green rush, its playfellow,—and yet, it is a spot

So small, that the inconstant butterfly

   Could steal the hoarded money from each flower

Ere it was noon, and still not satisfy

   Its over-greedy love,—within an hour

A sailor boy, were he but rude enow

To land and pluck a garland for his galley's painted prow,

Would almost leave the little meadow bare,

   For it knows nothing of great pageantry,

Only a few narcissi here and there

   Stand separate in sweet austerity,

Dotting the unmown grass with silver stars,

And here and there a daffodil waves tiny scimitars.

Hither the billow brought him, and was glad

   Of such dear servitude, and where the land

Was virgin of all waters laid the lad

   Upon the golden margent of the strand,

And like a lingering lover oft returned

To kiss those pallid limbs which once with intense fire burned,

Ere the wet seas had quenched that holocaust,

   That self-fed flame, that passionate lustihead,

Ere grisly death with chill and nipping frost

   Had withered up those lilies white and red

Which, while the boy would through the forest range,

Answered each other in a sweet antiphonal counter-change.

And when at dawn the wood-nymphs, hand-in-hand,

   Threaded the bosky dell, their satyr spied

The boy's pale body stretched upon the sand,

   And feared Poseidon's treachery, and cried,

And like bright sunbeams flitting through a glade

Each startled Dryad sought some safe and leafy ambuscade.

Save one white girl, who deemed it would not be

So dread a thing to feel a sea-god's arms

Crushing her breasts in amorous tyranny,

   And longed to listen to those subtle charms

Insidious lovers weave when they would win

Some fencèd fortress, and stole back again, nor thought it sin

To yield her treasure unto one so fair,

   And lay beside him, thirsty with love's drouth,

Called him soft names, played with his tangled hair,

   And with hot lips made havoc of his mouth

Afraid he might not wake, and then afraid

Lest he might wake too soon, fled back, and then, fond renegade,

Returned to fresh assault, and all day long

   Sat at his side, and laughed at her new toy,

And held his hand, and sang her sweetest song,

   Then frowned to see how froward was the boy

Who would not with her maidenhood entwine,

Nor knew that three days since his eyes had looked on Proserpine;

Nor knew what sacrilege his lips had done,

   But said, 'He will awake, I know him well,

He will awake at evening when the sun

Hangs his red shield on Corinth's citadel;

This sleep is but a cruel treachery

To make me love him more, and in some cavern of the sea

Deeper than ever falls the fisher's line

   Already a huge Triton blows his horn,

And weaves a garland from the crystalline

   And drifting ocean-tendrils to adorn

The emerald pillars of our bridal bed,

For sphered in foaming silver, and with coral crownèd head,

We two will sit upon a throne of pearl,

   And a blue wave will be our canopy,

And at our feet the water-snakes will curl

   In all their amethystine panoply

Of diamonded mail, and we will mark

The mullets swimming by the mast of some storm-foundered bark,

Vermilion-finned with eyes of bossy gold

   Like flakes of crimson light, and the great deep

His glassy-portaled chamber will unfold,

   And we will see the painted dolphins sleep

Cradled by murmuring halcyons on the rocks

Where Proteus in quaint suit of green pastures his monstrous flocks.

And tremulous opal-hued anemones

   Will wave their purple fringes where we tread

Upon the mirrored floor, and argosies

   Of fishes flecked with tawny scales will thread

The drifting cordage of the shattered wreck,

And honey-coloured amber beads our twining limbs will deck.'

But when that baffled Lord of War the Sun

   With gaudy pennon flying passed away

Into his brazen House, and one by one

   The little yellow stars began to stray

Across the field of heaven, ah! then indeed

She feared his lips upon her lips would never care to feed,

And cried, 'Awake, already the pale moon

   Washes the trees with silver, and the wave

Creeps grey and chilly up this sandy dune,

   The croaking frogs are out, and from the cave

The nightjar shrieks, the fluttering bats repass,

And the brown stoat with hollow flanks creeps through the dusky grass.

Nay, though thou art a god, be not so coy,

For in yon stream there is a little reed

That often whispers how a lovely boy

   Lay with her once upon a grassy mead,

Who when his cruel pleasure he had done

Spread wings of rustling gold and soared aloft into the sun.

Be not so coy, the laurel trembles still

   With great Apollo's kisses, and the fir

Whose clustering sisters fringe the seaward hill

   Hath many a tale of that bold ravisher

Whom men call Boreas, and I have seen

The mocking eyes of Hermes through the poplar's silvery sheen.

Even the jealous Naiads call me fair,

   And every morn a young and ruddy swain

Woos me with apples and with locks of hair,

   And seeks to soothe my virginal disdain

By all the gifts the gentle wood-nymphs love;

But yesterday he brought to me an iris-plumaged dove

With little crimson feet, which with its store

   Of seven spotted eggs the cruel lad

Had stolen from the lofty sycamore

113

At daybreak, when her amorous comrade had

Flown off in search of berried juniper

Which most they love; the fretful wasp, that earliest vintager

Of the blue grapes, hath not persistency

   So constant as this simple shepherd-boy

For my poor lips, his joyous purity

   And laughing sunny eyes might well decoy

A Dryad from her oath to Artemis;

For very beautiful is he, his mouth was made to kiss;

His argent forehead, like a rising moon

   Over the dusky hills of meeting brows,

Is crescent shaped, the hot and Tyrian noon

   Leads from the myrtle-grove no goodlier spouse

For Cytheræa, the first silky down

Fringes his blushing cheeks, and his young limbs are strong and brown;

And he is rich, and fat and fleecy herds

   Of bleating sheep upon his meadows lie,

And many an earthen bowl of yellow curds

   Is in his homestead for the thievish fly

To swim and drown in, the pink clover mead

Keeps its sweet store for him, and he can pipe on oaten reed.

And yet I love him not; it was for thee

    I kept my love; I knew that thou would'st come

To rid me of this pallid chastity,

    Thou fairest flower of the flowerless foam

Of all the wide Ægean, brightest star

Of ocean's azure heavens where the mirrored planets are!

I knew that thou would'st come, for when at first

    The dry wood burgeoned, and the sap of spring

Swelled in my green and tender bark or burst

    To myriad multitudinous blossoming

Which mocked the midnight with its mimic moons

That did not dread the dawn, and first the thrushes' rapturous tunes

Startled the squirrel from its granary,

    And cuckoo flowers fringed the narrow lane,

Through my young leaves a sensuous ecstasy

    Crept like new wine, and every mossy vein

Throbbed with the fitful pulse of amorous blood,

And the wild winds of passion shook my slim stem's maidenhood.

The trooping fawns at evening came and laid

Their cool black noses on my lowest boughs,

And on my topmost branch the blackbird made

   A little nest of grasses for his spouse,

And now and then a twittering wren would light

On a thin twig which hardly bare the weight of such delight.

I was the Attic shepherd's trysting place,

   Beneath my shadow Amaryllis lay,

And round my trunk would laughing Daphnis chase

   The timorous girl, till tired out with play

She felt his hot breath stir her tangled hair,

And turned, and looked, and fled no more from such delightful snare.

Then come away unto my ambuscade

   Where clustering woodbine weaves a canopy

For amorous pleasaunce, and the rustling shade

   Of Paphian myrtles seems to sanctify

The dearest rites of love; there in the cool

And green recesses of its farthest depth there is pool,

The ouzel's haunt, the wild bee's pasturage,

   For round its rim great creamy lilies float

Through their flat leaves in verdant anchorage,

Each cup a white-sailed golden-laden boat

Steered by a dragon-fly,—be not afraid

To leave this wan and wave-kissed shore, surely the place was made

For lovers such as we; the Cyprian Queen,

   One arm around her boyish paramour,

Strays often there at eve, and I have seen

   The moon strip off her misty vestiture

For young Endymion's eyes; be not afraid,

The panther feet of Dian never tread that secret glade.

Nay if thou will'st, back to the beating brine,

   Back to the boisterous billow let us go,

And walk all day beneath the hyaline

   Huge vault of Neptune's watery portico,

And watch the purple monsters of the deep

Sport in ungainly play, and from his lair keen Xiphias leap.

For if my mistress find me lying here

   She will not ruth or gentle pity show,

But lay her boar-spear down, and with austere

   Relentless fingers string the cornel bow,

And draw the feathered notch against her breast,

117

And loose the archèd cord; aye, even now upon the quest

I hear her hurrying feet,—awake, awake,

   Thou laggard in love's battle! once at least

Let me drink deep of passion's wine, and slake

   My parchèd being with the nectarous feast

Which even gods affect! O come, Love, come,

Still we have time to reach the cavern of thine azure home.'

Scarce had she spoken when the shuddering trees

   Shook, and the leaves divided, and the air

Grew conscious of a god, and the grey seas

   Crawled backward, and a long and dismal blare

Blew from some tasselled horn, a sleuth-hound bayed,

And like a flame a barbèd reed flew whizzing down the glade.

And where the little flowers of her breast

   Just brake into their milky blossoming,

This murderous paramour, this unbidden guest,

   Pierced and struck deep in horrid chambering,

And ploughed a bloody furrow with its dart,

And dug a long red road, and cleft with wingèd death her heart.

Sobbing her life out with a bitter cry

On the boy's body fell the Dryad maid,

Sobbing for incomplete virginity,

   And raptures unenjoyed, and pleasures dead,

And all the pain of things unsatisfied,

And the bright drops of crimson youth crept down her throbbing side.

Ah! pitiful it was to hear her moan,

   And very pitiful to see her die

Ere she had yielded up her sweets, or known

   The joy of passion, that dread mystery

Which not to know is not to live at all,

And yet to know is to be held in death's most deadly thrall.

But as it hapt the Queen of Cythere,

   Who with Adonis all night long had lain

Within some shepherd's hut in Arcady,

   On team of silver doves and gilded wain

Was journeying Paphos-ward, high up afar

From mortal ken between the mountains and the morning star,

And when low down she spied the hapless pair,

   And heard the Oread's faint despairing cry,

Whose cadence seemed to play upon the air

As though it were a viol, hastily

She bade her pigeons fold each straining plume,

And dropt to earth, and reached the strand, and saw their dolorous
doom.

For as a gardener turning back his head

   To catch the last notes of the linnet, mows

With careless scythe too near some flower bed,

   And cuts the thorny pillar of the rose,

And with the flower's loosened loneliness

Strews the brown mould; or as some shepherd lad in wantonness

Driving his little flock along the mead

   Treads down two daffodils, which side by aide

Have lured the lady-bird with yellow brede

   And made the gaudy moth forget its pride,

Treads down their brimming golden chalices

Under light feet which were not made for such rude ravages;

Or as a schoolboy tired of his book

   Flings himself down upon the reedy grass

And plucks two water-lilies from the brook,

   And for a time forgets the hour glass,

Then wearies of their sweets, and goes his way,

And lets the hot sun kill them, even go these lovers lay.

And Venus cried, 'It is dread Artemis
   Whose bitter hand hath wrought this cruelty,
Or else that mightier maid whose care it is
   To guard her strong and stainless majesty
Upon the hill Athenian,—alas!
That they who loved so well unloved into Death's house should pass.'

So with soft hands she laid the boy and girl
   In the great golden waggon tenderly
(Her white throat whiter than a moony pearl
   Just threaded with a blue vein's tapestry
Had not yet ceased to throb, and still her breast
Swayed like a wind-stirred lily in ambiguous unrest)

And then each pigeon spread its milky van,
   The bright car soared into the dawning sky,
And like a cloud the aerial caravan
   Passed over the Ægean silently,
Till the faint air was troubled with the song
From the wan mouths that call on bleeding Thammuz all night long.

But when the doves had reached their wonted goal

Where the wide stair of orbèd marble dips

Its snows into the sea, her fluttering soul

　Just shook the trembling petals of her lips

And passed into the void, and Venus knew

That one fair maid the less would walk amid her retinue,

And bade her servants carve a cedar chest

　With all the wonder of this history,

Within whose scented womb their limbs should rest

　Where olive-trees make tender the blue sky

On the low hills of Paphos, and the Faun

Pipes in the noonday, and the nightingale sings on till dawn.

Nor failed they to obey her hest, and ere

　The morning bee had stung the daffodil

With tiny fretful spear, or from its lair

　The waking stag had leapt across the rill

And roused the ouzel, or the lizard crept

Athwart the sunny rock, beneath the grass their bodies slept.

And when day brake, within that silver shrine

　Fed by the flames of cressets tremulous,

Queen Venus knelt and prayed to Proserpine

That she whose beauty made Death amorous

Should beg a guerdon from her pallid Lord,

And let Desire pass across dread Charon's icy ford.

III

In melancholy moonless Acheron,

   Farm for the goodly earth and joyous day

Where no spring ever buds, nor ripening sun

   Weighs down the apple trees, nor flowery May

Chequers with chestnut blooms the grassy floor,

Where thrushes never sing, and piping linnets mate no more,

There by a dim and dark Lethæan well

   Young Charmides was lying; wearily

He plucked the blossoms from the asphodel,

   And with its little rifled treasury

Strewed the dull waters of the dusky stream,

And watched the white stars founder, and the land was like a dream,

When as he gazed into the watery glass

   And through his brown hair's curly tangles scanned

His own wan face, a shadow seemed to pass

   Across the mirror, and a little hand

123

Stole into his, and warm lips timidly

Brushed his pale cheeks, and breathed their secret forth into a sigh.

Then turned he round his weary eyes and saw,

And ever nigher still their faces came,

And nigher ever did their young mouths draw

Until they seemed one perfect rose of flame,

And longing arms around her neck he cast,

And felt her throbbing bosom, and his breath came hot and fast,

And all his hoarded sweets were hers to kiss,

And all her maidenhood was his to slay,

And limb to limb in long and rapturous bliss

Their passion waxed and waned,—O why essay

To pipe again of love, too venturous reed!

Enough, enough that Eros laughed upon that flowerless mead.

Too venturous poesy, O why essay

To pipe again of passion! fold thy wings

O'er daring Icarus and bid thy lay

Sleep hidden in the lyre's silent strings

Till thou hast found the old Castalian rill,

Or from the Lesbian waters plucked drowned Sappho's golden quid!

Enough, enough that he whose life had been

   A fiery pulse of sin, a splendid shame,

Could in the loveless land of Hades glean

   One scorching harvest from those fields of flame

Where passion walks with naked unshod feet

And is not wounded,—ah! enough that once their lips could meet

In that wild throb when all existences

   Seemed narrowed to one single ecstasy

Which dies through its own sweetness and the stress

   Of too much pleasure, ere Persephone

Had bade them serve her by the ebon throne

Of the pale God who in the fields of Enna loosed her zone.

FLOWERS OF GOLD

IMPRESSIONS

I

LES SILHOUETTES

The sea is flecked with bars of grey,
The dull dead wind is out of tune,
And like a withered leaf the moon
Is blown across the stormy bay.

Etched clear upon the pallid sand
Lies the black boat: a sailor boy
Clambers aboard in careless joy
With laughing face and gleaming hand.

And overhead the curlews cry,
Where through the dusky upland grass
The young brown-throated reapers pass,
Like silhouettes against the sky.

II

LA FUITE DE LA LUNE

To outer senses there is peace,

A dreamy peace on either hand

Deep silence in the shadowy land,

Deep silence where the shadows cease.

Save for a cry that echoes shrill

From some lone bird disconsolate;

A corncrake calling to its mate;

The answer from the misty hill.

And suddenly the moon withdraws

Her sickle from the lightening skies,

And to her sombre cavern flies,

Wrapped in a veil of yellow gauze.

THE GRAVE OF KEATS

Rid of the world's injustice, and his pain,

He rests at last beneath God's veil of blue:

Taken from life when life and love were new

The youngest of the martyrs here is lain,

Fair as Sebastian, and as early slain.

No cypress shades his grave, no funeral yew,

But gentle violets weeping with the dew

Weave on his bones an ever-blossoming chain.

O proudest heart that broke for misery!

O sweetest lips since those of Mitylene!

O poet-painter of our English Land!

Thy name was writ in water—it shall stand:

And tears like mine will keep thy memory green,

As Isabella did her Basil-tree.

Rome.

THEOCRITUS: A VILLANELLE

O singer of Persephone!

In the dim meadows desolate

Dost thou remember Sicily?

Still through the ivy flits the bee

Where Amaryllis lies in state;

O Singer of Persephone!

Simætha calls on Hecate

And hears the wild dogs at the gate;

Dost thou remember Sicily?

Still by the light and laughing sea

Poor Polypheme bemoans his fate;

O Singer of Persephone!

And still in boyish rivalry
   Young Daphnis challenges his mate;
Dost thou remember Sicily?

Slim Lacon keeps a goat for thee,
   For thee the jocund shepherds wait;
O Singer of Persephone!
Dost thou remember Sicily?

IN THE GOLD ROOM: A HARMONY

Her ivory hands on the ivory keys
   Strayed in a fitful fantasy,
Like the silver gleam when the poplar trees
   Rustle their pale-leaves listlessly,
Or the drifting foam of a restless sea
When the waves show their teeth in the flying breeze.

Her gold hair fell on the wall of gold
   Like the delicate gossamer tangles spun
On the burnished disk of the marigold,
   Or the sunflower turning to meet the sun

129

When the gloom of the dark blue night is done,

And the spear of the lily is aureoled.

And her sweet red lips on these lips of mine

   Burned like the ruby fire set

In the swinging lamp of a crimson shrine,

   Or the bleeding wounds of the pomegranate,

   Or the heart of the lotus drenched and wet

With the spilt-out blood of the rose-red wine.

BALLADE DE MARGUERITE

(NORMANDE)

I am weary of lying within the chase

When the knights are meeting in market-place.

Nay, go not thou to the red-roofed town

Lest the hoofs of the war-horse tread thee down.

But I would not go where the Squires ride,

I would only walk by my Lady's side.

Alack! and alack! thou art overbold,

A Forester's son may not eat off gold.

Will she love me the less that my Father is seen

Each Martinmas day in a doublet green?

Perchance she is sewing at tapestrie,

Spindle and loom are not meet for thee.

Ah, if she is working the arras bright

I might ravel the threads by the fire-light.

Perchance she is hunting of the deer,

How could you follow o'er hill and mere?

Ah, if she is riding with the court,

I might run beside her and wind the morte.

Perchance she is kneeling in St. Denys,

(On her soul may our Lady have gramercy!)

Ah, if she is praying in lone chapelle,

I might swing the censer and ring the bell.

Come in, my son, for you look sae pale,

The father shall fill thee a stoup of ale.

But who are these knights in bright array?
Is it a pageant the rich folks play?

'T is the King of England from over sea,
Who has come unto visit our fair countrie.

But why does the curfew toll sae low?
And why do the mourners walk a-row?

O 't is Hugh of Amiens my sister's son
Who is lying stark, for his day is done.

Nay, nay, for I see white lilies clear,
It is no strong man who lies on the bier.

O 't is old Dame Jeannette that kept the hall,
I knew she would die at the autumn fall.

Dame Jeannette had not that gold-brown hair,
Old Jeannette was not a maiden fair.

O 't is none of our kith and none of our kin,

(Her soul may our Lady assoil from sin!)

But I hear the boy's voice chaunting sweet,
'Elle est morte, la Marguerite.'

Come in, my son, and lie on the bed,
And let the dead folk bury their dead.

O mother, you know I loved her true:
O mother, hath one grave room for two?

THE DOLE OF THE KING'S DAUGHTER
(BRETON)

Seven stars in the still water,
  And seven in the sky;
Seven sins on the King's daughter,
  Deep in her soul to lie.

Red roses are at her feet,
  (Roses are red in her red-gold hair)
And O where her bosom and girdle meet
  Red roses are hidden there.

Fair is the knight who lieth slain

Amid the rush and reed,

See the lean fishes that are fain

Upon dead men to feed.

Sweet is the page that lieth there,

(Cloth of gold is goodly prey,)

See the black ravens in the air,

Black, O black as the night are they.

What do they there so stark and dead?

(There is blood upon her hand)

Why are the lilies flecked with red?

(There is blood on the river sand.)

There are two that ride from the south and east,

And two from the north and west,

For the black raven a goodly feast,

For the King's daughter rest.

There is one man who loves her true,

(Red, O red, is the stain of gore!)

He hath duggen a grave by the darksome yew,

(One grave will do for four.)

No moon in the still heaven,

  In the black water none,

The sins on her soul are seven,

  The sin upon his is one.

AMOR INTELLECTUALIS

Oft have we trod the vales of Castaly

  And heard sweet notes of sylvan music blown

  From antique reeds to common folk unknown:

And often launched our bark upon that sea

Which the nine Muses hold in empery,

  And ploughed free furrows through the wave and foam,

  Nor spread reluctant sail for more safe home

Till we had freighted well our argosy.

Of which despoilèd treasures these remain,

  Sordello's passion, and the honeyed line

Of young Endymion, lordly Tamburlaine

  Driving his pampered jades, and more than these,

The seven-fold vision of the Florentine,

  And grave-browed Milton's solemn harmonies.

SANTA DECCA

The Gods are dead: no longer do we bring

To grey-eyed Pallas crowns of olive-leaves!

Demeter's child no more hath tithe of sheaves,

And in the noon the careless shepherds sing,

For Pan is dead, and all the wantoning

By secret glade and devious haunt is o'er:

Young Hylas seeks the water-springs no more;

Great Pan is dead, and Mary's son is King.

And yet—perchance in this sea-trancèd isle,

Chewing the bitter fruit of memory,

Some God lies hidden in the asphodel.

Ah Love! if such there be, then it were well

For us to fly his anger: nay, but see,

The leaves are stirring: let us watch awhile.

CORFU.

A VISION

Two crownèd Kings, and One that stood alone

With no green weight of laurels round his head,

But with sad eyes as one uncomforted,

And wearied with man's never-ceasing moan

For sins no bleating victim can atone,

And sweet long lips with tears and kisses fed.

Girt was he in a garment black and red,

And at his feet I marked a broken stone

Which sent up lilies, dove-like, to his knees.

Now at their sight, my heart being lit with flame,

I cried to Beatricé, 'Who are these?'

And she made answer, knowing well each name,

'Æschylos first, the second Sophokles,

And last (wide stream of tears!) Euripides.'

IMPRESSION DE VOYAGE

The sea was sapphire coloured, and the sky

Burned like a heated opal through the air;

We hoisted sail; the wind was blowing fair

For the blue lands that to the eastward lie.

From the steep prow I marked with quickening eye

Zakynthos, every olive grove and creek,

Ithaca's cliff, Lycaon's snowy peak,

And all the flower-strewn hills of Arcady.

The flapping of the sail against the mast,

The ripple of the water on the side,

The ripple of girls' laughter at the stern,

The only sounds:—when 'gan the West to burn,

And a red sun upon the seas to ride,

I stood upon the soil of Greece at last!

Katakolo.

THE GRAVE OF SHELLEY

Like burnt-out torches by a sick man's bed

    Gaunt cypress-trees stand round the sun-bleached stone;

    Here doth the little night-owl make her throne,

And the slight lizard show his jewelled head.

And, where the chaliced poppies flame to red,

    In the still chamber of yon pyramid

    Surely some Old-World Sphinx lurks darkly hid,

Grim warder of this pleasaunce of the dead.

Ah! sweet indeed to rest within the womb

    Of Earth, great mother of eternal sleep,

But sweeter far for thee a restless tomb

    In the blue cavern of an echoing deep,

Or where the tall ships founder in the gloom

    Against the rocks of some wave-shattered steep.

Rome.

BY THE ARNO

The oleander on the wall

Grows crimson in the dawning light,

Though the grey shadows of the night

Lie yet on Florence like a pall.

The dew is bright upon the hill,

And bright the blossoms overhead,

But ah! the grasshoppers have fled,

The little Attic song is still.

Only the leaves are gently stirred

By the soft breathing of the gale,

And in the almond-scented vale

The lonely nightingale is heard.

The day will make thee silent soon,

O nightingale sing on for love!

While yet upon the shadowy grove

Splinter the arrows of the moon.

Before across the silent lawn

In sea-green vest the morning steals,

And to love's frightened eyes reveals

The long white fingers of the dawn

Fast climbing up the eastern sky

To grasp and slay the shuddering night,

All careless of my heart's delight,

Or if the nightingale should die.

IMPRESSIONS DE THÉÂTRE

FABIEN DEI FRANCHI

To my Friend Henry Irving

The silent room, the heavy creeping shade,
　The dead that travel fast, the opening door,
　The murdered brother rising through the floor,
The ghost's white fingers on thy shoulders laid,
And then the lonely duel in the glade,
　The broken swords, the stifled scream, the gore,
　Thy grand revengeful eyes when all is o'er,—
These things are well enough,—but thou wert made
　For more august creation! frenzied Lear
　Should at thy bidding wander on the heath
　With the shrill fool to mock him, Romeo
For thee should lure his love, and desperate fear
Pluck Richard's recreant dagger from its sheath—
Thou trumpet set for Shakespeare's lips to blow!

PHÈDRE

To Sarah Bernhardt

How vain and dull this common world must seem

    To such a One as thou, who should'st have talked

At Florence with Mirandola, or walked

Through the cool olives of the Academe:

Thou should'st have gathered reeds from a green stream

    For Goat-foot Pan's shrill piping, and have played

    With the white girls in that Phæacian glade

Where grave Odysseus wakened from his dream.

Ah! surely once some urn of Attic clay

    Held thy wan dust, and thou hast come again

    Back to this common world so dull and vain,

For thou wert weary of the sunless day,

    The heavy fields of scentless asphodel,

    The loveless lips with which men kiss in Hell.

SONNETS WRITTEN AT THE LYCEUM THEATRE

I. PORTIA

To Ellen Terry

I marvel not Bassanio was so bold

    To peril all he had upon the lead,

Or that proud Aragon bent low his head

Or that Morocco's fiery heart grew cold:

For in that gorgeous dress of beaten gold

    Which is more golden than the golden sun

    No woman Veronesé looked upon

Was half so fair as thou whom I behold.

Yet fairer when with wisdom as your shield

    The sober-suited lawyer's gown you donned,

And would not let the laws of Venice yield

    Antonio's heart to that accursèd Jew—

    O Portia! take my heart: it is thy due:

I think I will not quarrel with the Bond.

II. QUEEN HENRIETTA MARIA

To Ellen Terry

In the lone tent, waiting for victory,

    She stands with eyes marred by the mists of pain,

    Like some wan lily overdrenched with rain:

The clamorous clang of arms, the ensanguined sky,

War's ruin, and the wreck of chivalry

    To her proud soul no common fear can bring:

    Bravely she tarrieth for her Lord the King,

Her soul a-flame with passionate ecstasy.

O Hair of Gold! O Crimson Lips! O Face

Made for the luring and the love of man!

With thee I do forget the toil and stress,

The loveless road that knows no resting place,

Time's straitened pulse, the soul's dread weariness,

My freedom, and my life republican!

III. CAMMA

To Ellen Terry

As one who poring on a Grecian urn

Scans the fair shapes some Attic hand hath made,

God with slim goddess, goodly man with maid,

And for their beauty's sake is loth to turn

And face the obvious day, must I not yearn

For many a secret moon of indolent bliss,

When in midmost shrine of Artemis

I see thee standing, antique-limbed, and stern?

And yet—methinks I'd rather see thee play

That serpent of old Nile, whose witchery

Made Emperors drunken,—come, great Egypt, shake

Our stage with all thy mimic pageants! Nay,

I am grown sick of unreal passions, make

The world thine Actium, me thine Anthony!

PANTHEA

Nay, let us walk from fire unto fire,
  From passionate pain to deadlier delight,—
I am too young to live without desire,
  Too young art thou to waste this summer night
Asking those idle questions which of old
Man sought of seer and oracle, and no reply was told.

For, sweet, to feel is better than to know,
  And wisdom is a childless heritage,
One pulse of passion—youth's first fiery glow,—
  Are worth the hoarded proverbs of the sage:
Vex not thy soul with dead philosophy,
Have we not lips to kiss with, hearts to love and eyes to see!

Dost thou not hear the murmuring nightingale,
  Like water bubbling from a silver jar,
So soft she sings the envious moon is pale,
  That high in heaven she is hung so far
She cannot hear that love-enraptured tune,—
  Mark how she wreathes each horn with mist, yon late and labouring
moon.

White lilies, in whose cups the gold bees dream,

   The fallen snow of petals where the breeze

Scatters the chestnut blossom, or the gleam

   Of boyish limbs in water,—are not these

Enough for thee, dost thou desire more?

Alas! the Gods will give nought else from their eternal store.

For our high Gods have sick and wearied grown

   Of all our endless sins, our vain endeavour

For wasted days of youth to make atone

   By pain or prayer or priest, and never, never,

Hearken they now to either good or ill,

But send their rain upon the just and the unjust at will.

They sit at ease, our Gods they sit at ease,

   Strewing with leaves of rose their scented wine,

They sleep, they sleep, beneath the rocking trees

   Where asphodel and yellow lotus twine,

Mourning the old glad days before they knew

What evil things the heart of man could dream, and dreaming do.

And far beneath the brazen floor they see

147

Like swarming flies the crowd of little men,

The bustle of small lives, then wearily

  Back to their lotus-haunts they turn again

Kissing each others' mouths, and mix more deep

The poppy-seeded draught which brings soft purple-lidded sleep.

There all day long the golden-vestured sun,

  Their torch-bearer, stands with his torch ablaze,

And, when the gaudy web of noon is spun

  By its twelve maidens, through the crimson haze

Fresh from Endymion's arms comes forth the moon,

And the immortal Gods in toils of mortal passions swoon.

There walks Queen Juno through some dewy mead,

  Her grand white feet flecked with the saffron dust

Of wind-stirred lilies, while young Ganymede

  Leaps in the hot and amber-foaming must,

His curls all tossed, as when the eagle bare

The frightened boy from Ida through the blue Ionian air.

There in the green heart of some garden close

  Queen Venus with the shepherd at her side,

Her warm soft body like the briar rose

Which would be white yet blushes at its pride,

Laughs low for love, till jealous Salmacis

Peers through the myrtle-leaves and sighs for pain of lonely bliss.

There never does that dreary north-wind blow

    Which leaves our English forests bleak and bare,

Nor ever falls the swift white-feathered snow,

    Nor ever doth the red-toothed lightning dare

To wake them in the silver-fretted night

When we lie weeping for some sweet sad sin, some dead delight.

Alas! they know the far Lethæan spring,

    The violet-hidden waters well they know,

Where one whose feet with tired wandering

    Are faint and broken may take heart and go,

And from those dark depths cool and crystalline

Drink, and draw balm, and sleep for sleepless souls, and anodyne.

But we oppress our natures, God or Fate

    Is our enemy, we starve and feed

On vain repentance—O we are born too late!

    What balm for us in bruisèd poppy seed

Who crowd into one finite pulse of time

The joy of infinite love and the fierce pain of infinite crime.

O we are wearied of this sense of guilt,

   Wearied of pleasure's paramour despair,

Wearied of every temple we have built,

   Wearied of every right, unanswered prayer,

For man is weak; God sleeps: and heaven is high:

One fiery-coloured moment: one great love; and lo! we die.

Ah! but no ferry-man with labouring pole

   Nears his black shallop to the flowerless strand,

No little coin of bronze can bring the soul

   Over Death's river to the sunless land,

Victim and wine and vow are all in vain,

The tomb is sealed; the soldiers watch; the dead rise not again.

We are resolved into the supreme air,

   We are made one with what we touch and see,

With our heart's blood each crimson sun is fair,

   With our young lives each spring-impassioned tree

Flames into green, the wildest beasts that range

The moor our kinsmen are, all life is one, and all is change.

With beat of systole and of diastole

One grand great life throbs through earth's giant heart,

And mighty waves of single Being roll

From nerveless germ to man, for we are part

Of every rock and bird and beast and hill,

One with the things that prey on us, and one with what we kill.

From lower cells of waking life we pass

To full perfection; thus the world grows old:

We who are godlike now were once a mass

Of quivering purple flecked with bars of gold,

Unsentient or of joy or misery,

And tossed in terrible tangles of some wild and wind-swept sea.

This hot hard flame with which our bodies burn

Will make some meadow blaze with daffodil,

Ay! and those argent breasts of thine will turn

To water-lilies; the brown fields men till

Will be more fruitful for our love to-night,

Nothing is lost in nature, all things live in Death's despite.

The boy's first kiss, the hyacinth's first bell,

The man's last passion, and the last red spear

That from the lily leaps, the asphodel

Which will not let its blossoms blow for fear

Of too much beauty, and the timid shame

Of the young bridegroom at his lover's eyes,—these with the same

One sacrament are consecrate, the earth

  Not we alone hath passions hymeneal,

The yellow buttercups that shake for mirth

  At daybreak know a pleasure not less real

Than we do, when in some fresh-blossoming wood,

We draw the spring into our hearts, and feel that life is good.

So when men bury us beneath the yew

  Thy crimson-stainèd mouth a rose will be,

And thy soft eyes lush bluebells dimmed with dew,

  And when the white narcissus wantonly

Kisses the wind its playmate some faint joy

Will thrill our dust, and we will be again fond maid and boy.

And thus without life's conscious torturing pain

  In some sweet flower we will feel the sun,

And from the linnet's throat will sing again,

  And as two gorgeous-mailèd snakes will run

Over our graves, or as two tigers creep

Through the hot jungle where the yellow-eyed huge lions sleep

And give them battle! How my heart leaps up
   To think of that grand living after death
In beast and bird and flower, when this cup,
   Being filled too full of spirit, bursts for breath,
And with the pale leaves of some autumn day
The soul earth's earliest conqueror becomes earth's last great prey.

O think of it! We shall inform ourselves
   Into all sensuous life, the goat-foot Faun,
The Centaur, or the merry bright-eyed Elves
   That leave their dancing rings to spite the dawn
Upon the meadows, shall not be more near
Than you and I to nature's mysteries, for we shall hear

The thrush's heart beat, and the daisies grow,
   And the wan snowdrop sighing for the sun
On sunless days in winter, we shall know
   By whom the silver gossamer is spun,
Who paints the diapered fritillaries,
On what wide wings from shivering pine to pine the eagle flies.

Ay! had we never loved at all, who knows

If yonder daffodil had lured the bee

Into its gilded womb, or any rose

   Had hung with crimson lamps its little tree!

Methinks no leaf would ever bud in spring,

But for the lovers' lips that kiss, the poets' lips that sing.

Is the light vanished from our golden sun,

   Or is this dædal-fashioned earth less fair,

That we are nature's heritors, and one

   With every pulse of life that beats the air?

Rather new suns across the sky shall pass,

New splendour come unto the flower, new glory to the grass.

And we two lovers shall not sit afar,

   Critics of nature, but the joyous sea

Shall be our raiment, and the bearded star

   Shoot arrows at our pleasure! We shall be

Part of the mighty universal whole,

And through all æons mix and mingle with the Kosmic Soul!

We shall be notes in that great Symphony

   Whose cadence circles through the rhythmic spheres,

And all the live World's throbbing heart shall be

One with our heart; the stealthy creeping years

Have lost their terrors now, we shall not die,

The Universe itself shall be our Immortality.

THE FOURTH MOVEMENT

IMPRESSION: LE RÉVEILLON

The sky is laced with fitful red,
The circling mists and shadows flee,
The dawn is rising from the sea,
Like a white lady from her bed.

And jagged brazen arrows fall
Athwart the feathers of the night,
And a long wave of yellow light
Breaks silently on tower and hall,

And spreading wide across the wold
Wakes into flight some fluttering bird,
And all the chestnut tops are stirred,
And all the branches streaked with gold.

AT VERONA

How steep the stairs within Kings' houses are
For exile-wearied feet as mine to tread,

And O how salt and bitter is the bread

Which falls from this Hound's table,—better far

That I had died in the red ways of war,

    Or that the gate of Florence bare my head,

    Than to live thus, by all things comraded

Which seek the essence of my soul to mar.

'Curse God and die: what better hope than this?

    He hath forgotten thee in all the bliss

    Of his gold city, and eternal day'—

Nay peace: behind my prison's blinded bars

    I do possess what none can take away

    My love, and all the glory of the stars.

APOLOGIA

Is it thy will that I should wax and wane,

    Barter my cloth of gold for hodden grey,

And at thy pleasure weave that web of pain

    Whose brightest threads are each a wasted day?

Is it thy will—Love that I love so well—

    That my Soul's House should be a tortured spot

Wherein, like evil paramours, must dwell

    The quenchless flame, the worm that dieth not?

157

Nay, if it be thy will I shall endure,

   And sell ambition at the common mart,

And let dull failure be my vesture,

   And sorrow dig its grave within my heart.

Perchance it may be better so—at least

   I have not made my heart a heart of stone,

Nor starved my boyhood of its goodly feast,

   Nor walked where Beauty is a thing unknown.

Many a man hath done so; sought to fence

   In straitened bonds the soul that should be free,

Trodden the dusty road of common sense,

   While all the forest sang of liberty,

Not marking how the spotted hawk in flight

   Passed on wide pinion through the lofty air,

To where some steep untrodden mountain height

   Caught the last tresses of the Sun God's hair.

Or how the little flower he trod upon,

   The daisy, that white-feathered shield of gold,

Followed with wistful eyes the wandering sun

    Content if once its leaves were aureoled.

But surely it is something to have been

    The best belovèd for a little while,

To have walked hand in hand with Love, and seen

    His purple wings flit once across thy smile.

Ay! though the gorgèd asp of passion feed

    On my boy's heart, yet have I burst the bars,

Stood face to face with Beauty, known indeed

    The Love which moves the Sun and all the stars!

QUIA MULTUM AMAVI

Dear Heart, I think the young impassioned priest

    When first he takes from out the hidden shrine

His God imprisoned in the Eucharist,

    And eats the bread, and drinks the dreadful wine,

Feels not such awful wonder as I felt

    When first my smitten eyes beat full on thee,

And all night long before thy feet I knelt

    Till thou wert wearied of Idolatry.

Ah! hadst thou liked me less and loved me more,

    Through all those summer days of joy and rain,

I had not now been sorrow's heritor,

    Or stood a lackey in the House of Pain.

Yet, though remorse, youth's white-faced seneschal,

    Tread on my heels with all his retinue,

I am most glad I loved thee—think of all

    The suns that go to make one speedwell blue!

SILENTIUM AMORIS

As often-times the too resplendent sun

    Hurries the pallid and reluctant moon

Back to her sombre cave, ere she hath won

    A single ballad from the nightingale,

    So doth thy Beauty make my lips to fail,

And all my sweetest singing out of tune.

And as at dawn across the level mead

    On wings impetuous some wind will come,

And with its too harsh kisses break the reed

    Which was its only instrument of song,

    So my too stormy passions work me wrong,

And for excess of Love my Love is dumb.

But surely unto Thee mine eyes did show

    Why I am silent, and my lute unstrung;

Else it were better we should part, and go,

    Thou to some lips of sweeter melody,

    And I to nurse the barren memory

Of unkissed kisses, and songs never sung.

HER VOICE

The wild bee reels from bough to bough

    With his furry coat and his gauzy wing,

Now in a lily-cup, and now

    Setting a jacinth bell a-swing,

      In his wandering;

Sit closer love: it was here I trow

      I made that vow,

Swore that two lives should be like one

    As long as the sea-gull loved the sea,

As long as the sunflower sought the sun,—

    It shall be, I said, for eternity

      'Twixt you and me!

Dear friend, those times are over and done;

Love's web is spun.

Look upward where the poplar trees

Sway and sway in the summer air,

Here in the valley never a breeze

Scatters the thistledown, but there

Great winds blow fair

From the mighty murmuring mystical seas,

And the wave-lashed leas.

Look upward where the white gull screams,

What does it see that we do not see?

Is that a star? or the lamp that gleams

On some outward voyaging argosy,—

Ah! can it be

We have lived our lives in a land of dreams!

How sad it seems.

Sweet, there is nothing left to say

But this, that love is never lost,

Keen winter stabs the breasts of May

Whose crimson roses burst his frost,

Ships tempest-tossed

Will find a harbour in some bay,

     And so we may.

And there is nothing left to do

  But to kiss once again, and part,

Nay, there is nothing we should rue,

  I have my beauty,—you your Art,

     Nay, do not start,

One world was not enough for two

     Like me and you.

MY VOICE

Within this restless, hurried, modern world

  We took our hearts' full pleasure—You and I,

And now the white sails of our ship are furled,

  And spent the lading of our argosy.

Wherefore my cheeks before their time are wan,

  For very weeping is my gladness fled,

Sorrow has paled my young mouth's vermilion,

  And Ruin draws the curtains of my bed.

But all this crowded life has been to thee

  No more than lyre, or lute, or subtle spell

163

Of viols, or the music of the sea

   That sleeps, a mimic echo, in the shell.

TÆDIUM VITÆ

To stab my youth with desperate knives, to wear

This paltry age's gaudy livery,

To let each base hand filch my treasury,

To mesh my soul within a woman's hair,

And be mere Fortune's lackeyed groom,—I swear

I love it not! these things are less to me

Than the thin foam that frets upon the sea,

Less than the thistledown of summer air

Which hath no seed: better to stand aloof

Far from these slanderous fools who mock my life

Knowing me not, better the lowliest roof

Fit for the meanest hind to sojourn in,

Than to go back to that hoarse cave of strife

Where my white soul first kissed the mouth of sin.

HUMANITAD

It is full winter now: the trees are bare,

   Save where the cattle huddle from the cold

Beneath the pine, for it doth never wear

   The autumn's gaudy livery whose gold

Her jealous brother pilfers, but is true

To the green doublet; bitter is the wind, as though it blew

From Saturn's cave; a few thin wisps of hay

   Lie on the sharp black hedges, where the wain

Dragged the sweet pillage of a summer's day

   From the low meadows up the narrow lane;

Upon the half-thawed snow the bleating sheep

Press close against the hurdles, and the shivering house-dogs creep

From the shut stable to the frozen stream

   And back again disconsolate, and miss

The bawling shepherds and the noisy team;

   And overhead in circling listlessness

The cawing rooks whirl round the frosted stack,

Or crowd the dripping boughs; and in the fen the ice-pools crack

Where the gaunt bittern stalks among the reeds

And flaps his wings, and stretches back his neck,

And hoots to see the moon; across the meads

Limps the poor frightened hare, a little speck;

And a stray seamew with its fretful cry

Flits like a sudden drift of snow against the dull grey sky.

Full winter: and the lusty goodman brings

His load of faggots from the chilly byre,

And stamps his feet upon the hearth, and flings

The sappy billets on the waning fire,

And laughs to see the sudden lightening scare

His children at their play, and yet,—the spring is in the air;

Already the slim crocus stirs the snow,

And soon yon blanchèd fields will bloom again

With nodding cowslips for some lad to mow,

For with the first warm kisses of the rain

The winter's icy sorrow breaks to tears,

And the brown thrushes mate, and with bright eyes the rabbit peers

From the dark warren where the fir-cones lie,

And treads one snowdrop under foot, and runs

Over the mossy knoll, and blackbirds fly

Across our path at evening, and the suns

Stay longer with us; ah! how good to see

Grass-girdled spring in all her joy of laughing greenery

Dance through the hedges till the early rose,

   (That sweet repentance of the thorny briar!)

Burst from its sheathèd emerald and disclose

   The little quivering disk of golden fire

Which the bees know so well, for with it come

Pale boy's-love, sops-in-wine, and daffadillies all in bloom.

Then up and down the field the sower goes,

   While close behind the laughing younker scares

With shrilly whoop the black and thievish crows,

   And then the chestnut-tree its glory wears,

And on the grass the creamy blossom falls

In odorous excess, and faint half-whispered madrigals

Steal from the bluebells' nodding carillons

   Each breezy morn, and then white jessamine,

That star of its own heaven, snap-dragons

   With lolling crimson tongues, and eglantine

In dusty velvets clad usurp the bed

And woodland empery, and when the lingering rose hath shed

Red leaf by leaf its folded panoply,
  And pansies closed their purple-lidded eyes,
Chrysanthemums from gilded argosy
  Unload their gaudy scentless merchandise,
And violets getting overbold withdraw
From their shy nooks, and scarlet berries dot the leafless haw.

O happy field! and O thrice happy tree!
  Soon will your queen in daisy-flowered smock
And crown of flower-de-luce trip down the lea,
  Soon will the lazy shepherds drive their flock
Back to the pasture by the pool, and soon
Through the green leaves will float the hum of murmuring bees at noon.

Soon will the glade be bright with bellamour,
  The flower which wantons love, and those sweet nuns
Vale-lilies in their snowy vestiture
  Will tell their beaded pearls, and carnations
With mitred dusky leaves will scent the wind,
And straggling traveller's-joy each hedge with yellow stars will bind.

Dear bride of Nature and most bounteous spring,

That canst give increase to the sweet-breath'd kine,

And to the kid its little horns, and bring

The soft and silky blossoms to the vine,

Where is that old nepenthe which of yore

Man got from poppy root and glossy-berried mandragore!

There was a time when any common bird

Could make me sing in unison, a time

When all the strings of boyish life were stirred

To quick response or more melodious rhyme

By every forest idyll;—do I change?

Or rather doth some evil thing through thy fair pleasaunce range?

Nay, nay, thou art the same: 'tis I who seek

To vex with sighs thy simple solitude,

And because fruitless tears bedew my cheek

Would have thee weep with me in brotherhood;

Fool! shall each wronged and restless spirit dare

To taint such wine with the salt poison of own despair!

Thou art the same: 'tis I whose wretched soul

Takes discontent to be its paramour,

And gives its kingdom to the rude control

Of what should be its servitor,—for sure

Wisdom is somewhere, though the stormy sea

Contain it not, and the huge deep answer "Tis not in me.'

To burn with one clear flame, to stand erect

  In natural honour, not to bend the knee

In profitless prostrations whose effect

  Is by itself condemned, what alchemy

Can teach me this? what herb Medea brewed

Will bring the unexultant peace of essence not subdued?

The minor chord which ends the harmony,

  And for its answering brother waits in vain

Sobbing for incompleted melody,

  Dies a swan's death; but I the heir of pain,

A silent Memnon with blank lidless eyes,

Wait for the light and music of those suns which never rise.

The quenched-out torch, the lonely cypress-gloom,

  The little dust stored in the narrow urn,

The gentle XAIPE of the Attic tomb,—

  Were not these better far than to return

To my old fitful restless malady,

Or spend my days within the voiceless cave of misery?

Nay! for perchance that poppy-crownèd god
  Is like the watcher by a sick man's bed
Who talks of sleep but gives it not; his rod
  Hath lost its virtue, and, when all is said,
Death is too rude, too obvious a key
To solve one single secret in a life's philosophy.

And Love! that noble madness, whose august
  And inextinguishable might can slay
The soul with honeyed drugs,—alas! I must
  From such sweet ruin play the runaway,
Although too constant memory never can
Forget the archèd splendour of those brows Olympian

Which for a little season made my youth
  So soft a swoon of exquisite indolence
That all the chiding of more prudent Truth
  Seemed the thin voice of jealousy,—O hence
Thou huntress deadlier than Artemis!
Go seek some other quarry! for of thy too perilous bliss.

My lips have drunk enough,—no more, no more,—

Though Love himself should turn his gilded prow

Back to the troubled waters of this shore

   Where I am wrecked and stranded, even now

The chariot wheels of passion sweep too near,

Hence! Hence! I pass unto a life more barren, more austere.

More barren—ay, those arms will never lean

   Down through the trellised vines and draw my soul

In sweet reluctance through the tangled green;

   Some other head must wear that aureole,

For I am hers who loves not any man

Whose white and stainless bosom bears the sign Gorgonian.

Let Venus go and chuck her dainty page,

   And kiss his mouth, and toss his curly hair,

With net and spear and hunting equipage

   Let young Adonis to his tryst repair,

But me her fond and subtle-fashioned spell

Delights no more, though I could win her dearest citadel.

Ay, though I were that laughing shepherd boy

   Who from Mount Ida saw the little cloud

Pass over Tenedos and lofty Troy

And knew the coming of the Queen, and bowed

In wonder at her feet, not for the sake

Of a new Helen would I bid her hand the apple take.

Then rise supreme Athena argent-limbed!

   And, if my lips be musicless, inspire

At least my life: was not thy glory hymned

   By One who gave to thee his sword and lyre

Like Æschylos at well-fought Marathon,

And died to show that Milton's England still could bear a son!

And yet I cannot tread the Portico

   And live without desire, fear and pain,

Or nurture that wise calm which long ago

   The grave Athenian master taught to men,

Self-poised, self-centred, and self-comforted,

To watch the world's vain phantasies go by with unbowed head.

Alas! that serene brow, those eloquent lips,

   Those eyes that mirrored all eternity,

Rest in their own Colonos, an eclipse

   Hath come on Wisdom, and Mnemosyne

Is childless; in the night which she had made

For lofty secure flight Athena's owl itself hath strayed.

Nor much with Science do I care to climb,

   Although by strange and subtle witchery

She drew the moon from heaven: the Muse Time

   Unrolls her gorgeous-coloured tapestry

To no less eager eyes; often indeed

In the great epic of Polymnia's scroll I love to read

How Asia sent her myriad hosts to war

   Against a little town, and panoplied

In gilded mail with jewelled scimitar,

   White-shielded, purple-crested, rode the Mede

Between the waving poplars and the sea

Which men call Artemisium, till he saw Thermopylæ

Its steep ravine spanned by a narrow wall,

   And on the nearer side a little brood

Of careless lions holding festival!

   And stood amazèd at such hardihood,

And pitched his tent upon the reedy shore,

And stayed two days to wonder, and then crept at midnight o'er

Some unfrequented height, and coming down

The autumn forests treacherously slew

What Sparta held most dear and was the crown

  Of far Eurotas, and passed on, nor knew

How God had staked an evil net for him

In the small bay at Salamis,—and yet, the page grows dim,

Its cadenced Greek delights me not, I feel

  With such a goodly time too out of tune

To love it much: for like the Dial's wheel

  That from its blinded darkness strikes the noon

Yet never sees the sun, so do my eyes

Restlessly follow that which from my cheated vision flies.

O for one grand unselfish simple life

  To teach us what is Wisdom! speak ye hills

Of lone Helvellyn, for this note of strife

  Shunned your untroubled crags and crystal rills,

Where is that Spirit which living blamelessly

Yet dared to kiss the smitten mouth of his own century!

Speak ye Rydalian laurels! where is he

  Whose gentle head ye sheltered, that pure soul

Whose gracious days of uncrowned majesty

Through lowliest conduct touched the lofty goal

Where love and duty mingle! Him at least

The most high Laws were glad of, he had sat at Wisdom's feast;

But we are Learning's changelings, know by rote

   The clarion watchword of each Grecian school

And follow none, the flawless sword which smote

   The pagan Hydra is an effete tool

Which we ourselves have blunted, what man now

Shall scale the august ancient heights and to old Reverence bow?

One such indeed I saw, but, Ichabod!

   Gone is that last dear son of Italy,

Who being man died for the sake of God,

   And whose unrisen bones sleep peacefully,

O guard him, guard him well, my Giotto's tower,

Thou marble lily of the lily town! let not the lour

Of the rude tempest vex his slumber, or

   The Arno with its tawny troubled gold

O'er-leap its marge, no mightier conqueror

   Clomb the high Capitol in the days of old

When Rome was indeed Rome, for Liberty

Walked like a bride beside him, at which sight pale Mystery

Fled shrieking to her farthest sombrest cell
   With an old man who grabbled rusty keys,
Fled shuddering, for that immemorial knell
   With which oblivion buries dynasties
Swept like a wounded eagle on the blast,
As to the holy heart of Rome the great triumvir passed.

He knew the holiest heart and heights of Rome,
   He drave the base wolf from the lion's lair,
And now lies dead by that empyreal dome
   Which overtops Valdarno hung in air
By Brunelleschi—O Melpomene
Breathe through thy melancholy pipe thy sweetest threnody!

Breathe through the tragic stops such melodies
   That Joy's self may grow jealous, and the Nine
Forget awhile their discreet emperies,
   Mourning for him who on Rome's lordliest shrine
Lit for men's lives the light of Marathon,
And bare to sun-forgotten fields the fire of the sun!

O guard him, guard him well, my Giotto's tower!

Let some young Florentine each eventide

Bring coronals of that enchanted flower

Which the dim woods of Vallombrosa hide,

And deck the marble tomb wherein he lies

Whose soul is as some mighty orb unseen of mortal eyes;

Some mighty orb whose cycled wanderings,

Being tempest-driven to the farthest rim

Where Chaos meets Creation and the wings

Of the eternal chanting Cherubim

Are pavilioned on Nothing, passed away

Into a moonless void,—and yet, though he is dust and clay,

He is not dead, the immemorial Fates

Forbid it, and the closing shears refrain.

Lift up your heads ye everlasting gates!

Ye argent clarions, sound a loftier strain

For the vile thing he hated lurks within

Its sombre house, alone with God and memories of sin.

Still what avails it that she sought her cave

That murderous mother of red harlotries?

At Munich on the marble architrave

   The Grecian boys die smiling, but the seas

Which wash Ægina fret in loneliness

Not mirroring their beauty; so our lives grow colourless

For lack of our ideals, if one star

   Flame torch-like in the heavens the unjust

Swift daylight kills it, and no trump of war

   Can wake to passionate voice the silent dust

Which was Mazzini once! rich Niobe

For all her stony sorrows hath her sons; but Italy,

What Easter Day shall make her children rise,

   Who were not Gods yet suffered? what sure feet

Shall find their grave-clothes folded? what clear eyes

   Shall see them bodily? O it were meet

To roll the stone from off the sepulchre

And kiss the bleeding roses of their wounds, in love of her,

Our Italy! our mother visible!

   Most blessed among nations and most sad,

For whose dear sake the young Calabrian fell

   That day at Aspromonte and was glad

That in an age when God was bought and sold

One man could die for Liberty! but we, burnt out and cold,

See Honour smitten on the cheek and gyves

   Bind the sweet feet of Mercy: Poverty

Creeps through our sunless lanes and with sharp knives

   Cuts the warm throats of children stealthily,

And no word said:—O we are wretched men

Unworthy of our great inheritance! where is the pen

Of austere Milton? where the mighty sword

   Which slew its master righteously? the years

Have lost their ancient leader, and no word

   Breaks from the voiceless tripod on our ears:

While as a ruined mother in some spasm

Bears a base child and loathes it, so our best enthusiasm

Genders unlawful children, Anarchy

   Freedom's own Judas, the vile prodigal

Licence who steals the gold of Liberty

   And yet has nothing, Ignorance the real

One Fraticide since Cain, Envy the asp

That stings itself to anguish, Avarice whose palsied grasp

Is in its extent stiffened, moneyed Greed

    For whose dull appetite men waste away

Amid the whirr of wheels and are the seed

    Of things which slay their sower, these each day

Sees rife in England, and the gentle feet

Of Beauty tread no more the stones of each unlovely street.

What even Cromwell spared is desecrated

    By weed and worm, left to the stormy play

Of wind and beating snow, or renovated

    By more destructful hands: Time's worst decay

Will wreathe its ruins with some loveliness,

But these new Vandals can but make a rain-proof barrenness.

Where is that Art which bade the Angels sing

    Through Lincoln's lofty choir, till the air

Seems from such marble harmonies to ring

    With sweeter song than common lips can dare

To draw from actual reed? ah! where is now

The cunning hand which made the flowering hawthorn branches bow

For Southwell's arch, and carved the House of One

Who loved the lilies of the field with all

Our dearest English flowers? the same sun

   Rises for us: the seasons natural

Weave the same tapestry of green and grey:

The unchanged hills are with us: but that Spirit hath passed away.

And yet perchance it may be better so,

   For Tyranny is an incestuous Queen,

Murder her brother is her bedfellow,

   And the Plague chambers with her: in obscene

And bloody paths her treacherous feet are set;

Better the empty desert and a soul inviolate!

For gentle brotherhood, the harmony

   Of living in the healthful air, the swift

Clean beauty of strong limbs when men are free

   And women chaste, these are the things which lift

Our souls up more than even Agnolo's

Gaunt blinded Sibyl poring o'er the scroll of human woes,

Or Titian's little maiden on the stair

   White as her own sweet lily and as tall,

Or Mona Lisa smiling through her hair,—

182

Ah! somehow life is bigger after all

Than any painted angel, could we see

The God that is within us! The old Greek serenity

Which curbs the passion of that level line

Of marble youths, who with untroubled eyes

And chastened limbs ride round Athena's shrine

And mirror her divine economies,

And balanced symmetry of what in man

Would else wage ceaseless warfare,—this at least within the span

Between our mother's kisses and the grave

Might so inform our lives, that we could win

Such mighty empires that from her cave

Temptation would grow hoarse, and pallid Sin

Would walk ashamed of his adulteries,

And Passion creep from out the House of Lust with startled eyes.

To make the body and the spirit one

With all right things, till no thing live in vain

From morn to noon, but in sweet unison

With every pulse of flesh and throb of brain

The soul in flawless essence high enthroned,

Against all outer vain attack invincibly bastioned,

Mark with serene impartiality
  The strife of things, and yet be comforted,
Knowing that by the chain causality
  All separate existences are wed
Into one supreme whole, whose utterance
Is joy, or holier praise! ah! surely this were governance

Of Life in most august omnipresence,
  Through which the rational intellect would find
In passion its expression, and mere sense,
  Ignoble else, lend fire to the mind,
And being joined with it in harmony
More mystical than that which binds the stars planetary,

Strike from their several tones one octave chord
  Whose cadence being measureless would fly
Through all the circling spheres, then to its Lord
  Return refreshed with its new empery
And more exultant power,—this indeed
Could we but reach it were to find the last, the perfect creed.

Ah! it was easy when the world was young

184

To keep one's life free and inviolate,

From our sad lips another song is rung,

By our own hands our heads are desecrate,

Wanderers in drear exile, and dispossessed

Of what should be our own, we can but feed on wild unrest.

Somehow the grace, the bloom of things has flown,

And of all men we are most wretched who

Must live each other's lives and not our own

For very pity's sake and then undo

All that we lived for—it was otherwise

When soul and body seemed to blend in mystic symphonies.

But we have left those gentle haunts to pass

With weary feet to the new Calvary,

Where we behold, as one who in a glass

Sees his own face, self-slain Humanity,

And in the dumb reproach of that sad gaze

Learn what an awful phantom the red hand of man can raise.

O smitten mouth! O forehead crowned with thorn!

O chalice of all common miseries!

Thou for our sakes that loved thee not hast borne

An agony of endless centuries,

And we were vain and ignorant nor knew

That when we stabbed thy heart it was our own real hearts we slew.

Being ourselves the sowers and the seeds,

　　The night that covers and the lights that fade,

The spear that pierces and the side that bleeds,

　　The lips betraying and the life betrayed;

The deep hath calm: the moon hath rest: but we

Lords of the natural world are yet our own dread enemy.

Is this the end of all that primal force

　　Which, in its changes being still the same,

From eyeless Chaos cleft its upward course,

　　Through ravenous seas and whirling rocks and flame,

Till the suns met in heaven and began

Their cycles, and the morning stars sang, and the Word was Man!

Nay, nay, we are but crucified, and though

　　The bloody sweat falls from our brows like rain

Loosen the nails—we shall come down I know,

　　Staunch the red wounds—we shall be whole again,

No need have we of hyssop-laden rod,

That which is purely human, that is godlike, that is God.

FLOWER OF LOVE

ΓΛΥΚΥΠΙΚΡΟΣ ΕΡΩΣ

Sweet, I blame you not, for mine the fault
    was, had I not been made of common clay
I had climbed the higher heights unclimbed
    yet, seen the fuller air, the larger day.

From the wildness of my wasted passion I had
    struck a better, clearer song,
Lit some lighter light of freer freedom, battled
    with some Hydra-headed wrong.

Had my lips been smitten into music by the
    kisses that but made them bleed,
You had walked with Bice and the angels on
    that verdant and enamelled mead.

I had trod the road which Dante treading saw
    the suns of seven circles shine,
Ay! perchance had seen the heavens opening,

as they opened to the Florentine.

And the mighty nations would have crowned

me, who am crownless now and without name,

And some orient dawn had found me kneeling

on the threshold of the House of Fame.

I had sat within that marble circle where the

oldest bard is as the young,

And the pipe is ever dropping honey, and the

lyre's strings are ever strung.

Keats had lifted up his hymeneal curls from out

the poppy-seeded wine,

With ambrosial mouth had kissed my forehead,

clasped the hand of noble love in mine.

And at springtide, when the apple-blossoms brush

the burnished bosom of the dove,

Two young lovers lying in an orchard would

have read the story of our love.

Would have read the legend of my passion,

known the bitter secret of my heart,

Kissed as we have kissed, but never parted as

we two are fated now to part.

For the crimson flower of our life is eaten by

the cankerworm of truth,

And no hand can gather up the fallen withered

petals of the rose of youth.

Yet I am not sorry that I loved you—ah! what

else had I a boy to do,—

For the hungry teeth of time devour, and the

silent-footed years pursue.

Rudderless, we drift athwart a tempest, and

when once the storm of youth is past,

Without lyre, without lute or chorus, Death

the silent pilot comes at last.

And within the grave there is no pleasure, for

the blindworm battens on the root,

And Desire shudders into ashes, and the tree of

Passion bears no fruit.

Ah! what else had I to do but love you, God's
    own mother was less dear to me,
And less dear the Cytheræan rising like an
    argent lily from the sea.

I have made my choice, have lived my poems,
    and, though youth is gone in wasted days,
I have found the lover's crown of myrtle better
    than the poet's crown of bays.

UNCOLLECTED POEMS

FROM SPRING DAYS TO WINTER
(FOR MUSIC)

In the glad springtime when leaves were green,
　O merrily the throstle sings!
I sought, amid the tangled sheen,
Love whom mine eyes had never seen,
　O the glad dove has golden wings!

Between the blossoms red and white,
　O merrily the throstle sings!
My love first came into my sight,
O perfect vision of delight,
　O the glad dove has golden wings!

The yellow apples glowed like fire,
　O merrily the throstle sings!
O Love too great for lip or lyre,
Blown rose of love and of desire,
　O the glad dove has golden wings!

But now with snow the tree is grey,

  Ah, sadly now the throstle sings!

My love is dead: ah! well-a-day,

See at her silent feet I lay

  A dove with broken wings!

  Ah, Love! ah, Love! that thou wert slain—

Fond Dove, fond Dove return again!

TRISTITÆ

Αἴλινον, αἴλινον εἰπέ, τὸ δ' εὖ νικάτω

O well for him who lives at ease

  With garnered gold in wide domain,

  Nor heeds the splashing of the rain,

The crashing down of forest trees.

O well for him who ne'er hath known

  The travail of the hungry years,

  A father grey with grief and tears,

A mother weeping all alone.

But well for him whose foot hath trod

  The weary road of toil and strife,

Yet from the sorrows of his life.

Builds ladders to be nearer God.

THE TRUE KNOWLEDGE

. . . ἀναγκαίως δ' ἔχει

Βίον θερίζειν ὥστε κάρπιμον στάχυν,

καὶ τὸν γὲν εἶναι τὸν δὲ γή.

Thou knowest all; I seek in vain

   What lands to till or sow with seed—

   The land is black with briar and weed,

Nor cares for falling tears or rain.

Thou knowest all; I sit and wait

   With blinded eyes and hands that fail,

   Till the last lifting of the veil

And the first opening of the gate.

Thou knowest all; I cannot see.

   I trust I shall not live in vain,

   I know that we shall meet again

In some divine eternity.

IMPRESSIONS

I. LE JARDIN

The lily's withered chalice falls
   Around its rod of dusty gold,
   And from the beech-trees on the wold
The last wood-pigeon coos and calls.

The gaudy leonine sunflower
   Hangs black and barren on its stalk,
   And down the windy garden walk
The dead leaves scatter,—hour by hour.

Pale privet-petals white as milk
   Are blown into a snowy mass:
   The roses lie upon the grass
Like little shreds of crimson silk.

II. LA MER

A white mist drifts across the shrouds,
   A wild moon in this wintry sky
   Gleams like an angry lion's eye
Out of a mane of tawny clouds.

The muffled steersman at the wheel

194

Is but a shadow in the gloom;—

And in the throbbing engine-room

Leap the long rods of polished steel.

The shattered storm has left its trace

Upon this huge and heaving dome,

For the thin threads of yellow foam

Float on the waves like ravelled lace.

UNDER THE BALCONY

O beautiful star with the crimson mouth!

O moon with the brows of gold!

Rise up, rise up, from the odorous south!

And light for my love her way,

Lest her little feet should stray

On the windy hill and the wold!

O beautiful star with the crimson mouth!

O moon with the brows of gold!

O ship that shakes on the desolate sea!

O ship with the wet, white sail!

Put in, put in, to the port to me!

For my love and I would go

To the land where the daffodils blow

In the heart of a violet dale!

O ship that shakes on the desolate sea!

O ship with the wet, white sail!

O rapturous bird with the low, sweet note!

O bird that sits on the spray!

Sing on, sing on, from your soft brown throat!

And my love in her little bed

Will listen, and lift her head

From the pillow, and come my way!

O rapturous bird with the low, sweet note!

O bird that sits on the spray!

O blossom that hangs in the tremulous air!

O blossom with lips of snow!

Come down, come down, for my love to wear!

You will die on her head in a crown,

You will die in a fold of her gown,

To her little light heart you will go!

O blossom that hangs in the tremulous air!

O blossom with lips of snow!

THE HARLOT'S HOUSE

We caught the tread of dancing feet,

We loitered down the moonlit street,

And stopped beneath the harlot's house.

Inside, above the din and fray,

We heard the loud musicians play

The 'Treues Liebes Herz' of Strauss.

Like strange mechanical grotesques,

Making fantastic arabesques,

The shadows raced across the blind.

We watched the ghostly dancers spin

To sound of horn and violin,

Like black leaves wheeling in the wind.

Like wire-pulled automatons,

Slim silhouetted skeletons

Went sidling through the slow quadrille,

Then took each other by the hand,

And danced a stately saraband;

Their laughter echoed thin and shrill.

Sometimes a clockwork puppet pressed

A phantom lover to her breast,

Sometimes they seemed to try to sing.

Sometimes a horrible marionette

Came out, and smoked its cigarette

Upon the steps like a live thing.

Then, turning to my love, I said,

'The dead are dancing with the dead,

The dust is whirling with the dust.'

But she—she heard the violin,

And left my side, and entered in:

Love passed into the house of lust.

Then suddenly the tune went false,

The dancers wearied of the waltz,

The shadows ceased to wheel and whirl.

And down the long and silent street,

The dawn, with silver-sandalled feet,

Crept like a frightened girl.

198

LE JARDIN DES TUILERIES

This winter air is keen and cold,
    And keen and cold this winter sun,
    But round my chair the children run
Like little things of dancing gold.

Sometimes about the painted kiosk
    The mimic soldiers strut and stride,
    Sometimes the blue-eyed brigands hide
In the bleak tangles of the bosk.

And sometimes, while the old nurse cons
    Her book, they steal across the square,
    And launch their paper navies where
Huge Triton writhes in greenish bronze.

And now in mimic flight they flee,
    And now they rush, a boisterous band—
    And, tiny hand on tiny hand,
Climb up the black and leafless tree.

Ah! cruel tree! if I were you,
    And children climbed me, for their sake

Though it be winter I would break

Into spring blossoms white and blue!

ON THE SALE BY AUCTION OF KEATS' LOVE LETTERS

These are the letters which Endymion wrote

　To one he loved in secret, and apart.

　And now the brawlers of the auction mart

Bargain and bid for each poor blotted note,

Ay! for each separate pulse of passion quote

　The merchant's price. I think they love not art

　Who break the crystal of a poet's heart

That small and sickly eyes may glare and gloat.

Is it not said that many years ago,

　In a far Eastern town, some soldiers ran

　With torches through the midnight, and began

To wrangle for mean raiment, and to throw

　Dice for the garments of a wretched man,

Not knowing the God's wonder, or His woe?

THE NEW REMORSE

The sin was mine; I did not understand.

　So now is music prisoned in her cave,

　Save where some ebbing desultory wave

Frets with its restless whirls this meagre strand.

And in the withered hollow of this land

   Hath Summer dug herself so deep a grave,

   That hardly can the leaden willow crave

One silver blossom from keen Winter's hand.

But who is this who cometh by the shore?

(Nay, love, look up and wonder!) Who is this

   Who cometh in dyed garments from the South?

It is thy new-found Lord, and he shall kiss

   The yet unravished roses of thy mouth,

And I shall weep and worship, as before.

FANTAISIES DÉCORATIVES

I. LE PANNEAU

Under the rose-tree's dancing shade

   There stands a little ivory girl,

   Pulling the leaves of pink and pearl

With pale green nails of polished jade.

The red leaves fall upon the mould,

   The white leaves flutter, one by one,

   Down to a blue bowl where the sun,

Like a great dragon, writhes in gold.

The white leaves float upon the air,
  The red leaves flutter idly down,
  Some fall upon her yellow gown,
And some upon her raven hair.

She takes an amber lute and sings,
  And as she sings a silver crane
  Begins his scarlet neck to strain,
And flap his burnished metal wings.

She takes a lute of amber bright,
  And from the thicket where he lies
  Her lover, with his almond eyes,
Watches her movements in delight.

And now she gives a cry of fear,
  And tiny tears begin to start:
  A thorn has wounded with its dart
The pink-veined sea-shell of her ear.

And now she laughs a merry note:

There has fallen a petal of the rose

Just where the yellow satin shows

The blue-veined flower of her throat.

With pale green nails of polished jade,

Pulling the leaves of pink and pearl,

There stands a little ivory girl

Under the rose-tree's dancing shade.

II. LES BALLONS

Against these turbid turquoise skies

The light and luminous balloons

Dip and drift like satin moons,

Drift like silken butterflies;

Reel with every windy gust,

Rise and reel like dancing girls,

Float like strange transparent pearls,

Fall and float like silver dust.

Now to the low leaves they cling,

Each with coy fantastic pose,

Each a petal of a rose

Straining at a gossamer string.

Then to the tall trees they climb,

    Like thin globes of amethyst,

    Wandering opals keeping tryst

With the rubies of the lime.

CANZONET

    I have no store

Of gryphon-guarded gold;

    Now, as before,

Bare is the shepherd's fold.

    Rubies nor pearls

Have I to gem thy throat;

    Yet woodland girls

Have loved the shepherd's note.

    Then pluck a reed

And bid me sing to thee,

    For I would feed

Thine ears with melody,

    Who art more fair

Than fairest fleur-de-lys,

    More sweet and rare

Than sweetest ambergris.

What dost thou fear?
Young Hyacinth is slain,
  Pan is not here,
And will not come again.
  No hornèd Faun
Treads down the yellow leas,
  No God at dawn
Steals through the olive trees.

  Hylas is dead,
Nor will he e'er divine
  Those little red
Rose-petalled lips of thine.
  On the high hill
No ivory dryads play,
  Silver and still
Sinks the sad autumn day.

SYMPHONY IN YELLOW

An omnibus across the bridge
  Crawls like a yellow butterfly,
  And, here and there, a passer-by
Shows like a little restless midge.

205

Big barges full of yellow hay

  Are moored against the shadowy wharf,

  And, like a yellow silken scarf,

The thick fog hangs along the quay.

The yellow leaves begin to fade

  And flutter from the Temple elms,

  And at my feet the pale green Thames

Lies like a rod of rippled jade.

IN THE FOREST

Out of the mid-wood's twilight

  Into the meadow's dawn,

Ivory limbed and brown-eyed,

  Flashes my Faun!

He skips through the copses singing,

  And his shadow dances along,

And I know not which I should follow,

  Shadow or song!

O Hunter, snare me his shadow!

  O Nightingale, catch me his strain!

Else moonstruck with music and madness

I track him in vain!

TO MY WIFE: WITH A COPY OF MY POEMS

I can write no stately proem

As a prelude to my lay;

From a poet to a poem

I would dare to say.

For if of these fallen petals

One to you seem fair,

Love will waft it till it settles

On your hair.

And when wind and winter harden

All the loveless land,

It will whisper of the garden,

You will understand.

WITH A COPY OF 'A HOUSE OF POMEGRANATES'

Go, little book,

To him who, on a lute with horns of pearl,

Sang of the white feet of the Golden Girl:

And bid him look

Into thy pages: it may hap that he

May find that golden maidens dance through thee.

ROSES AND RUE

(To L. L.)

Could we dig up this long-buried treasure,

   Were it worth the pleasure,

We never could learn love's song,

   We are parted too long.

Could the passionate past that is fled

   Call back its dead,

Could we live it all over again,

   Were it worth the pain!

I remember we used to meet

   By an ivied seat,

And you warbled each pretty word

   With the air of a bird;

And your voice had a quaver in it,

   Just like a linnet,

And shook, as the blackbird's throat
  With its last big note;

And your eyes, they were green and grey
  Like an April day,
But lit into amethyst
  When I stooped and kissed;

And your mouth, it would never smile
  For a long, long while,
Then it rippled all over with laughter
  Five minutes after.

You were always afraid of a shower,
  Just like a flower:
I remember you started and ran
  When the rain began.

I remember I never could catch you,
  For no one could match you,
You had wonderful, luminous, fleet,
  Little wings to your feet.

I remember your hair—did I tie it?

209

For it always ran riot—

Like a tangled sunbeam of gold:

   These things are old.

I remember so well the room,

   And the lilac bloom

That beat at the dripping pane

   In the warm June rain;

And the colour of your gown,

   It was amber-brown,

And two yellow satin bows

   From your shoulders rose.

And the handkerchief of French lace

   Which you held to your face—

Had a small tear left a stain?

   Or was it the rain?

On your hand as it waved adieu

   There were veins of blue;

In your voice as it said good-bye

   Was a petulant cry,

'You have only wasted your life.'

  (Ah, that was the knife!)

When I rushed through the garden gate

  It was all too late.

Could we live it over again,

  Were it worth the pain,

Could the passionate past that is fled

  Call back its dead!

Well, if my heart must break,

  Dear love, for your sake,

It will break in music, I know,

  Poets' hearts break so.

But strange that I was not told

  That the brain can hold

In a tiny ivory cell

  God's heaven and hell.

DÉSESPOIR

The seasons send their ruin as they go,

For in the spring the narciss shows its head

Nor withers till the rose has flamed to red,

And in the autumn purple violets blow,

And the slim crocus stirs the winter snow;

Wherefore yon leafless trees will bloom again

And this grey land grow green with summer rain

And send up cowslips for some boy to mow.

But what of life whose bitter hungry sea

Flows at our heels, and gloom of sunless night

Covers the days which never more return?

Ambition, love and all the thoughts that burn

We lose too soon, and only find delight

In withered husks of some dead memory.

PAN: DOUBLE VILLANELLE

I

O goat-foot God of Arcady!

This modern world is grey and old,

And what remains to us of thee?

No more the shepherd lads in glee

Throw apples at thy wattled fold,

O goat-foot God of Arcady!

Nor through the laurels can one see

Thy soft brown limbs, thy beard of gold,

And what remains to us of thee?

And dull and dead our Thames would be,

For here the winds are chill and cold,

O goat-foot God of Arcady!

Then keep the tomb of Helice,

Thine olive-woods, thy vine-clad wold,

And what remains to us of thee?

Though many an unsung elegy

Sleeps in the reeds our rivers hold,

O goat-foot God of Arcady!

Ah, what remains to us of thee?

II

Ah, leave the hills of Arcady,

Thy satyrs and their wanton play,

This modern world hath need of thee.

213

No nymph or Faun indeed have we,

For Faun and nymph are old and grey,

Ah, leave the hills of Arcady!

This is the land where liberty

Lit grave-browed Milton on his way,

This modern world hath need of thee!

A land of ancient chivalry

Where gentle Sidney saw the day,

Ah, leave the hills of Arcady!

This fierce sea-lion of the sea,

This England lacks some stronger lay,

This modern world hath need of thee!

Then blow some trumpet loud and free,

And give thine oaten pipe away,

Ah, leave the hills of Arcady!

This modern world hath need of thee!

214

THE SPHINX

TO

MARCEL SCHWOB

IN FRIENDSHIP

AND

IN ADMIRATION

THE SPHINX

In a dim corner of my room for longer than my fancy thinks
A beautiful and silent Sphinx has watched me through the shifting gloom.

Inviolate and immobile she does not rise she does not stir
For silver moons are naught to her and naught to her the suns that reel.

Red follows grey across the air, the waves of moonlight ebb and flow
But with the Dawn she does not go and in the night-time she is there.

Dawn follows Dawn and Nights grow old and all the while this curious cat
Lies couching on the Chinese mat with eyes of satin rimmed with gold.

Upon the mat she lies and leers and on the tawny throat of her
Flutters the soft and silky fur or ripples to her pointed ears.

Come forth, my lovely seneschal! so somnolent, so statuesque!
Come forth you exquisite grotesque! half woman and half animal!

Come forth my lovely languorous Sphinx! and put your head upon my knee!
And let me stroke your throat and see your body spotted like the Lynx!

And let me touch those curving claws of yellow ivory and grasp
The tail that like a monstrous Asp coils round your heavy velvet paws!

A thousand weary centuries are thine while I have hardly seen
Some twenty summers cast their green for Autumn's gaudy liveries.

But you can read the Hieroglyphs on the great sandstone obelisks,
And you have talked with Basilisks, and you have looked on Hippogriffs.

O tell me, were you standing by when Isis to Osiris knelt?
And did you watch the Egyptian melt her union for Antony

And drink the jewel-drunken wine and bend her head in mimic awe
To see the huge proconsul draw the salted tunny from the brine?

And did you mark the Cyprian kiss white Adon on his catafalque?

And did you follow Amenalk, the God of Heliopolis?

And did you talk with Thoth, and did you hear the moon-horned Io weep?

And know the painted kings who sleep beneath the wedge-shaped Pyramid?

Lift up your large black satin eyes which are like cushions where one sinks!

Fawn at my feet, fantastic Sphinx! and sing me all your memories!

Sing to me of the Jewish maid who wandered with the Holy Child,

And how you led them through the wild, and how they slept beneath your shade.

Sing to me of that odorous green eve when crouching by the marge

You heard from Adrian's gilded barge the laughter of Antinous

And lapped the stream and fed your drouth and watched with hot and hungry stare

The ivory body of that rare young slave with his pomegranate mouth!

Sing to me of the Labyrinth in which the twi-formed bull was stalled!

Sing to me of the night you crawled across the temple's granite plinth

When through the purple corridors the screaming scarlet Ibis flew

In terror, and a horrid dew dripped from the moaning Mandragores,

And the great torpid crocodile within the tank shed slimy tears,

And tare the jewels from his ears and staggered back into the Nile,

And the priests cursed you with shrill psalms as in your claws you seized their snake

And crept away with it to slake your passion by the shuddering palms.

Who were your lovers? who were they who wrestled for you in the dust?

Which was the vessel of your Lust? What Leman had you, every day?

Did giant Lizards come and crouch before you on the reedy banks?

Did Gryphons with great metal flanks leap on you in your trampled couch?

Did monstrous hippopotami come sidling toward you in the mist?

Did gilt-scaled dragons writhe and twist with passion as you passed them by?

And from the brick-built Lycian tomb what horrible Chimera came

With fearful heads and fearful flame to breed new wonders from your womb?

Or had you shameful secret quests and did you harry to your home

Some Nereid coiled in amber foam with curious rock crystal breasts?

Or did you treading through the froth call to the brown Sidonian

For tidings of Leviathan, Leviathan or Behemoth?

Or did you when the sun was set climb up the cactus-covered slope

To meet your swarthy Ethiop whose body was of polished jet?

Or did you while the earthen skiffs dropped down the grey Nilotic flats

At twilight and the flickering bats flew round the temple's triple glyphs

Steal to the border of the bar and swim across the silent lake

And slink into the vault and make the Pyramid your lúpanar

Till from each black sarcophagus rose up the painted swathèd dead?

Or did you lure unto your bed the ivory-horned Tragelaphos?

Or did you love the god of flies who plagued the Hebrews and was splashed

With wine unto the waist? or Pasht, who had green beryls for her eyes?

Or that young god, the Tyrian, who was more amorous than the dove

Of Ashtaroth? or did you love the god of the Assyrian

Whose wings, like strange transparent talc, rose high above his hawk-

219

faced head,

    Painted with silver and with red and ribbed with rods of Oreichalch?

    Or did huge Apis from his car leap down and lay before your feet

    Big blossoms of the honey-sweet and honey-coloured nenuphar?

    How subtle-secret is your smile! Did you love none then? Nay, I know

    Great Ammon was your bedfellow! He lay with you beside the Nile!

    The river-horses in the slime trumpeted when they saw him come

    Odorous with Syrian galbanum and smeared with spikenard and with thyme.

    He came along the river bank like some tall galley argent-sailed,

    He strode across the waters, mailed in beauty, and the waters sank.

    He strode across the desert sand: he reached the valley where you lay:

    He waited till the dawn of day: then touched your black breasts with his hand.

    You kissed his mouth with mouths of flame: you made the hornèd god your own:

    You stood behind him on his throne: you called him by his secret name.

220

You whispered monstrous oracles into the caverns of his ears:

With blood of goats and blood of steers you taught him monstrous miracles.

White Ammon was your bedfellow! Your chamber was the steaming Nile!

And with your curved archaic smile you watched his passion come and go.

With Syrian oils his brows were bright: and wide-spread as a tent at noon

His marble limbs made pale the moon and lent the day a larger light.

His long hair was nine cubits' span and coloured like that yellow gem

Which hidden in their garment's hem the merchants bring from Kurdistan.

His face was as the must that lies upon a vat of new-made wine:

The seas could not insapphirine the perfect azure of his eyes.

His thick soft throat was white as milk and threaded with thin veins of blue:

And curious pearls like frozen dew were broidered on his flowing silk.

On pearl and porphyry pedestalled he was too bright to look upon:

For on his ivory breast there shone the wondrous ocean-emerald,

That mystic moonlit jewel which some diver of the Colchian caves
Had found beneath the blackening waves and carried to the Colchian witch.

Before his gilded galiot ran naked vine-wreathed corybants,
And lines of swaying elephants knelt down to draw his chariot,

And lines of swarthy Nubians bare up his litter as he rode
Down the great granite-paven road between the nodding peacock-fans.

The merchants brought him steatite from Sidon in their painted ships:
The meanest cup that touched his lips was fashioned from a chrysolite.

The merchants brought him cedar chests of rich apparel bound with cords:
His train was borne by Memphian lords: young kings were glad to be
his guests.

Ten hundred shaven priests did bow to Ammon's altar day and night,
Ten hundred lamps did wave their light through Ammon's carven
house—and now

Foul snake and speckled adder with their young ones crawl from stone
to stone

222

For ruined is the house and prone the great rose-marble monolith!

Wild ass or trotting jackal comes and couches in the mouldering gates:
Wild satyrs call unto their mates across the fallen fluted drums.

And on the summit of the pile the blue-faced ape of Horus sits
And gibbers while the fig-tree splits the pillars of the peristyle

The god is scattered here and there: deep hidden in the windy sand
I saw his giant granite hand still clenched in impotent despair.

And many a wandering caravan of stately negroes silken-shawled,
Crossing the desert, halts appalled before the neck that none can span.

And many a bearded Bedouin draws back his yellow-striped burnous
To gaze upon the Titan thews of him who was thy paladin.

Go, seek his fragments on the moor and wash them in the evening dew,
And from their pieces make anew thy mutilated paramour!

Go, seek them where they lie alone and from their broken pieces make

Thy bruisèd bedfellow! And wake mad passions in the senseless stone!

Charm his dull ear with Syrian hymns! he loved your body! oh, be kind,
Pour spikenard on his hair, and wind soft rolls of linen round his limbs!

Wind round his head the figured coins! stain with red fruits those pallid lips!
Weave purple for his shrunken hips! and purple for his barren loins!

Away to Egypt! Have no fear. Only one God has ever died.
Only one God has let His side be wounded by a soldier's spear.

But these, thy lovers, are not dead. Still by the hundred-cubit gate
Dog-faced Anubis sits in state with lotus-lilies for thy head.

Still from his chair of porphyry gaunt Memnon strains his lidless eyes
Across the empty land, and cries each yellow morning unto thee.

And Nilus with his broken horn lies in his black and oozy bed
And till thy coming will not spread his waters on the withering corn.

Your lovers are not dead, I know. They will rise up and hear your voice
And clash their cymbals and rejoice and run to kiss your mouth! And so,

Set wings upon your argosies! Set horses to your ebon car!

Back to your Nile! Or if you are grown sick of dead divinities

Follow some roving lion's spoor across the copper-coloured plain,

Reach out and hale him by the mane and bid him be your paramour!

Couch by his side upon the grass and set your white teeth in his throat

And when you hear his dying note lash your long flanks of polished brass

And take a tiger for your mate, whose amber sides are flecked with black,

And ride upon his gilded back in triumph through the Theban gate,

And toy with him in amorous jests, and when he turns, and snarls, and gnaws,

O smite him with your jasper claws! and bruise him with your agate breasts!

Why are you tarrying? Get hence! I weary of your sullen ways,

I weary of your steadfast gaze, your somnolent magnificence.

Your horrible and heavy breath makes the light flicker in the lamp,

And on my brow I feel the damp and dreadful dews of night and death.

225

Your eyes are like fantastic moons that shiver in some stagnant lake,

Your tongue is like a scarlet snake that dances to fantastic tunes,

Your pulse makes poisonous melodies, and your black throat is like the hole

Left by some torch or burning coal on Saracenic tapestries.

Away! The sulphur-coloured stars are hurrying through the Western gate!

Away! Or it may be too late to climb their silent silver cars!

See, the dawn shivers round the grey gilt-dialled towers, and the rain

Streams down each diamonded pane and blurs with tears the wannish day.

What snake-tressed fury fresh from Hell, with uncouth gestures and unclean,

Stole from the poppy-drowsy queen and led you to a student's cell?

What songless tongueless ghost of sin crept through the curtains of the night,

And saw my taper burning bright, and knocked, and bade you enter in?

Are there not others more accursed, whiter with leprosies than I?

Are Abana and Pharphar dry that you come here to slake your thirst?

226

Get hence, you loathsome mystery! Hideous animal, get hence!
You wake in me each bestial sense, you make me what I would not be.

You make my creed a barren sham, you wake foul dreams of sensual life,
And Atys with his blood-stained knife were better than the thing I am.

False Sphinx! False Sphinx! By reedy Styx old Charon, leaning on his oar,
Waits for my coin. Go thou before, and leave me to my crucifix,

Whose pallid burden, sick with pain, watches the world with wearied eyes,
And weeps for every soul that dies, and weeps for every soul in vain.

THE BALLAD OF READING GAOL

IN MEMORIAM

C. T. W.

SOMETIME TROOPER OF THE ROYAL HORSE GUARDS

OBIIT H.M. PRISON, READING, BERKSHIRE

JULY 7, 1896

THE BALLAD OF READING GAOL

I

He did not wear his scarlet coat,
For blood and wine are red,
And blood and wine were on his hands
When they found him with the dead,
The poor dead woman whom he loved,
And murdered in her bed.

He walked amongst the Trial Men
In a suit of shabby grey;
A cricket cap was on his head,
And his step seemed light and gay;
But I never saw a man who looked

So wistfully at the day.

I never saw a man who looked
    With such a wistful eye
Upon that little tent of blue
    Which prisoners call the sky,
And at every drifting cloud that went
    With sails of silver by.

I walked, with other souls in pain,
    Within another ring,
And was wondering if the man had done
    A great or little thing,
When a voice behind me whispered low,
    'That fellow's got to swing.'

Dear Christ! the very prison walls
    Suddenly seemed to reel,
And the sky above my head became
    Like a casque of scorching steel;
And, though I was a soul in pain,
    My pain I could not feel.

I only knew what hunted thought

Quickened his step, and why
He looked upon the garish day
With such a wistful eye;
The man had killed the thing he loved,
And so he had to die.

Yet each man kills the thing he loves,
By each let this be heard,
Some do it with a bitter look,
Some with a flattering word,
The coward does it with a kiss,
The brave man with a sword!

Some kill their love when they are young,
And some when they are old;
Some strangle with the hands of Lust,
Some with the hands of Gold:
The kindest use a knife, because
The dead so soon grow cold.

Some love too little, some too long,
Some sell, and others buy;
Some do the deed with many tears,

And some without a sigh:

For each man kills the thing he loves,

   Yet each man does not die.

He does not die a death of shame

   On a day of dark disgrace,

Nor have a noose about his neck,

   Nor a cloth upon his face,

Nor drop feet foremost through the floor

   Into an empty space.

He does not sit with silent men

   Who watch him night and day;

Who watch him when he tries to weep,

   And when he tries to pray;

Who watch him lest himself should rob

   The prison of its prey.

He does not wake at dawn to see

   Dread figures throng his room,

The shivering Chaplain robed in white,

   The Sheriff stern with gloom,

And the Governor all in shiny black,

With the yellow face of Doom.

He does not rise in piteous haste

   To put on convict-clothes,

While some coarse-mouthed Doctor gloats, and notes

   Each new and nerve-twitched pose,

Fingering a watch whose little ticks

   Are like horrible hammer-blows.

He does not know that sickening thirst

   That sands one's throat, before

The hangman with his gardener's gloves

   Slips through the padded door,

And binds one with three leathern thongs,

   That the throat may thirst no more.

He does not bend his head to hear

   The Burial Office read,

Nor, while the terror of his soul

   Tells him he is not dead,

Cross his own coffin, as he moves

   Into the hideous shed.

He does not stare upon the air

Through a little roof of glass:

He does not pray with lips of clay

    For his agony to pass;

Nor feel upon his shuddering cheek

    The kiss of Caiaphas.

II

Six weeks our guardsman walked the yard,

    In the suit of shabby grey:

His cricket cap was on his head,

    And his step seemed light and gay,

But I never saw a man who looked

    So wistfully at the day.

I never saw a man who looked

    With such a wistful eye

Upon that little tent of blue

    Which prisoners call the sky,

And at every wandering cloud that trailed

    Its ravelled fleeces by.

He did not wring his hands, as do

    Those witless men who dare

To try to rear the changeling Hope

    In the cave of black Despair:

He only looked upon the sun,

    And drank the morning air.

He did not wring his hands nor weep,

    Nor did he peek or pine,

But he drank the air as though it held

    Some healthful anodyne;

With open mouth he drank the sun

    As though it had been wine!

And I and all the souls in pain,

    Who tramped the other ring,

Forgot if we ourselves had done

    A great or little thing,

And watched with gaze of dull amaze

    The man who had to swing.

And strange it was to see him pass

    With a step so light and gay,

And strange it was to see him look

    So wistfully at the day,

And strange it was to think that he
   Had such a debt to pay.

For oak and elm have pleasant leaves
   That in the springtime shoot:
But grim to see is the gallows-tree,
   With its adder-bitten root,
And, green or dry, a man must die
   Before it bears its fruit!

The loftiest place is that seat of grace
   For which all worldlings try:
But who would stand in hempen band
   Upon a scaffold high,
And through a murderer's collar take
   His last look at the sky?

It is sweet to dance to violins
   When Love and Life are fair:
To dance to flutes, to dance to lutes
   Is delicate and rare:
But it is not sweet with nimble feet
   To dance upon the air!

So with curious eyes and sick surmise

    We watched him day by day,

And wondered if each one of us

    Would end the self-same way,

For none can tell to what red Hell

    His sightless soul may stray.

At last the dead man walked no more

    Amongst the Trial Men,

And I knew that he was standing up

    In the black dock's dreadful pen,

And that never would I see his face

    In God's sweet world again.

Like two doomed ships that pass in storm

    We had crossed each other's way:

But we made no sign, we said no word,

    We had no word to say;

For we did not meet in the holy night,

    But in the shameful day.

A prison wall was round us both,

Two outcast men we were:

The world had thrust us from its heart,

And God from out His care:

And the iron gin that waits for Sin

Had caught us in its snare.

III

In Debtors' Yard the stones are hard,

And the dripping wall is high,

So it was there he took the air

Beneath the leaden sky,

And by each side a Warder walked,

For fear the man might die.

Or else he sat with those who watched

His anguish night and day;

Who watched him when he rose to weep,

And when he crouched to pray;

Who watched him lest himself should rob

Their scaffold of its prey.

The Governor was strong upon

The Regulations Act:

The Doctor said that Death was but
    A scientific fact:
And twice a day the Chaplain called,
    And left a little tract.

And twice a day he smoked his pipe,
    And drank his quart of beer:
His soul was resolute, and held
    No hiding-place for fear;
He often said that he was glad
    The hangman's hands were near.

But why he said so strange a thing
    No Warder dared to ask:
For he to whom a watcher's doom
    Is given as his task,
Must set a lock upon his lips,
    And make his face a mask.

Or else he might be moved, and try
    To comfort or console:
And what should Human Pity do
    Pent up in Murderers' Hole?

What word of grace in such a place

   Could help a brother's soul?

With slouch and swing around the ring

   We trod the Fools' Parade!

We did not care: we knew we were

   The Devil's Own Brigade:

And shaven head and feet of lead

   Make a merry masquerade.

We tore the tarry rope to shreds

   With blunt and bleeding nails;

We rubbed the doors, and scrubbed the floors,

   And cleaned the shining rails:

And, rank by rank, we soaped the plank,

   And clattered with the pails.

We sewed the sacks, we broke the stones,

   We turned the dusty drill:

We banged the tins, and bawled the hymns,

   And sweated on the mill:

But in the heart of every man

   Terror was lying still.

So still it lay that every day

    Crawled like a weed-clogged wave:

And we forgot the bitter lot

    That waits for fool and knave,

Till once, as we tramped in from work,

    We passed an open grave.

With yawning mouth the yellow hole

    Gaped for a living thing;

The very mud cried out for blood

    To the thirsty asphalte ring:

And we knew that ere one dawn grew fair

    Some prisoner had to swing.

Right in we went, with soul intent

    On Death and Dread and Doom:

The hangman, with his little bag,

    Went shuffling through the gloom:

And each man trembled as he crept

    Into his numbered tomb.

That night the empty corridors

Were full of forms of Fear,

And up and down the iron town

Stole feet we could not hear,

And through the bars that hide the stars

White faces seemed to peer.

He lay as one who lies and dreams

In a pleasant meadow-land,

The watchers watched him as he slept,

And could not understand

How one could sleep so sweet a sleep

With a hangman close at hand.

But there is no sleep when men must weep

Who never yet have wept:

So we—the fool, the fraud, the knave—

That endless vigil kept,

And through each brain on hands of pain

Another's terror crept.

Alas! it is a fearful thing

To feel another's guilt!

For, right within, the sword of Sin

Pierced to its poisoned hilt,

And as molten lead were the tears we shed

For the blood we had not spilt.

The Warders with their shoes of felt

Crept by each padlocked door,

And peeped and saw, with eyes of awe,

Grey figures on the floor,

And wondered why men knelt to pray

Who never prayed before.

All through the night we knelt and prayed,

Mad mourners of a corse!

The troubled plumes of midnight were

The plumes upon a hearse:

And bitter wine upon a sponge

Was the savour of Remorse.

The grey cock crew, the red cock crew,

But never came the day:

And crooked shapes of Terror crouched,

In the corners where we lay:

And each evil sprite that walks by night

    Before us seemed to play.

They glided past, they glided fast,

    Like travellers through a mist:

They mocked the moon in a rigadoon

    Of delicate turn and twist,

And with formal pace and loathsome grace

    The phantoms kept their tryst.

With mop and mow, we saw them go,

    Slim shadows hand in hand:

About, about, in ghostly rout

    They trod a saraband:

And the damned grotesques made arabesques,

    Like the wind upon the sand!

With the pirouettes of marionettes,

    They tripped on pointed tread:

But with flutes of Fear they filled the ear,

    As their grisly masque they led,

And loud they sang, and long they sang,

    For they sang to wake the dead.

'Oho!' they cried, 'The world is wide,
*   But fettered limbs go lame!*
And once, or twice, to throw the dice
*   Is a gentlemanly game,*
But he does not win who plays with Sin
*   In the secret House of Shame.'*

No things of air these antics were,
    That frolicked with such glee:
To men whose lives were held in gyves,
    And whose feet might not go free,
Ah! wounds of Christ! they were living things,
    Most terrible to see.

Around, around, they waltzed and wound;
    Some wheeled in smirking pairs;
With the mincing step of a demirep
    Some sidled up the stairs:
And with subtle sneer, and fawning leer,
    Each helped us at our prayers.

The morning wind began to moan,

But still the night went on:

Through its giant loom the web of gloom

  Crept till each thread was spun:

And, as we prayed, we grew afraid

  Of the Justice of the Sun.

The moaning wind went wandering round

  The weeping prison-wall:

Till like a wheel of turning steel

  We felt the minutes crawl:

O moaning wind! what had we done

  To have such a seneschal?

At last I saw the shadowed bars,

  Like a lattice wrought in lead,

Move right across the whitewashed wall

  That faced my three-plank bed,

And I knew that somewhere in the world

  God's dreadful dawn was red.

At six o'clock we cleaned our cells,

  At seven all was still,

But the sough and swing of a mighty wing

The prison seemed to fill,
For the Lord of Death with icy breath
   Had entered in to kill.

He did not pass in purple pomp,
   Nor ride a moon-white steed.
Three yards of cord and a sliding board
   Are all the gallows' need:
So with rope of shame the Herald came
   To do the secret deed.

We were as men who through a fen
   Of filthy darkness grope:
We did not dare to breathe a prayer,
   Or to give our anguish scope:
Something was dead in each of us,
   And what was dead was Hope.

For Man's grim Justice goes its way,
   And will not swerve aside:
It slays the weak, it slays the strong,
   It has a deadly stride:
With iron heel it slays the strong,

The monstrous parricide!

We waited for the stroke of eight:
  Each tongue was thick with thirst:
For the stroke of eight is the stroke of Fate
  That makes a man accursed,
And Fate will use a running noose
  For the best man and the worst.

We had no other thing to do,
  Save to wait for the sign to come:
So, like things of stone in a valley lone,
  Quiet we sat and dumb:
But each man's heart beat thick and quick,
  Like a madman on a drum!

With sudden shock the prison-clock
  Smote on the shivering air,
And from all the gaol rose up a wail
  Of impotent despair,
Like the sound that frightened marshes hear
  From some leper in his lair.

And as one sees most fearful things

In the crystal of a dream,

We saw the greasy hempen rope

   Hooked to the blackened beam,

And heard the prayer the hangman's snare

   Strangled into a scream.

And all the woe that moved him so

   That he gave that bitter cry,

And the wild regrets, and the bloody sweats,

   None knew so well as I:

For he who lives more lives than one

   More deaths than one must die.

IV

There is no chapel on the day

   On which they hang a man:

The Chaplain's heart is far too sick,

   Or his face is far too wan,

Or there is that written in his eyes

   Which none should look upon.

So they kept us close till nigh on noon,

   And then they rang the bell,

248

And the Warders with their jingling keys
    Opened each listening cell,
And down the iron stair we tramped,
    Each from his separate Hell.

Out into God's sweet air we went,
    But not in wonted way,
For this man's face was white with fear,
    And that man's face was grey,
And I never saw sad men who looked
    So wistfully at the day.

I never saw sad men who looked
    With such a wistful eye
Upon that little tent of blue
    We prisoners called the sky,
And at every careless cloud that passed
    In happy freedom by.

But there were those amongst us all
    Who walked with downcast head,
And knew that, had each got his due,
    They should have died instead:

He had but killed a thing that lived,
  Whilst they had killed the dead.

For he who sins a second time
  Wakes a dead soul to pain,
And draws it from its spotted shroud,
  And makes it bleed again,
And makes it bleed great gouts of blood,
  And makes it bleed in vain!

Like ape or clown, in monstrous garb
  With crooked arrows starred,
Silently we went round and round
  The slippery asphalte yard;
Silently we went round and round,
  And no man spoke a word.

Silently we went round and round,
  And through each hollow mind
The Memory of dreadful things
  Rushed like a dreadful wind,
And Horror stalked before each man,
  And Terror crept behind.

250

The Warders strutted up and down,

    And kept their herd of brutes,

Their uniforms were spick and span,

    And they wore their Sunday suits,

But we knew the work they had been at,

    By the quicklime on their boots.

For where a grave had opened wide,

    There was no grave at all:

Only a stretch of mud and sand

    By the hideous prison-wall,

And a little heap of burning lime,

    That the man should have his pall.

For he has a pall, this wretched man,

    Such as few men can claim:

Deep down below a prison-yard,

    Naked for greater shame,

He lies, with fetters on each foot,

    Wrapt in a sheet of flame!

And all the while the burning lime

Eats flesh and bone away,

It eats the brittle bone by night,

And the soft flesh by day,

It eats the flesh and bone by turns,

But it eats the heart alway.

For three long years they will not sow

Or root or seedling there:

For three long years the unblessed spot

Will sterile be and bare,

And look upon the wondering sky

With unreproachful stare.

They think a murderer's heart would taint

Each simple seed they sow.

It is not true! God's kindly earth

Is kindlier than men know,

And the red rose would but blow more red,

The white rose whiter blow.

Out of his mouth a red, red rose!

Out of his heart a white!

For who can say by what strange way,

Christ brings His will to light,

Since the barren staff the pilgrim bore

   Bloomed in the great Pope's sight?

But neither milk-white rose nor red

   May bloom in prison-air;

The shard, the pebble, and the flint,

   Are what they give us there:

For flowers have been known to heal

   A common man's despair.

So never will wine-red rose or white,

   Petal by petal, fall

On that stretch of mud and sand that lies

   By the hideous prison-wall,

To tell the men who tramp the yard

   That God's Son died for all.

Yet though the hideous prison-wall

   Still hems him round and round,

And a spirit may not walk by night

   That is with fetters bound,

And a spirit may but weep that lies

In such unholy ground,

He is at peace—this wretched man—
   At peace, or will be soon:
There is no thing to make him mad,
   Nor does Terror walk at noon,
For the lampless Earth in which he lies
   Has neither Sun nor Moon.

They hanged him as a beast is hanged:
   They did not even toll
A requiem that might have brought
   Rest to his startled soul,
But hurriedly they took him out,
   And hid him in a hole.

They stripped him of his canvas clothes,
   And gave him to the flies:
They mocked the swollen purple throat,
   And the stark and staring eyes:
And with laughter loud they heaped the shroud
   In which their convict lies.

The Chaplain would not kneel to pray

By his dishonoured grave:
Nor mark it with that blessed Cross
That Christ for sinners gave,
Because the man was one of those
Whom Christ came down to save.

Yet all is well; he has but passed
To Life's appointed bourne:
And alien tears will fill for him
Pity's long-broken urn,
For his mourners will be outcast men,
And outcasts always mourn

V

I know not whether Laws be right,
Or whether Laws be wrong;
All that we know who lie in gaol
Is that the wall is strong;
And that each day is like a year,
A year whose days are long.

But this I know, that every Law
That men have made for Man,

Since first Man took his brother's life,

    And the sad world began,

But straws the wheat and saves the chaff

    With a most evil fan.

This too I know—and wise it were

    If each could know the same—

That every prison that men build

    Is built with bricks of shame,

And bound with bars lest Christ should see

    How men their brothers maim.

With bars they blur the gracious moon,

    And blind the goodly sun:

And they do well to hide their Hell,

    For in it things are done

That Son of God nor son of Man

    Ever should look upon!

The vilest deeds like poison weeds,

    Bloom well in prison-air;

It is only what is good in Man

    That wastes and withers there:

Pale Anguish keeps the heavy gate,

    And the Warder is Despair.

For they starve the little frightened child

    Till it weeps both night and day:

And they scourge the weak, and flog the fool,

    And gibe the old and grey,

And some grow mad, and all grow bad,

    And none a word may say.

Each narrow cell in which we dwell

    Is a foul and dark latrine,

And the fetid breath of living Death

    Chokes up each grated screen,

And all, but Lust, is turned to dust

    In Humanity's machine.

The brackish water that we drink

    Creeps with a loathsome slime,

And the bitter bread they weigh in scales

    Is full of chalk and lime,

And Sleep will not lie down, but walks

    Wild-eyed, and cries to Time.

But though lean Hunger and green Thirst

    Like asp with adder fight,

We have little care of prison fare,

    For what chills and kills outright

Is that every stone one lifts by day

    Becomes one's heart by night.

With midnight always in one's heart,

    And twilight in one's cell,

We turn the crank, or tear the rope,

    Each in his separate Hell,

And the silence is more awful far

    Than the sound of a brazen bell.

And never a human voice comes near

    To speak a gentle word:

And the eye that watches through the door

    Is pitiless and hard:

And by all forgot, we rot and rot,

    With soul and body marred.

And thus we rust Life's iron chain

Degraded and alone:

And some men curse, and some men weep,

And some men make no moan:

But God's eternal Laws are kind

And break the heart of stone.

And every human heart that breaks,

In prison-cell or yard,

Is as that broken box that gave

Its treasure to the Lord,

And filled the unclean leper's house

With the scent of costliest nard.

Ah! happy they whose hearts can break

And peace of pardon win!

How else may man make straight his plan

And cleanse his soul from Sin?

How else but through a broken heart

May Lord Christ enter in?

And he of the swollen purple throat,

And the stark and staring eyes,

Waits for the holy hands that took

The Thief to Paradise;

And a broken and a contrite heart

The Lord will not despise.

The man in red who reads the Law

Gave him three weeks of life,

Three little weeks in which to heal

His soul of his soul's strife,

And cleanse from every blot of blood

The hand that held the knife.

And with tears of blood he cleansed the hand,

The hand that held the steel:

For only blood can wipe out blood,

And only tears can heal:

And the crimson stain that was of Cain

Became Christ's snow-white seal.

VI

In Reading gaol by Reading town

There is a pit of shame,

And in it lies a wretched man

Eaten by teeth of flame,

In a burning winding-sheet he lies,

And his grave has got no name.

And there, till Christ call forth the dead,

In silence let him lie:

No need to waste the foolish tear,

Or heave the windy sigh:

The man had killed the thing he loved,

And so he had to die.

And all men kill the thing they love,

By all let this be heard,

Some do it with a bitter look,

Some with a flattering word,

The coward does it with a kiss,

The brave man with a sword!

RAVENNA

Newdigate Prize Poem

Recited in the Sheldonian Theatre

Oxford

June 26th, 1878

TO MY FRIEND

GEORGE FLEMING

AUTHOR OF

'THE NILE NOVEL' AND 'MIRAGE'

Ravenna, March 1877

Oxford, March 1878

RAVENNA

I.

A year ago I breathed the Italian air,—

And yet, methinks this northern Spring is fair,—

These fields made golden with the flower of March,

The throstle singing on the feathered larch,

The cawing rooks, the wood-doves fluttering by,

The little clouds that race across the sky;

And fair the violet's gentle drooping head,

The primrose, pale for love uncomforted,

The rose that burgeons on the climbing briar,

The crocus-bed, (that seems a moon of fire

Round-girdled with a purple marriage-ring);

And all the flowers of our English Spring,

Fond snowdrops, and the bright-starred daffodil.

Up starts the lark beside the murmuring mill,

And breaks the gossamer-threads of early dew;

And down the river, like a flame of blue,

Keen as an arrow flies the water-king,

While the brown linnets in the greenwood sing.

A year ago!—it seems a little time

Since last I saw that lordly southern clime,

Where flower and fruit to purple radiance blow,

And like bright lamps the fabled apples glow.

Full Spring it was—and by rich flowering vines,

Dark olive-groves and noble forest-pines,

I rode at will; the moist glad air was sweet,

The white road rang beneath my horse's feet,

And musing on Ravenna's ancient name,

I watched the day till, marked with wounds of flame,

The turquoise sky to burnished gold was turned.

O how my heart with boyish passion burned,

When far away across the sedge and mere

I saw that Holy City rising clear,

Crowned with her crown of towers!—On and on

I galloped, racing with the setting sun,

And ere the crimson after-glow was passed,

I stood within Ravenna's walls at last!

II.

How strangely still! no sound of life or joy

Startles the air; no laughing shepherd-boy

Pipes on his reed, nor ever through the day

Comes the glad sound of children at their play:

O sad, and sweet, and silent! surely here

A man might dwell apart from troublous fear,

Watching the tide of seasons as they flow

From amorous Spring to Winter's rain and snow,

And have no thought of sorrow;—here, indeed,

Are Lethe's waters, and that fatal weed

Which makes a man forget his fatherland.

Ay! amid lotus-meadows dost thou stand,

Like Proserpine, with poppy-laden head,

Guarding the holy ashes of the dead.

For though thy brood of warrior sons hath ceased,

Thy noble dead are with thee!—they at least

Are faithful to thine honour:—guard them well,

O childless city! for a mighty spell,

To wake men's hearts to dreams of things sublime,

Are the lone tombs where rest the Great of Time.

III.

Yon lonely pillar, rising on the plain,

Marks where the bravest knight of France was slain,—

The Prince of chivalry, the Lord of war,

Gaston de Foix: for some untimely star

Led him against thy city, and he fell,

As falls some forest-lion fighting well.

Taken from life while life and love were new,

He lies beneath God's seamless veil of blue;

Tall lance-like reeds wave sadly o'er his head,

And oleanders bloom to deeper red,

Where his bright youth flowed crimson on the ground.

265

Look farther north unto that broken mound,—

There, prisoned now within a lordly tomb

Raised by a daughter's hand, in lonely gloom,

Huge-limbed Theodoric, the Gothic king,

Sleeps after all his weary conquering.

Time hath not spared his ruin,—wind and rain

Have broken down his stronghold; and again

We see that Death is mighty lord of all,

And king and clown to ashen dust must fall

Mighty indeed their glory! yet to me

Barbaric king, or knight of chivalry,

Or the great queen herself, were poor and vain,

Beside the grave where Dante rests from pain.

His gilded shrine lies open to the air;

And cunning sculptor's hands have carven there

The calm white brow, as calm as earliest morn,

The eyes that flashed with passionate love and scorn,

The lips that sang of Heaven and of Hell,

The almond-face which Giotto drew so well,

The weary face of Dante;—to this day,

Here in his place of resting, far away

266

From Arno's yellow waters, rushing down
Through the wide bridges of that fairy town,
Where the tall tower of Giotto seems to rise
A marble lily under sapphire skies!

Alas! my Dante! thou hast known the pain
Of meaner lives,—the exile's galling chain,
How steep the stairs within kings' houses are,
And all the petty miseries which mar
Man's nobler nature with the sense of wrong.
Yet this dull world is grateful for thy song;
Our nations do thee homage,—even she,
That cruel queen of vine-clad Tuscany,
Who bound with crown of thorns thy living brow,
Hath decked thine empty tomb with laurels now,
And begs in vain the ashes of her son.

O mightiest exile! all thy grief is done:
Thy soul walks now beside thy Beatrice;
Ravenna guards thine ashes: sleep in peace.

IV.

How lone this palace is; how grey the walls!

No minstrel now wakes echoes in these halls.

The broken chain lies rusting on the door,

And noisome weeds have split the marble floor:

Here lurks the snake, and here the lizards run

By the stone lions blinking in the sun.

Byron dwelt here in love and revelry

For two long years—a second Anthony,

Who of the world another Actium made!

Yet suffered not his royal soul to fade,

Or lyre to break, or lance to grow less keen,

'Neath any wiles of an Egyptian queen.

For from the East there came a mighty cry,

And Greece stood up to fight for Liberty,

And called him from Ravenna: never knight

Rode forth more nobly to wild scenes of fight!

None fell more bravely on ensanguined field,

Borne like a Spartan back upon his shield!

O Hellas! Hellas! in thine hour of pride,

Thy day of might, remember him who died

To wrest from off thy limbs the trammelling chain:

O Salamis! O lone Platæan plain!

O tossing waves of wild Euboean sea!

O wind-swept heights of lone Thermopylæ!

He loved you well—ay, not alone in word,

Who freely gave to thee his lyre and sword,

Like Æschylos at well-fought Marathon:

  And England, too, shall glory in her son,

Her warrior-poet, first in song and fight.

No longer now shall Slander's venomed spite

Crawl like a snake across his perfect name,

Or mar the lordly scutcheon of his fame.

  For as the olive-garland of the race,

Which lights with joy each eager runner's face,

As the red cross which saveth men in war,

As a flame-bearded beacon seen from far

By mariners upon a storm-tossed sea,—

Such was his love for Greece and Liberty!

  Byron, thy crowns are ever fresh and green:

Red leaves of rose from Sapphic Mitylene

Shall bind thy brows; the myrtle blooms for thee,

In hidden glades by lonely Castaly;

The laurels wait thy coming: all are thine,

And round thy head one perfect wreath will twine.

V.

The pine-tops rocked before the evening breeze

With the hoarse murmur of the wintry seas,

And the tall stems were streaked with amber bright;—

I wandered through the wood in wild delight,

Some startled bird, with fluttering wings and fleet,

Made snow of all the blossoms; at my feet,

Like silver crowns, the pale narcissi lay,

And small birds sang on every twining spray.

O waving trees, O forest liberty!

Within your haunts at least a man is free,

And half forgets the weary world of strife:

The blood flows hotter, and a sense of life

Wakes i' the quickening veins, while once again

The woods are filled with gods we fancied slain.

Long time I watched, and surely hoped to see

Some goat-foot Pan make merry minstrelsy

Amid the reeds! some startled Dryad-maid

In girlish flight! or lurking in the glade,

The soft brown limbs, the wanton treacherous face

Of woodland god! Queen Dian in the chase,

White-limbed and terrible, with look of pride,

And leash of boar-hounds leaping at her side!

Or Hylas mirrored in the perfect stream.

O idle heart! O fond Hellenic dream!

Ere long, with melancholy rise and swell,

The evening chimes, the convent's vesper bell,

Struck on mine ears amid the amorous flowers.

Alas! alas! these sweet and honied hours

Had whelmed my heart like some encroaching sea,

And drowned all thoughts of black Gethsemane.

VI.

O lone Ravenna! many a tale is told

Of thy great glories in the days of old:

Two thousand years have passed since thou didst see

Cæsar ride forth to royal victory.

Mighty thy name when Rome's lean eagles flew

From Britain's isles to far Euphrates blue;

And of the peoples thou wast noble queen,

Till in thy streets the Goth and Hun were seen.

Discrowned by man, deserted by the sea,

271

Thou sleepest, rocked in lonely misery!

No longer now upon thy swelling tide,

Pine-forest-like, thy myriad galleys ride!

For where the brass-beaked ships were wont to float,

The weary shepherd pipes his mournful note;

And the white sheep are free to come and go

Where Adria's purple waters used to flow.

O fair! O sad! O Queen uncomforted!

In ruined loveliness thou liest dead,

Alone of all thy sisters; for at last

Italia's royal warrior hath passed

Rome's lordliest entrance, and hath worn his crown

In the high temples of the Eternal Town!

The Palatine hath welcomed back her king,

And with his name the seven mountains ring!

And Naples hath outlived her dream of pain,

And mocks her tyrant! Venice lives again,

New risen from the waters! and the cry

Of Light and Truth, of Love and Liberty,

Is heard in lordly Genoa, and where

The marble spires of Milan wound the air,

Rings from the Alps to the Sicilian shore,

And Dante's dream is now a dream no more.

But thou, Ravenna, better loved than all,

Thy ruined palaces are but a pall

That hides thy fallen greatness! and thy name

Burns like a grey and flickering candle-flame

Beneath the noonday splendour of the sun

Of new Italia! for the night is done,

The night of dark oppression, and the day

Hath dawned in passionate splendour: far away

The Austrian hounds are hunted from the land,

Beyond those ice-crowned citadels which stand

Girdling the plain of royal Lombardy,

From the far West unto the Eastern sea.

I know, indeed, that sons of thine have died

In Lissa's waters, by the mountain-side

Of Aspromonte, on Novara's plain,—

Nor have thy children died for thee in vain:

And yet, methinks, thou hast not drunk this wine

From grapes new-crushed of Liberty divine,

Thou hast not followed that immortal Star

273

Which leads the people forth to deeds of war.

Weary of life, thou liest in silent sleep,

As one who marks the lengthening shadows creep,

Careless of all the hurrying hours that run,

Mourning some day of glory, for the sun

Of Freedom hath not shewn to thee his face,

And thou hast caught no flambeau in the race.

   Yet wake not from thy slumbers,—rest thee well,

Amidst thy fields of amber asphodel,

Thy lily-sprinkled meadows,—rest thee there,

To mock all human greatness: who would dare

To vent the paltry sorrows of his life

Before thy ruins, or to praise the strife

Of kings' ambition, and the barren pride

Of warring nations! wert not thou the Bride

Of the wild Lord of Adria's stormy sea!

The Queen of double Empires! and to thee

Were not the nations given as thy prey!

And now—thy gates lie open night and day,

The grass grows green on every tower and hall,

The ghastly fig hath cleft thy bastioned wall;

And where thy mailèd warriors stood at rest

The midnight owl hath made her secret nest.

O fallen! fallen! from thy high estate,

O city trammelled in the toils of Fate,

Doth nought remain of all thy glorious days,

But a dull shield, a crown of withered bays!

   Yet who beneath this night of wars and fears,

From tranquil tower can watch the coming years;

Who can foretell what joys the day shall bring,

Or why before the dawn the linnets sing?

Thou, even thou, mayst wake, as wakes the rose

To crimson splendour from its grave of snows;

As the rich corn-fields rise to red and gold

From these brown lands, now stiff with Winter's cold;

As from the storm-rack comes a perfect star!

   O much-loved city! I have wandered far

From the wave-circled islands of my home;

Have seen the gloomy mystery of the Dome

Rise slowly from the drear Campagna's way,

Clothed in the royal purple of the day:

I from the city of the violet crown

Have watched the sun by Corinth's hill go down,

And marked the 'myriad laughter' of the sea

From starlit hills of flower-starred Arcady;

Yet back to thee returns my perfect love,

As to its forest-nest the evening dove.

O poet's city! one who scarce has seen

Some twenty summers cast their doublets green

For Autumn's livery, would seek in vain

To wake his lyre to sing a louder strain,

Or tell thy days of glory;—poor indeed

Is the low murmur of the shepherd's reed,

Where the loud clarion's blast should shake the sky,

And flame across the heavens! and to try

Such lofty themes were folly: yet I know

That never felt my heart a nobler glow

Than when I woke the silence of thy street

With clamorous trampling of my horse's feet,

And saw the city which now I try to sing,

After long days of weary travelling.

VII.

Adieu, Ravenna! but a year ago,

I stood and watched the crimson sunset glow

From the lone chapel on thy marshy plain:

The sky was as a shield that caught the stain

Of blood and battle from the dying sun,

And in the west the circling clouds had spun

A royal robe, which some great God might wear,

While into ocean-seas of purple air

Sank the gold galley of the Lord of Light.

   Yet here the gentle stillness of the night

Brings back the swelling tide of memory,

And wakes again my passionate love for thee:

Now is the Spring of Love, yet soon will come

On meadow and tree the Summer's lordly bloom;

And soon the grass with brighter flowers will blow,

And send up lilies for some boy to mow.

Then before long the Summer's conqueror,

Rich Autumn-time, the season's usurer,

Will lend his hoarded gold to all the trees,

And see it scattered by the spendthrift breeze;

And after that the Winter cold and drear.

So runs the perfect cycle of the year.

And so from youth to manhood do we go,

And fall to weary days and locks of snow.

277

Love only knows no winter; never dies:

Nor cares for frowning storms or leaden skies

And mine for thee shall never pass away,

Though my weak lips may falter in my lay.

Adieu! Adieu! yon silent evening star,

The night's ambassador, doth gleam afar,

And bid the shepherd bring his flocks to fold.

Perchance before our inland seas of gold

Are garnered by the reapers into sheaves,

Perchance before I see the Autumn leaves,

I may behold thy city; and lay down

Low at thy feet the poet's laurel crown.

Adieu! Adieu! yon silver lamp, the moon,

Which turns our midnight into perfect noon,

Doth surely light thy towers, guarding well

Where Dante sleeps, where Byron loved to dwell.

SALOMÉ: A TRAGEDY IN ONE ACT

THE PERSONS OF THE PLAY.

HEROD ANTIPAS, TETRARCH OF JUDÆA.

JOKANAAN, THE PROPHET.

THE YOUNG SYRIAN, CAPTAIN of the GUARD.

TIGELLINUS, A YOUNG ROMAN.

A CAPPADOCIAN.

A NUBIAN.

FIRST SOLDIER.

SECOND SOLDIER.

THE PAGE OF HERODIAS. JEWS, NAZARENES, ETC.

A SLAVE.

NAAMAN, THE EXECUTIONER.

HERODIAS, WIFE OF THE TETRARCH.

SALOMÉ, DAUGHTER OF HERODIAS.

THE SLAVES OF SALOMÉ.

A NOTE ON "SALOMÉ."

"SALOMÉ" has made the author's name a household word wherever the English language is not spoken. Few English plays have such a peculiar history. Written in French in 1892 it was in full rehearsal by Madame Bernhardt at the Palace Theatre when it was prohibited by the Censor. Oscar Wilde immediately announced his intention of changing his nationality, a characteristic jest, which was only taken seriously, oddly enough, in Ireland. The interference of the Censor has seldom been more popular or more heartily endorsed by English critics. On its publication in book form "Salomé" was greeted by a chorus of ridicule, and it may be noted in passing that at least two of the more violent reviews were from the pens of unsuccessful dramatists, while all those whose French never went beyond Ollendorff were glad to find in that venerable school classic an unsuspected asset in their education—a handy missile with which to pelt "Salomé" and its author. The correctness of the French was, of course, impugned, although the scrip had been passed by a distinguished French writer, to whom I have heard the whole work attributed. The Times, while depreciating the drama, gave its author credit for a tour de force, in being capable of writing a French play for Madame Bernhardt, and this drew from him the following letter:—

The Times, Thursday, March 2, 1893, p. 4.

MR. OSCAR WILDE ON "SALOMÉ."

To the Editor of The Times.

Sir, My attention has been drawn to a review of "Salomé" which was published in your columns last week. The opinions of English critics on a French work of mine have, of course, little, if any, interest for me. I write simply to ask you to allow me to correct a misstatement that appears in the review in question.

The fact that the greatest tragic actress of any stage now living saw in my play such beauty that she was anxious to produce it, to take herself the part of the heroine, to lend to the entire poem the glamour of her personality, and to my prose the music of her flute-like voice—this was naturally, and always will be, a source of pride and pleasure to me, and I look forward with delight to seeing Mme. Bernhardt present my play in Paris, that vivid centre of art, where religious dramas are often performed. But my play was in no sense of the words written for this great actress. I have never written a play for any actor or actress, nor shall I ever do so. Such work is for the artisan in literature—not for the artist.

I remain, Sir, your obedient servant,

OSCAR WILDE.

When "Salomé" was translated into English by Lord Alfred Douglas, the illustrator, Aubrey Beardsley, shared some of the obloquy heaped on Wilde. It is interesting that he should have found inspiration for his finest work in a play he never admired and by a writer he cordially disliked. The motives are, of course, made to his hand, and never was there a more suitable material for that odd tangent art in which there are no tactile values. The amusing caricatures of Wilde which appear in the Frontispiece, "Enter Herodias" and "The Eyes of Herod," are the only pieces of vraisemblance in these exquisite designs. The colophon is a real masterpiece and a witty criticism of the play as well.

On the production of "Salomé" by the New Stage Club in May, 1905,[1] the dramatic critics again expressed themselves vehemently, vociferating their regrets that the play had been dragged from its obscurity. The obscure drama, however, had become for five years past part of the literature of Europe. It is performed regularly or intermittently in Holland, Sweden, Italy, France, and Russia, and it has been translated into every European language, including the Czech. It forms part of the repertoire of the German stage, where it is performed more often than any play by any English writer except Shakespeare. Owing, perhaps, to what I must call its obscure popularity in the continental theatres, Dr. Strauss was preparing his remarkable opera at the very moment when there appeared the criticisms to which I refer, and since the production of the opera in Dresden in December, 1905, English musical journalists and correspondents always refer to the work as founded on Wilde's drama. That is the only way in which they can evade an awkward truth—a palpable contravention to their own wishes and theories. The music, however, has been set to the actual words of "Salomé" in Madame Hedwig Lachmann's admirable translation. The words have not been transfigured into ordinary operatic nonsense to suit the score, or the susceptibilities of the English people. I observe that admirers of Dr. Strauss are a little mortified that the great master should have found an occasion for composition in a play which they long ago consigned to oblivion and the shambles of Aubrey Beardsley. Wilde himself, in a rhetorical period, seems to have contemplated the possibility of his prose drama for a musical theme. In "De Profundis" he says: "The refrains, whose recurring motifs make 'Salomé' so like a piece of music, and bind it together as a ballad."

He was still incarcerated in 1896, when Mons. Luigne Poë produced the play for the first time at the Théâtre Libre in Paris, with Lina Muntz in the title role. A rather pathetic reference to this occasion occurs in a letter Wilde wrote to me from Reading:—

"Please say how gratified I was at the performance of my play, and have my thanks conveyed to Luigne Poë. It is something that at a time of disgrace and shame I should still be regarded as an artist. I wish I could feel more pleasure, but I seem dead to all emotions except those of anguish and despair. However, please let Luigne Poë know that I am sensible of the honour he has done me. He is a poet himself. Write to me in answer to this, and try and see what Lemaitre, Bauer, and Sarcey said of 'Salomé.'"

The bias of personal friendship precludes me from praising or defending "Salomé," even if it were necessary to do so. Nothing I might say would add to the reputation of its detractors. Its sources are obvious; particularly Flaubert and Maeterlinck, in whose peculiar and original style it is an essay. A critic, for whom I have a greater regard than many of his contemporaries, says that "Salomé" is only a catalogue; but a catalogue can be intensely dramatic, as we know when the performance takes place at Christie's; few plays are more exciting than an auction in King Street when the stars are fighting for Sisera.

287

It has been remarked that Wilde confuses Herod the Great (Mat. xi. 1), Herod Antipas (Mat. xiv. 3), and Herod Agrippa (Acts xiii), but the confusion is intentional, as in mediæval mystery plays Herod is taken for a type, not an historical character, and the criticism is about as valuable as that of people who laboriously point out the anachronisms in Beardsley's designs. With reference to the charge of plagiarism brought against "Salomé" and its author, I venture to mention a personal recollection.

Wilde complained to me one day that someone in a well-known novel had stolen an idea of his. I pleaded in defence of the culprit that Wilde himself was a fearless literary thief. "My dear fellow," he said, with his usual drawling emphasis, "when I see a monstrous tulip with four wonderful petals in someone else's garden, I am impelled to grow a monstrous tulip with five wonderful petals, but that is no reason why someone should grow a tulip with only three petals." THAT WAS OSCAR WILDE.

ROBERT ROSS.

[1] A more recent performance of "Salomé" (1906), by the Literary Theatre Club, has again produced an ebullition of rancour and deliberate misrepresentation on the part of the dramatic critics, the majority of whom are anxious to parade their ignorance of the continental stage. The production was remarkable on account of the beautiful dresses and mounting, for which Mr. Charles Ricketts was responsible, and the marvellous impersonation of Herod by Mr. Robert Farquharson. Wilde used to say that "Salomé" was a mirror in which everyone could see himself. The artist, art; the dull, dulness; the vulgar, vulgarity.

Cast of the Performance of "Salomé," represented in England for the first time.

NEW STAGE CLUB.

"SALOMÉ,"

BY OSCAR WILDE.

May 10th and 13th 1905.

A YOUNG SYRIAN CAPTAIN — MR. HERBERT ALEXANDER.

PAGE OF HERODIAS — MRS. GWENDOLEN BISHOP.

FIRST SOLDIER — MR. CHARLES GEE.

SECOND SOLDIER — MR. RALPH DE ROHAN.

CAPPADOCIAN — MR. CHARLES DALMON.

JOKANAAN — MR. VINCENT NELLO.

NAAMAN, THE EXECUTIONER — MR. W. EVELYN OSBORN.

SALOMÉ — Miss MILLICENT MURBY.

SLAVE — Miss CARRIE KEITH.

HEROD — MR. ROBERT FARQUHARSON.

HERODIAS — Miss LOUISE SALOM.

TIGELLINUS — MR. C.L. DELPH.

SLAVE — Miss STANSFELD.

FIRST JEW — MR. F. STANLEY SMITH.

SECOND JEW — MR. BERNHARD SMITH.

THIRD JEW — MR. JOHN BATE.

FOURTH JEW — STEPHEN BAGEHOT

FIFTH JEW — FREDERICK LAWRENCE.

Scene—THE GREAT TERRACE OUTSIDE THE PALACE.

289

SCENE.—*A great terrace in the Palace of Herod, set above the banqueting-hall. Some soldiers are leaning over the balcony. To the right there is a gigantic staircase, to the left, at the back, an old cistern surrounded by a wall of green bronze. Moonlight.*

THE YOUNG SYRIAN

How beautiful is the Princess Salomé to-night!

THE PAGE OF HERODIAS

Look at the moon! How strange the moon seems! She is like a woman rising from a tomb. She is like a dead woman. You would fancy she was looking for dead things.

THE YOUNG SYRIAN

She has a strange look. She is like a little princess who wears a yellow veil, and whose feet are of silver. She is like a princess who has little white doves for feet. You would fancy she was dancing.

THE PAGE OF HERODIAS

She is like a woman who is dead. She moves very slowly.

[*Noise in the banqueting-hall.*]

FIRST SOLDIER

What an uproar! Who are those wild beasts howling?

SECOND SOLDIER

The Jews. They are always like that. They are disputing about their religion.

FIRST SOLDIER

Why do they dispute about their religion?

SECOND SOLDIER

I cannot tell. They are always doing it. The Pharisees, for instance, say

290

that there are angels, and the Sadducees declare that angels do not exist.

FIRST SOLDIER

I think it is ridiculous to dispute about such things.

THE YOUNG SYRIAN

How beautiful is the Princess Salomé to-night!

THE PAGE OF HERODIAS

You are always looking at her. You look at her too much. It is dangerous to look at people in such fashion. Something terrible may happen.

THE YOUNG SYRIAN

She is very beautiful to-night.

FIRST SOLDIER

The Tetrarch has a sombre look.

SECOND SOLDIER

Yes; he has a sombre look.

FIRST SOLDIER

He is looking at something.

SECOND SOLDIER

He is looking at some one.

FIRST SOLDIER

At whom is he looking?

SECOND SOLDIER

I cannot tell.

THE YOUNG SYRIAN

How pale the Princess is! Never have I seen her so pale. She is like the shadow of a white rose in a mirror of silver.

THE PAGE OF HERODIAS

You must not look at her. You look too much at her.

FIRST SOLDIER

Herodias has filled the cup of the Tetrarch.

THE CAPPADOCIAN

Is that the Queen Herodias, she who wears a black mitre sewn with pearls, and whose hair is powdered with blue dust?

FIRST SOLDIER

Yes; that is Herodias, the Tetrarch's wife.

SECOND SOLDIER

The Tetrarch is very fond of wine. He has wine of three sorts. One which is brought from the Island of Samothrace, and is purple like the cloak of Cæsar.

THE CAPPADOCIAN

I have never seen Cæsar.

SECOND SOLDIER

Another that comes from a town called Cyprus, and is yellow like gold.

THE CAPPADOCIAN

I love gold.

SECOND SOLDIER

And the third is a wine of Sicily. That wine is red like blood.

THE NUBIAN

The gods of my country are very fond of blood. Twice in the year we sacrifice to them young men and maidens; fifty young men and a hundred maidens. But it seems we never give them quite enough, for they are very harsh to us.

THE CAPPADOCIAN

In my country there are no gods left. The Romans have driven them out. There are some who say that they have hidden themselves in the mountains, but I do not believe it. Three nights I have been on the mountains seeking them everywhere. I did not find them. And at last I called them by their names, and they did not come. I think they are dead.

FIRST SOLDIER

The Jews worship a God that you cannot see.

THE CAPPADOCIAN

I cannot understand that.

FIRST SOLDIER

In fact, they only believe in things that you cannot see.

THE CAPPADOCIAN

That seems to me altogether ridiculous.

THE VOICE OF JOKANAAN

After me shall come another mightier than I. I am not worthy so much as to unloose the latchet of his shoes. When he cometh, the solitary places shall be glad. They shall blossom like the lily. The eyes of the blind shall see the day, and the ears of the deaf shall be opened. The new-born child shall put his hand upon the dragon's lair, he shall lead the lions by their manes.

SECOND SOLDIER

Make him be silent. He is always saying ridiculous things.

FIRST SOLDIER

No, no. He is a holy man. He is very gentle, too. Every day, when I give him to eat he thanks me.

THE CAPPADOCIAN

Who is he?

FIRST SOLDIER

A prophet.

THE CAPPADOCIAN

What is his name?

FIRST SOLDIER

Jokanaan.

THE CAPPADOCIAN

Whence comes he?

FIRST SOLDIER

From the desert, where he fed on locusts and wild honey. He was clothed in camel's hair, and round his loins he had a leathern belt. He was very terrible to look upon. A great multitude used to follow him. He even had disciples.

THE CAPPADOCIAN

What is he talking of?

FIRST SOLDIER

We can never tell. Sometimes he says terrible things, but it is impossible to understand what he says.

THE CAPPADOCIAN

May one see him?

FIRST SOLDIER

No. The Tetrarch has forbidden it.

THE YOUNG SYRIAN

The Princess has hidden her face behind her fan! Her little white hands are fluttering like doves that fly to their dove-cots. They are like white butterflies. They are just like white butterflies.

THE PAGE OF HERODIAS

What is that to you? Why do you look at her? You must not look at her.... Something terrible may happen.

THE CAPPADOCIAN

[*Pointing to the cistern.*]

What a strange prison!

SECOND SOLDIER

It is an old cistern.

THE CAPPADOCIAN

An old cistern! It must be very unhealthy.

SECOND SOLDIER

Oh no! For instance, the Tetrarch's brother, his elder brother, the first husband of Herodias the Queen, was imprisoned there for twelve years. It did not kill him. At the end of the twelve years he had to be strangled.

THE CAPPADOCIAN

Strangled? Who dared to do that?

SECOND SOLDIER

[*Pointing to the Executioner, a huge Negro.*]

That man yonder, Naaman.

THE CAPPADOCIAN

He was not afraid?

SECOND SOLDIER

Oh no! The Tetrarch sent him the ring.

THE CAPPADOCIAN

What ring?

SECOND SOLDIER

The death-ring. So he was not afraid.

THE CAPPADOCIAN

Yet it is a terrible thing to strangle a king.

FIRST SOLDIER

Why? Kings have but one neck, like other folk.

THE CAPPADOCIAN

I think it terrible.

THE YOUNG SYRIAN

The Princess rises! She is leaving the table! She looks very troubled. Ah, she is coming this way. Yes, she is coming towards us. How pale she is! Never have I seen her so pale.

THE PAGE OF HERODIAS

Do not look at her. I pray you not to look at her.

THE YOUNG SYRIAN

She is like a dove that has strayed.... She is like a narcissus trembling in the wind.... She is like a silver flower.

[*Enter Salomé.*]

SALOMÉ

I will not stay. I cannot stay. Why does the Tetrarch look at me all the while with his mole's eyes under his shaking eyelids? It is strange that the husband of my mother looks at me like that. I know not what it means. In truth, yes, I know it.

THE YOUNG SYRIAN

You have just left the feast, Princess?

SALOMÉ

How sweet the air is here! I can breathe here! Within there are Jews from Jerusalem who are tearing each other in pieces over their foolish ceremonies, and barbarians who drink and drink, and spill their wine on the pavement, and Greeks from Smyrna with painted eyes and painted cheeks, and frizzed hair curled in twisted coils, and silent, subtle Egyptians, with long nails of jade and russett cloaks, and Romans brutal and coarse, with their uncouth jargon. Ah! how I loathe the Romans! They are rough and common, and they give themselves the airs of noble lords.

THE YOUNG SYRIAN

Will you be seated, Princess?

THE PAGE OF HERODIAS

Why do you speak to her? Why do you look at her? Oh! something terrible will happen.

SALOMÉ

How good to see the moon! She is like a little piece of money, you would think she was a little silver flower. The moon is cold and chaste. I am sure she is a virgin, she has a virgin's beauty. Yes, she is a virgin. She has never defiled herself. She has never abandoned herself to men, like the other goddesses.

THE VOICE OF JOKANAAN

The Lord hath come. The son of man hath come. The centaurs have hidden themselves in the rivers, and the sirens have left the rivers, and are lying beneath the leaves of the forest.

SALOMÉ

Who was that who cried out?

SECOND SOLDIER

The prophet, Princess.

SALOMÉ

Ah, the prophet! He of whom the Tetrarch is afraid?

SECOND SOLDIER

We know nothing of that, Princess. It was the prophet Jokanaan who cried out.

THE YOUNG SYRIAN

Is it your pleasure that I bid them bring your litter, Princess? The night is fair in the garden.

SALOMÉ

He says terrible things about my mother, does he not?

SECOND SOLDIER

We never understand what he says, Princess.

SALOMÉ

Yes; he says terrible things about her.

[*Enter a Slave.*]

THE SLAVE

Princess, the Tetrarch prays you to return to the feast.

SALOMÉ

I will not go back.

THE YOUNG SYRIAN

Pardon me, Princess, but if you do not return some misfortune may happen.

SALOMÉ

Is he an old man, this prophet?

THE YOUNG SYRIAN

Princess, it were better to return. Suffer me to lead you in.

SALOMÉ

This prophet ... is he an old man?

FIRST SOLDIER

No, Princess, he is quite a young man.

SECOND SOLDIER

You cannot be sure. There are those who say he is Elias.

SALOMÉ

Who is Elias?

SECOND SOLDIER

A very ancient prophet of this country, Princess.

THE SLAVE

What answer may I give the Tetrarch from the Princess?

THE VOICE OF JOKANAAN

Rejoice not thou, land of Palestine, because the rod of him who smote thee is broken. For from the seed of the serpent shall come forth a basilisk, and that which is born of it shall devour the birds.

SALOMÉ

What a strange voice! I would speak with him.

FIRST SOLDIER

I fear it is impossible, Princess. The Tetrarch does not wish any one to speak with him. He has even forbidden the high priest to speak with him.

SALOMÉ

I desire to speak with him.

FIRST SOLDIER

It is impossible, Princess.

SALOMÉ

I will speak with him.

THE YOUNG SYRIAN

Would it not be better to return to the banquet?

SALOMÉ

Bring forth this prophet.

[*Exit the slave.*]

FIRST SOLDIER

We dare not, Princess.

SALOMÉ

[*Approaching the cistern and looking down into it.*]

How black it is, down there! It must be terrible to be in so black a pit! It is like a tomb.... [*To the soldiers.*] Did you not hear me? Bring out the prophet. I wish to see him.

SECOND SOLDIER

Princess, I beg you do not require this of us.

SALOMÉ

You keep me waiting!

FIRST SOLDIER

Princess, our lives belong to you, but we cannot do what you have asked of us. And indeed, it is not of us that you should ask this thing.

SALOMÉ

[*Looking at the young Syrian.*]

Ah!

THE PAGE OF HERODIAS

Oh! what is going to happen? I am sure that some misfortune will happen.

SALOMÉ

[*Going up to the young Syrian.*]

You will do this tiling for me, will you not, Narraboth? You will do this thing for me. I have always been kind to you. You will do it for me. I would but look at this strange prophet. Men have talked so much of him. Often have I heard the Tetrarch talk of him. I think the Tetrarch is afraid of him. Are you, even you, also afraid of him, Narraboth?

THE YOUNG SYRIAN

I fear him not, Princess; there is no man I fear. But the Tetrarch has formally forbidden that any man should raise the cover of this well.

SALOMÉ

You will do this thing for me, Narraboth, and to-morrow when I pass in my litter beneath the gateway of the idol-sellers I will let fall for you a little flower, a little green flower.

THE YOUNG SYRIAN

Princess, I cannot, I cannot.

SALOMÉ

[*Smiling.*]

You will do this thing for me, Narraboth. You know that you will do this thing for me. And to-morrow when I pass in my litter by the bridge of the idol-buyers, I will look at you through the muslin veils, I will look at you, Narraboth, it may be I will smile at you. Look at me, Narraboth, look at me. Ah! you know that you will do what I ask of you. You know it well.... I know that you will do this thing.

THE YOUNG SYRIAN

[*Signing to the third soldier.*]

Let the prophet come forth.... The Princess Salomé desires to see him.

SALOMÉ

Ah!

THE PAGE OF HERODIAS

Oh! How strange the moon looks. You would think it was the hand of a dead woman who is seeking to cover herself with a shroud.

THE YOUNG SYRIAN

She has a strange look! She is like a little princess, whose eyes are eyes of amber. Through the clouds of muslin she is smiling like a little princess.

[*The prophet comes out of the cistern. Salomé looks at him and steps slowly back.*]

JOKANAAN

Where is he whose cup of abominations is now full? Where is he, who in a robe of silver shall one day die in the face of all the people? Bid him come forth, that he may hear the voice of him who hath cried in the waste places and in the houses of kings.

SALOMÉ

Of whom is he speaking?

THE YOUNG SYRIAN

You can never tell, Princess.

JOKANAAN

Where is she who having seen the images of men painted on the walls, the images of the Chaldeans limned in colours, gave herself up unto the lust of her eyes, and sent ambassadors into Chaldea?

SALOMÉ

It is of my mother that he speaks.

THE YOUNG SYRIAN

Oh, no, Princess.

SALOMÉ

Yes; it is of my mother that he speaks.

JOKANAAN

Where is she who gave herself unto the Captains of Assyria, who have baldricks on their loins, and tiaras of divers colours on their heads? Where is she who hath given herself to the young men of Egypt, who are clothed in fine linen and purple, whose shields are of gold, whose helmets are of silver, whose bodies are mighty? Bid her rise up from the bed of her abominations, from the bed of her incestuousness, that she may hear the words of him who prepareth the way of the Lord, that she may repent her of her iniquities. Though she will never repent, but will stick fast in her abominations; bid her come, for the fan of the Lord is in His hand.

SALOMÉ

But he is terrible, he is terrible!

THE YOUNG SYRIAN

Do not stay here, Princess, I beseech you.

SALOMÉ

It is his eyes above all that are terrible. They are like black holes burned by torches in a Tyrian tapestry. They are like black caverns where dragons dwell. They are like the black caverns of Egypt in which the dragons make their lairs. They are like black lakes troubled by fantastic moons.... Do you think he will speak again?

THE YOUNG SYRIAN

Do not stay here, Princess. I pray you do not stay here.

SALOMÉ

How wasted he is! He is like a thin ivory statue. He is like an image of silver. I am sure he is chaste as the moon is. He is like a moonbeam, like a shaft of silver. His flesh must be cool like ivory. I would look closer at him.

THE YOUNG SYRIAN

No, no, Princess.

SALOMÉ

I must look at him closer.

THE YOUNG SYRIAN

Princess! Princess!

JOKANAAN

Who is this woman who is looking at me? I will not have her look at me. Wherefore doth she look at me with her golden eyes, under her gilded eyelids? I know not who she is. I do not wish to know who she is. Bid her begone. It is not to her that I would speak.

SALOMÉ

I am Salomé, daughter of Herodias, Princess of Judæa.

JOKANAAN

Back! daughter of Babylon! Come not near the chosen of the Lord. Thy mother hath filled the earth with the wine of her iniquities, and the cry of her sins hath come up to the ears of God.

SALOMÉ

Speak again, Jokanaan. Thy voice is wine to me.

THE YOUNG SYRIAN

Princess! Princess! Princess!

SALOMÉ

Speak again! Speak again, Jokanaan, and tell me what I must do.

JOKANAAN

Daughter of Sodom, come not near me! But cover thy face with a veil, and scatter ashes upon thine head, and get thee to the desert and seek out the Son of Man.

SALOMÉ

Who is he, the Son of Man? Is he as beautiful as thou art, Jokanaan?

JOKANAAN

Get thee behind me! I hear in the palace the beating of the wings of the angel of death.

THE YOUNG SYRIAN

Princess, I beseech thee to go within.

JOKANAAN

Angel of the Lord God, what dost thou here with thy sword? Whom seekest thou in this foul palace? The day of him who shall die in a robe of silver has not yet come.

SALOMÉ

Jokanaan!

JOKANAAN

Who speaketh?

SALOMÉ

Jokanaan, I am amorous of thy body! Thy body is white like the lilies of a field that the mower hath never mowed. Thy body is white like the snows that lie on the mountains, like the snows that lie on the mountains of Judæa, and come down into the valleys. The roses in the garden of the Queen of Arabia are not so white as thy body. Neither the roses in the garden of the Queen of Arabia, the perfumed garden of spices of the Queen of Arabia, nor the feet of the dawn when they light on the leaves, nor the breast of the moon when she lies on the breast of the sea.... There is nothing in the world so white as thy body. Let me touch thy body.

JOKANAAN

Back! daughter of Babylon! By woman came evil into the world. Speak not to me. I will not listen to thee. I listen but to the voice of the Lord God.

SALOMÉ

Thy body is hideous. It is like the body of a leper. It is like a plastered wall where vipers have crawled; like a plastered wall where the scorpions have made their nest. It is like a whitened sepulchre full of loathsome things. It is horrible, thy body is horrible. It is of thy hair that I am enamoured, Jokanaan. Thy hair is like clusters of grapes, like the clusters of black grapes that hang from the vine-trees of Edom in the land of the Edomites. Thy hair is like the cedars of Lebanon, like the great cedars of Lebanon that give their shade to the lions and to the robbers who would hide themselves by day. The long black nights, when the moon hides her face, when the stars are afraid, are not so black. The silence that dwells in the forest is not so black. There is nothing in the world so black as thy hair.... Let me touch thy hair.

JOKANAAN

Back, daughter of Sodom! Touch me not. Profane not the temple of the Lord God.

306

SALOMÉ

Thy hair is horrible. It is covered with mire and dust. It is like a crown of thorns which they have placed on thy forehead. It is like a knot of black serpents writhing round thy neck. I love not thy hair.... It is thy mouth that I desire, Jokanaan. Thy mouth is like a band of scarlet on a tower of ivory. It is like a pomegranate cut with a knife of ivory. The pomegranate-flowers that blossom in the gardens of Tyre, and are redder than roses, are not so red. The red blasts of trumpets that herald the approach of kings, and make afraid the enemy, are not so red. Thy mouth is redder than the feet of those who tread the wine in the wine-press. Thy mouth is redder than the feet of the doves who haunt the temples and are fed by the priests. It is redder than the feet of him who cometh from a forest where he hath slain a lion, and seen gilded tigers. Thy mouth is like a branch of coral that fishers have found in the twilight of the sea, the coral that they keep for the kings!... It is like the vermilion that the Moabites find in the mines of Moab, the vermilion that the kings take from them. It is like the bow of the King of the Persians, that is painted with vermilion, and is tipped with coral. There is nothing in the world so red as thy mouth.... Let me kiss thy mouth.

JOKANAAN

Never! daughter of Babylon! Daughter of Sodom! Never.

SALOMÉ

I will kiss thy mouth, Jokanaan. I will kiss thy mouth.

THE YOUNG SYRIAN

Princess, Princess, thou who art like a garden of myrrh, thou who art the dove of all doves, look not at this man, look not at him! Do not speak such words to him. I cannot suffer them.... Princess, Princess, do not speak these things.

SALOMÉ

I will kiss thy mouth, Jokanaan.

THE YOUNG SYRIAN

Ah! [*He kills himself and falls between Salomé and Jokanaan.*]

THE PAGE OF HERODIAS

The young Syrian has slain himself! The young captain has slain himself! He has slain himself who was my friend! I gave him a little box of perfumes and ear-rings wrought in silver, and now he has killed himself! Ah, did he not foretell that some misfortune would happen? I, too, foretold it, and it has happened. Well I knew that the moon was seeking a dead thing, but I knew not that it was he whom she sought. Ah! why did I not hide him from the moon? If I had hidden him in a cavern she would not have seen him.

FIRST SOLDIER

Princess, the young captain has just killed himself.

SALOMÉ

Let me kiss thy mouth, Jokanaan.

JOKANAAN

Art thou not afraid, daughter of Herodias? Did I not tell thee that I had heard in the palace the beatings of the wings of the angel of death, and hath he not come, the angel of death?

SALOMÉ

Let me kiss thy mouth.

JOKANAAN

Daughter of adultery, there is but one who can save thee, it is He of whom I spake. Go seek Him. He is in a boat on the sea of Galilee, and He talketh with His disciples. Kneel down on the shore of the sea, and call unto Him by His name. When He cometh to thee (and to all who call on Him He cometh), bow thyself at His feet and ask of Him the remission of thy sins.

SALOMÉ

Let me kiss thy mouth.

JOKANAAN

Cursed be thou! daughter of an incestuous mother, be thou accursed!

SALOMÉ

I will kiss thy mouth, Jokanaan.

JOKANAAN

I do no wish to look at thee. I will not look at thee, thou art accursed, Salomé, thou art accursed. [He goes down into the cistern.]

SALOMÉ

I will kiss thy mouth, Jokanaan; I will kiss thy mouth.

FIRST SOLDIER

We must bear away the body to another place. The Tetrarch does not care to see dead bodies, save the bodies of those whom he himself has slain.

THE PAGE OF HERODIAS

He was my brother, and nearer to me than a brother. I gave him a little box full of perfumes, and a ring of agate that he wore always on his hand. In the evening we used to walk by the river, among the almond trees, and he would tell me of the things of his country. He spake ever very low. The sound of his voice was like the sound of the flute, of a flute player. Also he much loved to gaze at himself in the river. I used to reproach him for that.

SECOND SOLDIER

You are right; we must hide the body. The Tetrarch must not see it.

FIRST SOLDIER

The Tetrarch will not come to this place. He never comes on the terrace. He is too much afraid of the prophet.

[*Enter Herod, Herodias, and all the Court.*]

HEROD

309

Where is Salomé? Where is the Princess? Why did she not return to the banquet as I commanded her? Ah! there she is!

HERODIAS

You must not look at her! You are always looking at her!

HEROD

The moon has a strange look to-night. Has she not a strange look? She is like a mad woman, a mad woman who is seeking everywhere for lovers. She is naked too. She is quite naked. The clouds are seeking to clothe her nakedness, but she will not let them. She shows herself naked in the sky. She reels through the clouds like a drunken woman.... I am sure she is looking for lovers. Does she not reel like a drunken woman? She is like a mad woman, is she not?

HERODIAS

No; the moon is like the moon, that is all. Let us go within.... You have nothing to do here.

HEROD

I will stay here! Manesseh, lay carpets there. Light torches, bring forth the ivory tables, and the tables of jasper. The air here is delicious. I will drink more wine with my guests. We must show all honours to the ambassadors of Cæsar.

HERODIAS

It is not because of them that you remain.

HEROD

Yes; the air is delicious. Come, Herodias, our guests await us. Ah! I have slipped! I have slipped in blood! It is an ill omen. It is a very evil omen. Wherefore is there blood here?... and this body, what does this body here? Think you I am like the King of Egypt, who gives no feast to his guests but that he shows them a corpse? Whose is it? I will not look on it.

310

FIRST SOLDIER

It is our captain, sire. He is the young Syrian whom you made captain only three days ago.

HEROD

I gave no order that he should be slain.

SECOND SOLDIER

He killed himself, sire.

HEROD

For what reason? I had made him captain.

SECOND SOLDIER

We do not know, sire. But he killed himself.

HEROD

That seems strange to me. I thought it was only the Roman philosophers who killed themselves. Is it not true, Tigellinus, that the philosophers at Rome kill themselves?

TIGELLINUS

There are some who kill themselves, sire. They are the Stoics. The Stoics are coarse people. They are ridiculous people. I myself regard them as being perfectly ridiculous.

HEROD

I also. It is ridiculous to kill oneself.

TIGELLINUS

Everybody at Rome laughs at them. The Emperor has written a satire against them. It is recited everywhere.

HEROD

Ah! he has written a satire against them? Cæsar is wonderful. He can do everything.... It is strange that the young Syrian has killed himself. I am sorry he has killed himself. I am very sorry; for he was fair to look upon. He was even very fair. He had very languorous eyes. I remember that I saw that he looked languorously at Salomé. Truly, I thought he looked too much at her.

HERODIAS

There are others who look at her too much.

HEROD

His father was a king. I drove him from his kingdom. And you made a slave of his mother, who was a queen, Herodias. So he was here as my guest, as it were, and for that reason I made him my captain. I am sorry he is dead. Ho! why have you left the body here? I will not look at it—away with it! [They take away the body.] It is cold here. There is a wind blowing. Is there not a wind blowing?

HERODIAS

No; there is no wind.

HEROD

I tell you there is a wind that blows.... And I hear in the air something that is like the beating of wings, like the beating of vast wings. Do you not hear it?

HERODIAS

I hear nothing.

HEROD

I hear it no longer. But I heard it. It was the blowing of the wind, no doubt. It has passed away. But no, I hear it again. Do you not hear it? It is just like the beating of wings.

HERODIAS

I tell you there is nothing. You are ill. Let us go within.

312

HEROD

I am not ill. It is your daughter who is sick. She has the mien of a sick person. Never have I seen her so pale.

HERODIAS

I have told you not to look at her.

HEROD

Pour me forth wine [*wine is brought*]. Salomé, come drink a little wine with me. I have here a wine that is exquisite. Cæsar himself sent it me. Dip into it thy little red lips, that I may drain the cup.

SALOMÉ

I am not thirsty, Tetrarch.

HEROD

You hear how she answers me, this daughter of yours?

HERODIAS

She does right. Why are you always gazing at her?

HEROD

Bring me ripe fruits [*fruits are brought*]. Salomé, come and eat fruit with me. I love to see in a fruit the mark of thy little teeth. Bite but a little of this fruit and then I will eat what is left.

SALOMÉ

I am not hungry, Tetrarch.

HEROD

[*To Herodias.*] You see how you have brought up this daughter of yours.

HERODIAS

My daughter and I come of a royal race. As for thee, thy father was a camel driver! He was also a robber!

HEROD

Thou liest!

HERODIAS

Thou knowest well that it is true.

HEROD

Salomé, come and sit next to me. I will give thee the throne of thy mother.

SALOMÉ

I am not tired, Tetrarch.

HERODIAS

You see what she thinks of you.

HEROD

Bring me—what is it that I desire? I forget. Ah! ah! I remember.

 THE VOICE OF JOKANAAN

Lo! the time is come! That which I foretold has come to pass, saith the Lord God. Lo! the day of which I spoke.

HERODIAS

Bid him be silent. I will not listen to his voice. This man is for ever vomiting insults against me.

HEROD

He has said nothing against you. Besides, he is a very great prophet.

HERODIAS

I do not believe in prophets. Can a man tell what will come to pass?

No man knows it. Moreover, he is for ever insulting me. But I think you are afraid of him.... I know well that you are afraid of him.

HEROD

I am not afraid of him. I am afraid of no man.

HERODIAS

I tell you, you are afraid of him. If you are not afraid of him why do you not deliver him to the Jews, who for these six months past have been clamouring for him?

A JEW

Truly, my lord, it were better to deliver him into our hands.

HEROD

Enough on this subject. I have already given you my answer. I will not deliver him into your hands. He is a holy man. He is a man who has seen God.

A JEW

That cannot be. There is no man who hath seen God since the prophet Elias. He is the last man who saw God. In these days God doth not show Himself. He hideth Himself. Therefore great evils have come upon the land.

ANOTHER JEW

Verily, no man knoweth if Elias the prophet did indeed see God. Peradventure it was but the shadow of God that he saw.

A THIRD JEW

God is at no time hidden. He showeth Himself at all times and in everything. God is in what is evil even as He is in what is good.

A FOURTH JEW

That must not be said. It is a very dangerous doctrine. It is a doctrine that cometh from the schools at Alexandria, where men teach the philosophy of the Greeks. And the Greeks are Gentiles: They are not even circumcised.

A FIFTH JEW

No one can tell how God worketh. His ways are very mysterious. It may be that the things which we call evil are good, and that the things which we call good are evil. There is no knowledge of any thing. We must needs submit to everything, for God is very strong. He breaketh in pieces the strong together with the weak, for He regardeth not any man.

FIRST JEW

Thou speaketh truly. God is terrible; He breaketh the strong and the weak as a man brays corn in a mortar. But this man hath never seen God. No man hath seen God since the prophet Elias.

HERODIAS

Make them be silent. They weary me.

HEROD

But I have heard it said that Jokanaan himself is your prophet Elias.

THE JEW

That cannot be. It is more than three hundred years since the days of the prophet Elias.

HEROD

There be some who say that this man is the prophet Elias.

A NAZARENE

I am sure that he is the prophet Elias.

THE JEW

Nay, but he is not the prophet Elias.

THE VOICE OF JOKANAAN

So the day is come, the day of the Lord, and I hear upon the mountains the feet of Him who shall be the Saviour of the world.

HEROD

What does that mean? The Saviour of the world.

TIGELLINUS

It is a title that Cæsar takes.

HEROD

But Cæsar is not coming into Judæa. Only yesterday I received letters from Rome. They contained nothing concerning this matter. And you, Tigellinus, who were at Rome during the winter, you heard nothing concerning this matter, did you?

TIGELLINUS

Sire, I heard nothing concerning the matter. I was explaining the title. It is one of Cæsar's titles.

HEROD

But Cæsar cannot come. He is too gouty. They say that his feet are like the feet of an elephant. Also there are reasons of State. He who leaves Rome loses Rome. He will not come. Howbeit, Cæsar is lord, he will come if he wishes. Nevertheless, I do not think he will come.

FIRST NAZARENE

It was not concerning Cæsar that the prophet spake these words, sire.

HEROD

Not of Cæsar?

FIRST NAZARENE

No, sire.

HEROD

Concerning whom then did he speak?

FIRST NAZARENE

Concerning Messias who has come.

A JEW

Messiah hath not come.

FIRST NAZARENE

He hath come, and everywhere He worketh miracles.

HERODIAS Ho! ho! miracles! I do not believe in miracles. I have seen too many. [To the page.] My fan!

FIRST NAZARENE

This man worketh true miracles. Thus, at a marriage which took place in a little town of Galilee, a town of some importance, He changed water into wine. Certain persons who were present related it to me. Also He healed two lepers that were seated before the Gate of Capernaum simply by touching them.

SECOND NAZARENE

Nay, it was blind men that he healed at Capernaum.

FIRST NAZARENE

Nay; they were lepers. But He hath healed blind people also, and He was seen on a mountain talking with angels.

A SADDUCEE

Angels do not exist.

A PHARISEE

Angels exist, but I do not believe that this Man has talked with them.

FIRST NAZARENE

He was seen by a great multitude of people talking with angels.

A SADDUCEE

Not with angels.

HERODIAS

How these men weary me! They are ridiculous! [To the page.] Well! my fan! [The page gives her the fan.] You have a dreamer's look; you must not dream. It is only sick people who dream. [She strikes the page with her fan.]

SECOND NAZARENE

There is also the miracle of the daughter of Jairus.

FIRST NAZARENE

Yes, that is sure. No man can gainsay it.

HERODIAS

These men are mad. They have looked too long on the moon. Command them to be silent.

HEROD

What is this miracle of the daughter of Jairus?

FIRST NAZARENE

The daughter of Jairus was dead. He raised her from the dead.

HEROD

He raises the dead?

FIRST NAZARENE

Yea, sire, He raiseth the dead.

HEROD

I do not wish Him to do that. I forbid Him to do that. I allow no man to raise the dead. This Man must be found and told that I forbid Him to raise the dead. Where is this Man at present?

SECOND NAZARENE

He is in every place, my lord, but it is hard to find Him.

FIRST NAZARENE

It is said that He is now in Samaria.

A JEW

It is easy to see that this is not Messias, if He is in Samaria. It is not to the Samaritans that Messias shall come. The Samaritans are accursed. They bring no offerings to the Temple.

SECOND NAZARENE

He left Samaria a few days since. I think that at the present moment He is in the neighbourhood of Jerusalem.

FIRST NAZARENE

No; He is not there. I have just come from Jerusalem. For two months they have had no tidings of Him.

HEROD

No matter! But let them find Him, and tell Him from me, I will not allow him to raise the dead! To change water into wine, to heal the lepers and the blind.... He may do these things if He will. I say nothing against these things. In truth I hold it a good deed to heal a leper. But I allow no man to raise the dead. It would be terrible if the dead came back.

THE VOICE OF JOKANAAN

Ah! the wanton! The harlot! Ah! the daughter of Babylon with her golden eyes and her gilded eyelids!—Thus saith the Lord God, Let there come up against her a multitude of men. Let the people take stones and stone her....

HERODIAS

Command him to be silent.

THE VOICE OF JOKANAAN

Let the war captains pierce her with their swords, let them crush her beneath their shields.

HERODIAS

Nay, but it is infamous.

THE VOICE OF JOKANAAN

It is thus that I will wipe out all wickedness from the earth, and that all women shall learn not to imitate her abominations.

HERODIAS

You hear what he says against me? You allow him to revile your wife?

HEROD

He did not speak your name.

HERODIAS

What does that matter? You know well that it is I whom he seeks to revile. And I am your wife, am I not?

HEROD

Of a truth, dear and noble Herodias, you are my wife, and before that you were the wife of my brother.

HERODIAS

It was you who tore me from his arms.

HEROD

Of a truth I was stronger.... But let us not talk of that matter. I do not desire to talk of it. It is the cause of the terrible words that the prophet has spoken. Peradventure on account of it a misfortune will come. Let us not speak of this matter. Noble Herodias, we are not mindful of our guests. Fill thou my cup, my well-beloved. Fill with wine the great goblets of silver, and the great goblets of glass. I will drink to Cæsar. There are Romans here, we must drink to Cæsar.

ALL

Cæsar! Cæsar!

HEROD

Do you not see your daughter, how pale she is?

HERODIAS

What is it to you if she be pale or not?

HEROD

Never have I seen her so pale.

HERODIAS

You must not look at her.

THE VOICE OF JOKANAAN

In that day the sun shall become black like sackcloth of hair, and the moon shall become like blood, and the stars of the heavens shall fall upon the earth like ripe figs that fall from the fig-tree, and the kings of the earth shall be afraid.

HERODIAS

Ah! Ah! I should like to see that day of which he speaks, when the moon shall become like blood, and when the stars shall fall upon the earth like ripe figs. This prophet talks like a drunken man ... but I cannot suffer the sound of his voice. I hate his voice. Command him to be silent.

HEROD

I will not. I cannot understand what it is that he saith, but it may be an omen.

HERODIAS

I do not believe in omens. He speaks like a drunken man.

HEROD

It may be he is drunk with the wine of God.

HERODIAS

What wine is that, the wine of God? From what vineyards is it gathered? In what wine-press may one find it?

HEROD

[*From this point he looks all the while at Salomé.*]

Tigellinus, when you were at Rome of late, did the Emperor speak with you on the subject of...?

TIGELLINUS

On what subject, sire?

HEROD

On what subject? Ah! I asked you a question, did I not? I have forgotten what I would have asked you.

HERODIAS

You are looking again at my daughter. You must not look at her. I have already said so.

HEROD

You say nothing else.

HERODIAS

I say it again.

HEROD

And that restoration of the Temple about which they have talked so much, will anything be done? They say the veil of the Sanctuary has disappeared, do they not?

HERODIAS

It was thyself didst steal it. Thou speakest at random. I will not stay here. Let us go within.

HEROD

Dance for me, Salomé.

HERODIAS

I will not have her dance.

SALOMÉ

I have no desire to dance, Tetrarch.

HEROD

Salomé, daughter of Herodias, dance for me.

HERODIAS

Let her alone.

HEROD

I command thee to dance, Salomé.

SALOMÉ

I will not dance, Tetrarch.

HERODIAS

[*Laughing*].

You see how she obeys you.

HEROD

What is it to me whether she dance or not? It is naught to me. To-night I am happy, I am exceeding happy. Never have I been so happy.

FIRST SOLDIER

The Tetrarch has a sombre look. Has he not a sombre look?

SECOND SOLDIER

Yes, he has a sombre look.

HEROD

Wherefore should I not be happy? Cæsar, who is lord of the world, who is lord of all things, loves me well. He has just sent me most precious gifts. Also he has promised me to summon to Rome the King of Cappadocia, who is my enemy. It may be that at Rome he will crucify him, for he is able to do all things that he wishes. Verily, Cæsar is lord. Thus you see I have a right to be happy. Indeed, I am happy. I have never been so happy. There is nothing in the world that can mar my happiness.

THE VOICE OF JOKANAAN

He shall be seated on this throne. He shall be clothed in scarlet and purple. In his hand he shall bear a golden cup full of his blasphemies. And the angel of the Lord shall smite him. He shall be eaten of worms.

HERODIAS

You hear what he says about you. He says that you will be eaten of worms.

HEROD

It is not of me that he speaks. He speaks never against me. It is of the King of Cappadocia that he speaks; the King of Cappadocia, who is mine enemy. It is he who shall be eaten of worms. It is not I. Never has he spoken word against me, this prophet, save that I sinned in taking to wife the wife of my brother. It may be he is right. For, of a truth, you are sterile.

HERODIAS

I am sterile, I? You say that, you that are ever looking at my daughter, you that would have her dance for your pleasure? It is absurd to say that. I have borne a child. You have gotten no child, no, not even from one of your slaves. It is you who are sterile, not I.

HEROD

Peace, woman! I say that you are sterile. You have borne me no child, and the prophet says that our marriage is not a true marriage. He says that it is an incestuous marriage, a marriage that will bring evils.... I fear he is right; I am sure that he is right. But it is not the moment to speak of such things. I would be happy at this moment. Of a truth, I am happy. There is nothing I lack.

HERODIAS

I am glad you are of so fair a humour to-night. It is not your custom. But it is late. Let us go within. Do not forget that we hunt at sunrise. All honours must be shown to Cæsar's ambassadors, must they not?

SECOND SOLDIER

What a sombre look the Tetrarch wears.

FIRST SOLDIER

Yes, he wears a sombre look.

HEROD

Salomé, Salomé, dance for me. I pray thee dance for me. I am sad to-night. Yes; I am passing sad to-night. When I came hither I slipped in blood, which is an evil omen; and I heard, I am sure I heard in the air a beating of wings, a beating of giant wings. I cannot tell what they mean ... I am sad to-night. Therefore dance for me. Dance for me, Salomé, I beseech you. If you dance for me you may ask of me what you will, and I will give it you, even unto the half of my kingdom.

SALOMÉ

[*Rising.*] Will you indeed give me whatsoever I shall ask, Tetrarch?

326

HERODIAS

Do not dance, my daughter.

HEROD

Everything, even the half of my kingdom.

SALOMÉ

You swear it, Tetrarch?

HEROD

I swear it, Salomé.

HERODIAS

Do not dance, my daughter.

SALOMÉ

By what will you swear, Tetrarch?

HEROD

By my life, by my crown, by my gods. Whatsoever you desire I will give it you, even to the half of my kingdom, if you will but dance for me. O, Salomé, Salomé, dance for me!

SALOMÉ

You have sworn, Tetrarch.

HEROD

I have sworn, Salomé.

SALOMÉ

All this I ask, even the half of your kingdom.

HERODIAS

My daughter, do not dance.

HEROD

Even to the half of my kingdom. Thou wilt be passing fair as a queen, Salomé, if it please thee to ask for the half of my kingdom. Will she not be fair as a queen? Ah! it is cold here! There is an icy wind, and I hear ... wherefore do I hear in the air this beating of wings? Ah! one might fancy a bird, a huge black bird that hovers over the terrace. Why can I not see it, this bird? The beat of its wings is terrible. The breath of the wind of its wings is terrible. It is a chill wind. Nay, but it is not cold, it is hot. I am choking. Pour water on my hands. Give me snow to eat. Loosen my mantle. Quick! quick! loosen my mantle. Nay, but leave it. It is my garland that hurts me, my garland of roses. The flowers are like fire. They have burned my forehead. [He tears the wreath from his head and throws it on the table.] Ah! I can breathe now. How red those petals are! They are like stains of blood on the cloth. That does not matter. You must not find symbols in everything you see. It makes life impossible. It were better to say that stains of blood are as lovely as rose petals. It were better far to say that.... But we will not speak of this. Now I am happy, I am passing happy. Have I not the right to be happy? Your daughter is going to dance for me. Will you not dance for me, Salomé? You have promised to dance for me.

HERODIAS

I will not have her dance.

SALOMÉ

I will dance for you, Tetrarch.

HEROD

You hear what your daughter says. She is going to dance for me. You do well to dance for me, Salomé. And when you have danced for me, forget not to ask of me whatsoever you wish. Whatsoever you wish I will give it you, even to the half of my kingdom. I have sworn it, have I not?

SALOMÉ

You have sworn it, Tetrarch.

328

HEROD

And I have never broken my word. I am not of those who break their oaths. I know not how to lie. I am the slave of my word, and my word is the word of a king. The King of Cappadocia always lies, but he is no true king. He is a coward. Also he owes me money that he will not repay. He has even insulted my ambassadors. He has spoken words that were wounding. But Cæsar will crucify him when he comes to Rome. I am sure that Cæsar will crucify him. And if not, yet will he die, being eaten of worms. The prophet has prophesied it. Well! wherefore dost thou tarry, Salomé?

SALOMÉ

I am awaiting until my slaves bring perfumes to me and the seven veils, and take off my sandals. [Slaves bring perfumes and the seven veils, and take off the sandals of Salomé.]

HEROD

Ah, you are going to dance with naked feet. 'Tis well!—'Tis well. Your little feet will be like white doves. They will be like little white flowers that dance upon the trees.... No, no, she is going to dance on blood. There is blood spilt on the ground. She must not dance on blood. It were an evil omen.

HERODIAS

What is it to you if she dance on blood? Thou hast waded deep enough therein....

HEROD

What is it to me? Ah! look at the moon! She has become red. She has become red as blood. Ah! the prophet prophesied truly. He prophesied that the moon would become red as blood. Did he not prophesy it? All of you heard him. And now the moon has become red as blood. Do ye not see it?

HERODIAS

Oh, yes, I see it well, and the stars are falling like ripe figs, are they not? and the sun is becoming black like sackcloth of hair, and the kings of the

329

earth are afraid. That at least one can see. The prophet, for once in his life, was right, the kings of the earth are afraid.... Let us go within. You are sick. They will say at Rome that you are mad. Let us go within, I tell you.

THE VOICE OF JOKANAAN

Who is this who cometh from Edom, who is this who cometh from Bozra, whose raiment is dyed with purple, who shineth in the beauty of his garments, who walketh mighty in his greatness? Wherefore is thy raiment stained with scarlet?

HERODIAS

Let us go within. The voice of that man maddens me. I will not have my daughter dance while he is continually crying out. I will not have her dance while you look at her in this fashion. In a word, I will not have her dance.

HEROD

Do not rise, my wife, my queen, it will avail thee nothing. I will not go within till she hath danced. Dance, Salomé, dance for me.

HERODIAS

Do not dance, my daughter.

SALOMÉ

I am ready, Tetrarch.

[*Salomé dances the dance of the seven veils.*]

HEROD

Ah! wonderful! wonderful! You see that she has danced for me, your daughter. Come near, Salomé, come near, that I may give you your reward. Ah! I pay the dancers well. I will pay thee royally. I will give thee whatsoever thy soul desireth. What wouldst thou have? Speak.

SALOMÉ

[*Kneeling*].

330

I would that they presently bring me in a silver charger....

HEROD

[*Laughing.*]

In a silver charger? Surely yes, in a silver charger. She is charming, is she not? What is it you would have in a silver charger, O sweet and fair Salomé, you who are fairer than all the daughters of Judæa? What would you have them bring thee in a silver charger? Tell me. Whatsoever it may be, they shall give it you. My treasures belong to thee. What is it, Salomé?

SALOMÉ

[*Rising*].

The head of Jokanaan.

HERODIAS

Ah! that is well said, my daughter.

HEROD

No, no!

HERODIAS

That is well said, my daughter.

HEROD

No, no, Salomé. You do not ask me that. Do not listen to your mother's voice. She is ever giving you evil counsel. Do not heed her.

SALOMÉ

I do not heed my mother. It is for mine own pleasure that I ask the head of Jokanaan in a silver charger. You hath sworn, Herod. Forget not that you have sworn an oath.

HEROD

I know it. I have sworn by my gods. I know it well. But I pray you,

Salomé, ask of me something else. Ask of me the half of my kingdom, and I will give it you. But ask not of me what you have asked.

SALOMÉ

I ask of you the head of Jokanaan.

HEROD

No, no, I do not wish it.

SALOMÉ

You have sworn, Herod.

HERODIAS

Yes, you have sworn. Everybody heard you. You swore it before everybody.

HEROD

Be silent! It is not to you I speak.

HERODIAS

My daughter has done well to ask the head of Jokanaan. He has covered me with insults. He has said monstrous things against me. One can see that she loves her mother well. Do not yield, my daughter. He has sworn, he has sworn.

HEROD

Be silent, speak not to me!... Come, Salomé, be reasonable. I have never been hard to you. I have ever loved you.... It may be that I have loved you too much. Therefore ask not this thing of me. This is a terrible thing, an awful thing to ask of me. Surely, I think thou art jesting. The head of a man that is cut from his body is ill to look upon, is it not? It is not meet that the eyes of a virgin should look upon such a thing. What pleasure could you have in it? None. No, no, it is not what you desire. Hearken to me. I have an emerald, a great round emerald, which Cæsar's minion sent me. If you look through this emerald you can see things which happen at a great distance. Cæsar himself carries such an emerald when he goes to the circus. But my emerald is larger. I know well that it is larger. It is the largest emerald in the whole world. You would like that, would you not? Ask it of me and I will give it you.

SALOMÉ

I demand the head of Jokanaan.

HEROD

You are not listening. You are not listening. Suffer me to speak, Salomé.

SALOMÉ

The head of Jokanaan.

HEROD

No, no, you would not have that. You say that to trouble me, because I have looked at you all this evening. It is true, I have looked at you all this evening. Your beauty troubled me. Your beauty has grievously troubled me, and I have looked at you too much. But I will look at you no more. Neither at things, nor at people should one look. Only in mirrors should one look, for mirrors do but show us masks. Oh! oh! bring wine! I thirst.... Salomé, Salomé, let us be friends. Come now!... Ah! what would I say? What was't? Ah! I remember!... Salomé—nay, but come nearer to me; I fear you will not hear me—Salomé, you know my white peacocks, my beautiful white peacocks, that walk in the garden between the myrtles and the tall cypress trees. Their beaks are gilded with gold, and the grains that they eat are gilded with gold also, and their feet are stained with purple. When they cry out the rain comes, and the moon shows herself in the heavens when they spread their tails. Two by two they walk between the cypress trees and the black myrtles, and each has a slave to tend it. Sometimes they fly across the trees, and anon they crouch in the grass, and round the lake. There are not in all the world birds so wonderful. There is no king in all the world who possesses such wonderful birds. I am sure that Cæsar himself has no birds so fair as my birds. I will give you fifty of my peacocks. They will follow you whithersoever you go, and in the midst of them you will be like the moon in the midst of a great white cloud.... I will give them all to you. I have but a hundred, and in the whole world there is no king who has peacocks like unto my peacocks. But I will give them all to you. Only you must loose me from my oath, and must not ask of me that which you have asked of me.

[*He empties the cup of wine.*]

SALOMÉ

Give me the head of Jokanaan.

HERODIAS

Well said, my daughter! As for you, you are ridiculous with your peacocks.

HEROD

Be silent! You cry out always; you cry out like a beast of prey. You must not. Your voice wearies me. Be silent, I say Salomé, think of what you are doing. This man comes perchance from God. He is a holy man. The finger of God has touched him. God has put into his mouth terrible words. In the palace as in the desert God is always with him.... At least it is possible. One does not know. It is possible that God is for him and with him. Furthermore, if he died some misfortune might happen to me. In any case, he said that the day he dies a misfortune will happen to some one. That could only be to me. Remember, I slipped in blood when I entered. Also, I heard a beating of wings in the air, a beating of mighty wings. These are very evil omens, and there were others. I am sure there were others though I did not see them. Well, Salomé, you do not wish a misfortune to happen to me? You do not wish that. Listen to me, then.

SALOMÉ

Give me the head of Jokanaan.

HEROD

Ah! you are not listening to me. Be calm. I—I am calm. I am quite calm.

334

Listen. I have jewels hidden in this place—jewels that your mother even has never seen; jewels that are marvellous. I have a collar of pearls, set in four rows. They are like unto moons chained with rays of silver. They are like fifty moons caught in a golden net. On the ivory of her breast a queen has worn it. Thou shalt be as fair as a queen when thou wearest it. I have amethysts of two kinds, one that is black like wine, and one that is red like wine which has been coloured with water. I have topazes, yellow as are the eyes of tigers, and topazes that are pink as the eyes of a wood-pigeon, and green topazes that are as the eyes of cats. I have opals that burn always, with an icelike flame, opals that make sad men's minds, and are fearful of the shadows. I have onyxes like the eyeballs of a dead woman. I have moonstones that change when the moon changes, and are wan when they see the sun. I have sapphires big like eggs, and as blue as blue flowers. The sea wanders within them and the moon comes never to trouble the blue of their waves. I have chrysolites and beryls and chrysoprases and rubies. I have sardonyx and hyacinth stones, and stones of chalcedony, and I will give them all to you, all, and other things will I add to them. The King of the Indies has but even now sent me four fans fashioned from the feathers of parrots, and the King of Numidia a garment of ostrich feathers. I have a crystal, into which it is not lawful for a woman to look, nor may young men behold it until they have been beaten with rods. In a coffer of nacre I have three wondrous turquoises. He who wears them on his forehead can imagine things which are not, and he who carries them in his hand can make women sterile. These are great treasures above all price. They are treasures without price. But this is not all. In an ebony coffer I have two cups of amber, that are like apples of gold. If an enemy pour poison into these cups, they become like an apple of silver. In a coffer incrusted with amber I have sandals incrusted with glass. I have mantles that have been brought from the land of the Seres, and bracelets decked about with carbuncles and with jade that come from the city of Euphrates.... What desirest thou more than this, Salomé? Tell me the thing that thou desirest, and I will give it thee. All that thou askest I will give thee, save one thing. I will give thee all that is mine, save one life. I will give thee the mantle of the high priest. I will give thee the veil of the sanctuary.

THE JEWS

Oh! oh!

SALOMÉ

Give me the head of Jokanaan.

HEROD

[*Sinking back in his seat*]. Let her be given what she asks! Of a truth she is her mother's child! [*The first Soldier approaches. Herodias draws from the hand of the Tetrarch the ring of death and gives it to the Soldier, who straightway bears it to the Executioner. The Executioner looks scared.*] Who has taken my ring? There was a ring on my right hand. Who has drunk my wine? There was wine in my cup. It was full of wine. Someone has drunk it! Oh! surely some evil will befall some one. [*The Executioner goes down into the cistern.*] Ah! Wherefore did I give my oath? Kings ought never to pledge their word. If they keep it not, it is terrible, and if they keep it, it is terrible also.

HERODIAS

My daughter has done well.

HEROD

I am sure that some misfortune will happen.

SALOMÉ

[*She leans over the cistern and listens.*]

There is no sound. I hear nothing. Why does he not cry out, this man? Ah! if any man sought to kill me, I would cry out, I would struggle, I would not suffer.... Strike, strike, Naaman, strike, I tell you.... No, I hear nothing. There is a silence, a terrible silence. Ah! something has fallen upon the ground. I heard something fall. It is the sword of the headsman. He is afraid, this slave. He has let his sword fall. He dare not kill him. He is a coward, this slave! Let soldiers be sent. [*She sees the Page of Herodias and addresses him.*] Come hither, thou wert the friend of him who is dead, is it not so? Well, I tell thee, there are not dead men enough. Go to the soldiers and bid them go down and bring me the thing I ask, the thing the Tetrarch has promised me, the thing that is mine. [*The Page recoils. She turns to the soldiers.*] Hither, ye soldiers. Get ye down into this cistern and bring me the head of this man. [*The Soldiers recoil.*] Tetrarch, Tetrarch, command your soldiers that they bring me the head of Jokanaan.

[*A huge black arm, the arm of the Executioner, comes forth from the cistern, bearing on a silver shield the head of Jokanaan. Salomé seizes it. Herod hides his face with his cloak. Herodias smiles and fans herself. The Nazarenes fall on their knees and begin to pray.*]

Ah! thou wouldst not suffer me to kiss thy mouth, Jokanaan. Well! I will kiss it now. I will bite it with my teeth as one bites a ripe fruit. Yes, I will kiss thy mouth, Jokanaan. I said it; did I not say it? I said it. Ah! I will kiss it now.... But, wherefore dost thou not look at me, Jokanaan? Thine eyes that were so terrible, so full of rage and scorn, are shut now. Wherefore are they shut? Open thine eyes! Lift up thine eyelids, Jokanaan! Wherefore dost thou not look at me? Art thou afraid of me, Jokanaan, that thou wilt not look at me?... And thy tongue, that was like a red snake darting poison, it moves no more, it says nothing now, Jokanaan, that scarlet viper that spat its venom upon me. It is strange, is it not? How is it that the red viper stirs no longer?... Thou wouldst have none of me, Jokanaan. Thou didst reject me. Thou didst speak evil words against me. Thou didst treat me as a harlot, as a wanton, me, Salomé, daughter of Herodias, Princess of Judæa! Well, Jokanaan, I still live, but thou, thou art dead, and thy head belongs to me. I can do with it what I will. I can throw it to the dogs and to the birds of the air. That which the dogs leave, the birds of the air shall devour.... Ah, Jokanaan, Jokanaan, thou wert the only man that I have loved. All other men are hateful to me. But thou, thou wert beautiful! Thy body was a column of ivory set on a silver socket. It was a garden full of doves and of silver lilies. It was a tower of silver decked with shields of ivory. There was nothing in the world so white as thy body. There was nothing in the world so black as thy hair. In the whole world there was nothing so red as thy mouth. Thy voice was a censer that scattered strange perfumes, and when I looked on thee I heard a strange music. Ah! wherefore didst thou not look at me, Jokanaan? Behind thine hands and thy curses thou didst hide thy face. Thou didst put upon thine eyes the covering of him who would see his God. Well, thou hast seen thy God, Jokanaan, but me, me, thou didst never see. If thou hadst seen me thou wouldst have loved me. I, I saw thee, Jokanaan, and I loved thee. Oh, how I loved thee! I love thee yet, Jokanaan, I love thee only.... I am athirst for thy beauty; I am hungry for thy body; and neither wine nor fruits can appease my desire. What shall I do now, Jokanaan? Neither the floods nor the great waters can quench my passion. I was a princess, and thou didst scorn me. I was a virgin, and thou didst take my virginity from me. I was chaste, and thou didst fill my veins with fire.... Ah! ah! wherefore didst thou not look at me, Jokanaan? If thou hadst looked at me thou hadst loved me. Well I know that thou wouldst have loved me, and the mystery of love is greater than the mystery of death. Love only should one consider.

HEROD

She is monstrous, thy daughter, she is altogether monstrous. In truth, what she has done is a great crime. I am sure that it was a crime against an unknown God.

HERODIAS

I approve of what my daughter has done. And I will stay here now.

HEROD

[*Rising*].

Ah! There speaks the incestuous wife! Come! I will not stay here. Come, I tell thee. Surely some terrible thing will befall. Manasseh, Issachar, Ozias, put out the torches. I will not look at things, I will not suffer things to look at me. Put out the torches! Hide the moon! Hide the stars! Let us hide ourselves in our palace, Herodias. I begin to be afraid.

[*The slaves put out the torches. The stars disappear. A great black cloud crosses the moon and conceals it completely. The stage becomes very dark. The Tetrarch begins to climb the staircase.*]

THE VOICE OF SALOMÉ

Ah! I have kissed thy mouth, Jokanaan, I have kissed thy mouth. There

338

was a bitter taste on thy lips. Was it the taste of blood?... But perchance it is the taste of love.... They say that love hath a bitter taste.... But what of that? what of that? I have kissed thy mouth, Jokanaan.

[*A moonbeam falls on Salomé covering her with light.*]

HEROD

[*Turning round and seeing Salomé.*]

Kill that woman!

[*The soldiers rush forward and crush beneath their shields Salomé, daughter of Herodias, Princess of Judæa.*]

CURTAIN.

About Author

Oscar Fingal O'Flahertie Wills Wilde (16 October 1854 – 30 November 1900) was an Irish poet and playwright. After writing in different forms throughout the 1880s, the early 1890s saw him become one of the most popular playwrights in London. He is best remembered for his epigrams and plays, his novel The Picture of Dorian Gray, and the circumstances of his criminal conviction for "gross indecency", imprisonment, and early death at age 46.

Wilde's parents were successful Anglo-Irish intellectuals in Dublin. A young Wilde learned to speak fluent French and German. At university, Wilde read Greats; he demonstrated himself to be an exceptional classicist, first at Trinity College Dublin, then at Oxford. He became associated with the emerging philosophy of aestheticism, led by two of his tutors, Walter Pater and John Ruskin. After university, Wilde moved to London into fashionable cultural and social circles.

As a spokesman for aestheticism, he tried his hand at various literary activities: he published a book of poems, lectured in the United States and Canada on the new "English Renaissance in Art" and interior decoration, and then returned to London where he worked prolifically as a journalist. Known for his biting wit, flamboyant dress and glittering conversational skill, Wilde became one of the best-known personalities of his day. At the turn of the 1890s, he refined his ideas about the supremacy of art in a series of dialogues and essays, and incorporated themes of decadence, duplicity, and beauty into what would be his only novel, The Picture of Dorian Gray (1890). The opportunity to construct aesthetic details precisely, and combine them with larger social themes, drew Wilde to write drama. He wrote Salome (1891) in French while in Paris but it was refused a licence for England due to an absolute prohibition on the portrayal of Biblical subjects on the English stage. Unperturbed, Wilde produced four society comedies in the early 1890s, which made him one of the most successful playwrights of late-Victorian London.

At the height of his fame and success, while The Importance of Being Earnest (1895) was still being performed in London, Wilde had the Marquess of Queensberry prosecuted for criminal libel. The Marquess was the father of Wilde's lover, Lord Alfred Douglas. The libel trial unearthed evidence that caused Wilde to drop his charges and led to his own arrest and trial for gross indecency with men. After two more trials he was convicted and sentenced to two years' hard labour, the maximum penalty, and was jailed from 1895 to 1897. During his last year in prison, he wrote De Profundis (published posthumously in 1905), a long letter which discusses his spiritual journey through his trials, forming a dark counterpoint to his earlier philosophy of pleasure. On his release, he left immediately for France, never to return to Ireland or Britain. There he wrote his last work, The Ballad of Reading Gaol (1898), a long poem commemorating the harsh rhythms of prison life.

Early life

Oscar Wilde was born at 21 Westland Row, Dublin (now home of the Oscar Wilde Centre, Trinity College), the second of three children born to Anglo-Irish Sir William Wilde and Jane Wilde, two years behind his brother William ("Willie"). Wilde's mother had distant Italian ancestry,and under the pseudonym "Speranza" (the Italian word for 'hope'), wrote poetry for the revolutionary Young Irelanders in 1848; she was a lifelong Irish nationalist. She read the Young Irelanders' poetry to Oscar and Willie, inculcating a love of these poets in her sons. Lady Wilde's interest in the neo-classical revival showed in the paintings and busts of ancient Greece and Rome in her home.

William Wilde was Ireland's leading oto-ophthalmologic (ear and eye) surgeon and was knighted in 1864 for his services as medical adviser and assistant commissioner to the censuses of Ireland. He also wrote books about Irish archaeology and peasant folklore. A renowned philanthropist, his dispensary for the care of the city's poor at the rear of Trinity College, Dublin, was the forerunner of the Dublin Eye and Ear Hospital, now located at Adelaide Road. On his father's side Wilde was descended from a Dutchman, Colonel de Wilde, who went to Ireland with King William of Orange's invading army in 1690, and numerous Anglo-Irish ancestors. On his mother's side, Wilde's ancestors included a bricklayer from County Durham, who emigrated to Ireland sometime in the 1770s.

Wilde was baptised as an infant in St. Mark's Church, Dublin, the local Church of Ireland (Anglican) church. When the church was closed, the records were moved to the nearby St. Ann's Church, Dawson Street. Davis Coakley mentions a second baptism by a Catholic priest, Father Prideaux Fox, who befriended Oscar's mother circa 1859. According to Fox's testimony in Donahoe's Magazine in 1905, Jane Wilde would visit his chapel in Glencree, County Wicklow, for Mass and would take her sons with her. She asked Father Fox in this period to baptise her sons.

Fox described it in this way:

> "I am not sure if she ever became a Catholic herself but it was not long before she asked me to instruct two of her children, one of them being the future erratic genius, Oscar Wilde. After a few weeks I baptized these two children, Lady Wilde herself being present on the occasion.

In addition to his children with his wife, Sir William Wilde was the father of three children born out of wedlock before his marriage: Henry Wilson, born in 1838 to one woman, and Emily and Mary Wilde, born in 1847 and 1849, respectively, to a second woman. Sir William acknowledged paternity of his illegitimate or "natural" children and provided for their education, arranging for them to be reared by his relatives rather than with his legitimate children in his family household with his wife.

In 1855, the family moved to No. 1 Merrion Square, where Wilde's sister, Isola, was born in 1857. The Wildes' new home was larger. With both his parents' success and delight in social life, the house soon became the site of a "unique medical and cultural milieu". Guests at their salon included Sheridan Le Fanu, Charles Lever, George Petrie, Isaac Butt, William Rowan Hamilton and Samuel Ferguson.

Until he was nine, Oscar Wilde was educated at home, where a French nursemaid and a German governess taught him their languages. He attended Portora Royal School in Enniskillen, County Fermanagh, from 1864 to 1871. Until his early twenties, Wilde summered at the villa, Moytura House, which his father had built in Cong, County Mayo. There the young Wilde and his brother Willie played with George Moore.

343

Isola died at age nine of meningitis. Wilde's poem "Requiescat" is written to her memory.

"Tread lightly, she is near

Under the snow

Speak gently, she can hear

the daisies grow"

University education: 1870s

Trinity College, Dublin

Wilde left Portora with a royal scholarship to read classics at Trinity College, Dublin, from 1871 to 1874, sharing rooms with his older brother Willie Wilde. Trinity, one of the leading classical schools, placed him with scholars such as R. Y. Tyrell, Arthur Palmer, Edward Dowden and his tutor, Professor J. P. Mahaffy, who inspired his interest in Greek literature. As a student Wilde worked with Mahaffy on the latter's book Social Life in Greece. Wilde, despite later reservations, called Mahaffy "my first and best teacher" and "the scholar who showed me how to love Greek things".For his part, Mahaffy boasted of having created Wilde; later, he said Wilde was "the only blot on my tutorship".

The University Philosophical Society also provided an education, as members discussed intellectual and artistic subjects such as Dante Gabriel Rossetti and Algernon Charles Swinburne weekly. Wilde quickly became an established member – the members' suggestion book for 1874 contains two pages of banter (sportingly) mocking Wilde's emergent aestheticism. He presented a paper titled "Aesthetic Morality". At Trinity, Wilde established himself as an outstanding student: he came first in his class in his first year, won a scholarship by competitive examination in his second and, in his finals, won the Berkeley Gold Medal in Greek, the University's highest academic award. He was encouraged to compete for a demyship to Magdalen College, Oxford – which he won easily, having already studied Greek for over nine years.

344

Magdalen College, Oxford

At Magdalen, he read Greats from 1874 to 1878, and from there he applied to join the Oxford Union, but failed to be elected.

Attracted by its dress, secrecy, and ritual, Wilde petitioned the Apollo Masonic Lodge at Oxford, and was soon raised to the "Sublime Degree of Master Mason".During a resurgent interest in Freemasonry in his third year, he commented he "would be awfully sorry to give it up if I secede from the Protestant Heresy". Wilde's active involvement in Freemasonry lasted only for the time he spent at Oxford; he allowed his membership of the Apollo University Lodge to lapse after failing to pay subscriptions.

Catholicism deeply appealed to him, especially its rich liturgy, and he discussed converting to it with clergy several times. In 1877, Wilde was left speechless after an audience with Pope Pius IX in Rome.He eagerly read the books of Cardinal Newman, a noted Anglican priest who had converted to Catholicism and risen in the church hierarchy. He became more serious in 1878, when he met the Reverend Sebastian Bowden, a priest in the Brompton Oratory who had received some high-profile converts. Neither his father, who threatened to cut off his funds, nor Mahaffy thought much of the plan; but mostly Wilde, the supreme individualist, balked at the last minute from pledging himself to any formal creed. On the appointed day of his baptism, Wilde sent Father Bowden a bunch of altar lilies instead. Wilde did retain a lifelong interest in Catholic theology and liturgy.

While at Magdalen College, Wilde became particularly well known for his role in the aesthetic and decadent movements. He wore his hair long, openly scorned "manly" sports though he occasionally boxed, and he decorated his rooms with peacock feathers, lilies, sunflowers, blue china and other objets d'art. He once remarked to friends, whom he entertained lavishly, "I find it harder and harder every day to live up to my blue china." The line quickly became famous, accepted as a slogan by aesthetes but used against them by critics who sensed in it a terrible vacuousness. Some elements disdained the aesthetes, but their languishing attitudes and showy costumes became a recognised pose. Wilde was once physically attacked by a group of four fellow students, and dealt with them single-handedly, surprising critics. By his third year Wilde had truly begun to develop himself and his myth, and considered his learning to be more expansive than what was within the prescribed texts. This attitude resulted in his being rusticated for one term, after he had returned late to a college term from a trip to Greece with Mahaffy.

Wilde did not meet Walter Pater until his third year, but had been enthralled by his Studies in the History of the Renaissance, published during Wilde's final year in Trinity. Pater argued that man's sensibility to beauty should be refined above all else, and that each moment should be felt to its fullest extent. Years later, in De Profundis, Wilde described Pater's Studies... as "that book that has had such a strange influence over my life".He learned tracts of the book by heart, and carried it with him on travels in later years. Pater gave Wilde his sense of almost flippant devotion to art, though he gained a purpose for it through the lectures and writings of critic John Ruskin. Ruskin despaired at the self-validating aestheticism of Pater, arguing that the importance of art lies in its potential for the betterment of society. Ruskin admired beauty, but believed it must be allied with, and applied to, moral good. When Wilde eagerly attended Ruskin's lecture series The Aesthetic and Mathematic Schools of Art in Florence, he learned about aesthetics as the non-mathematical elements of painting. Despite being given to neither early rising nor manual labour, Wilde volunteered for Ruskin's project to convert a swampy country lane into a smart road neatly edged with flowers.

Wilde won the 1878 Newdigate Prize for his poem "Ravenna", which reflected on his visit there the year before, and he duly read it at Encaenia. In November 1878, he graduated with a double first in his B.A. of Classical Moderations and Literae Humaniores (Greats). Wilde wrote to a friend, "The dons are 'astonied' beyond words – the Bad Boy doing so well in the end!"

Apprenticeship of an aesthete: 1880s

Debut in society

After graduation from Oxford, Wilde returned to Dublin, where he met again Florence Balcombe, a childhood sweetheart. She became engaged to Bram Stoker and they married in 1878. Wilde was disappointed but stoic:

he wrote to her, remembering "the two sweet years – the sweetest years of all my youth" during which they had been close. He also stated his intention to "return to England, probably for good." This he did in 1878, only briefly visiting Ireland twice after that.

Unsure of his next step, Wilde wrote to various acquaintances enquiring about Classics positions at Oxford or Cambridge. The Rise of Historical Criticism was his submission for the Chancellor's Essay prize of 1879, which, though no longer a student, he was still eligible to enter. Its subject, "Historical Criticism among the Ancients" seemed ready-made for Wilde – with both his skill in composition and ancient learning – but he struggled to find his voice with the long, flat, scholarly style. Unusually, no prize was awarded that year.

With the last of his inheritance from the sale of his father's houses, he set himself up as a bachelor in London. The 1881 British Census listed Wilde as a boarder at 1 (now 44) Tite Street, Chelsea, where Frank Miles, a society painter, was the head of the household. Wilde spent the next six years in London and Paris, and in the United States, where he travelled to deliver lectures.

He had been publishing lyrics and poems in magazines since entering Trinity College, especially in Kottabos and the Dublin University Magazine. In mid-1881, at 27 years old, he published Poems, which collected, revised and expanded his poems.

The book was generally well received, and sold out its first print run of 750 copies. Punch was less enthusiastic, saying "The poet is Wilde, but his poetry's tame". By a tight vote, the Oxford Union condemned the book for alleged plagiarism. The librarian, who had requested the book for the library, returned the presentation copy to Wilde with a note of apology. Biographer Richard Ellmann argues that Wilde's poem "Hélas!" was a sincere, though flamboyant, attempt to explain the dichotomies the poet saw in himself; one line reads: "To drift with every passion till my soul

Is a stringed lute on which all winds can play".

The book had further printings in 1882. It was bound in a rich, enamel parchment cover (embossed with gilt blossom) and printed on hand-made Dutch paper; over the next few years, Wilde presented many copies to the dignitaries and writers who received him during his lecture tours.

America: 1882

Aestheticism was sufficiently in vogue to be caricatured by Gilbert and Sullivan in Patience (1881). Richard D'Oyly Carte, an English impresario, invited Wilde to make a lecture tour of North America, simultaneously priming the pump for the US tour of Patience and selling this most charming aesthete to the American public. Wilde journeyed on the SS Arizona, arriving 2 January 1882, and disembarking the following day. Originally planned to last four months, it continued for almost a year due to the commercial success. Wilde sought to transpose the beauty he saw in art into daily life. This was a practical as well as philosophical project: in Oxford he had surrounded himself with blue china and lilies, and now one of his lectures was on interior design.

When asked to explain reports that he had paraded down Piccadilly in London carrying a lily, long hair flowing, Wilde replied, "It's not whether I did it or not that's important, but whether people believed I did it". Wilde believed that the artist should hold forth higher ideals, and that pleasure and beauty would replace utilitarian ethics.

Wilde and aestheticism were both mercilessly caricatured and criticised in the press; the Springfield Republican, for instance, commented on Wilde's behaviour during his visit to Boston to lecture on aestheticism, suggesting that Wilde's conduct was more a bid for notoriety rather than devotion to beauty and the aesthetic. T. W. Higginson, a cleric and abolitionist, wrote in "Unmanly Manhood" of his general concern that Wilde, "whose only distinction is that he has written a thin volume of very mediocre verse", would improperly influence the behaviour of men and women.

According to biographer Michèle Mendelssohn, Wilde was the subject of anti-Irish caricature and was portrayed as a monkey, a blackface performer and a Christy's Minstrel throughout his career. "Harper's Weekly put a sunflower-worshipping monkey dressed as Wilde on the front of the January 1882 issue. The magazine didn't let its reputation for quality impede its expression of what are now considered odious ethnic and racial ideologies. The drawing stimulated other American maligners and, in England, had a full-page reprint in the Lady's Pictorial. ... When the National Republican discussed Wilde, it was to explain 'a few items as to the animal's pedigree.' And on 22 January 1882 the Washington Post illustrated the Wild Man of Borneo alongside Oscar Wilde of England and asked 'How far is it from this to this?' "Though his press reception was hostile, Wilde was well received in diverse settings across America; he drank whiskey with miners in Leadville, Colorado, and was fêted at the most fashionable salons in many cities he visited.

London life and marriage

His earnings, plus expected income from The Duchess of Padua, allowed him to move to Paris between February and mid-May 1883. While there he met Robert Sherard, whom he entertained constantly. "We are dining on the Duchess tonight", Wilde would declare before taking him to an expensive restaurant. In August he briefly returned to New York for the production of Vera, his first play, after it was turned down in London. He reportedly entertained the other passengers with "Ave Imperatrix!, A Poem on England", about the rise and fall of empires. E. C. Stedman, in Victorian Poets, describes this "lyric to England" as "manly verse – a poetic and eloquent invocation". The play was initially well received by the audience, but when the critics wrote lukewarm reviews, attendance fell sharply and the play closed a week after it had opened.

Wilde had to return to England, where he continued to lecture on topics including Personal Impressions of America, The Value of Art in Modern Life, and Dress.

In London, he had been introduced in 1881 to Constance Lloyd, daughter of Horace Lloyd, a wealthy Queen's Counsel, and his wife. She happened to be visiting Dublin in 1884, when Wilde was lecturing at the Gaiety Theatre. He proposed to her, and they married on 29 May 1884 at the Anglican St James's Church, Paddington, in London. Although Constance had an annual allowance of £250, which was generous for a young woman (equivalent to about £25,600 in current value), the Wildes had relatively luxurious tastes. They had preached to others for so long on the subject of design that people expected their home to set new standards. No. 16, Tite Street was duly renovated in seven months at considerable expense. The couple had two sons together, Cyril (1885) and Vyvyan (1886). Wilde became the sole literary signatory of George Bernard Shaw's petition for a pardon of the anarchists arrested (and later executed) after the Haymarket massacre in Chicago in 1886.

Robert Ross had read Wilde's poems before they met at Oxford in 1886. He seemed unrestrained by the Victorian prohibition against homosexuality, and became estranged from his family. By Richard Ellmann's account, he was a precocious seventeen-year-old who "so young and yet so knowing, was determined to seduce Wilde". According to Daniel Mendelsohn, Wilde, who had long alluded to Greek love, was "initiated into homosexual sex" by Ross, while his "marriage had begun to unravel after his wife's second pregnancy, which left him physically repelled".

Prose writing: 1886–91

Journalism and editorship: 1886–89

Criticism over artistic matters in The Pall Mall Gazette provoked a letter in self-defence, and soon Wilde was a contributor to that and other journals during 1885–87. He enjoyed reviewing and journalism; the form suited his style. He could organise and share his views on art, literature and life, yet in a format less tedious than lecturing. Buoyed up, his reviews were largely chatty and positive. Wilde, like his parents before him, also supported the cause of Irish nationalism. When Charles Stewart Parnell was falsely accused of inciting murder, Wilde wrote a series of astute columns defending him in the Daily Chronicle.

His flair, having previously been put mainly into socialising, suited journalism and rapidly attracted notice. With his youth nearly over, and a family to support, in mid-1887 Wilde became the editor of The Lady's World magazine, his name prominently appearing on the cover. He promptly renamed it as The Woman's World and raised its tone, adding serious articles on parenting, culture, and politics, while keeping discussions of fashion and arts. Two pieces of fiction were usually included, one to be read to children, the other for the ladies themselves. Wilde worked hard to solicit good contributions from his wide artistic acquaintance, including those of Lady Wilde and his wife Constance, while his own "Literary and Other Notes" were themselves popular and amusing.

The initial vigour and excitement which he brought to the job began to fade as administration, commuting and office life became tedious. At the same time as Wilde's interest flagged, the publishers became concerned anew about circulation: sales, at the relatively high price of one shilling, remained low. Increasingly sending instructions to the magazine by letter, Wilde began a new period of creative work and his own column appeared less regularly.In October 1889, Wilde had finally found his voice in prose and, at the end of the second volume, Wilde left The Woman's World. The magazine outlasted him by one issue.

If Wilde's period at the helm of the magazine was a mixed success from an organizational point of view, it played a pivotal role in his development as a writer and facilitated his ascent to fame. Whilst Wilde the journalist supplied articles under the guidance of his editors, Wilde the editor was forced to learn to manipulate the literary marketplace on his own terms.

During the late 1880s, Wilde was a close friend of the artist James NcNeill Whistler and they dined together on many occasions. At one of these dinners, Whistler said a bon mot that Wilde found particularly witty, Wilde exclaimed that he wished that he had said it, and Whistler retorted "You will, Oscar, you will".Herbert Vivian—a mutual friend of Wilde and Whistler—attended the dinner and recorded it in his article The Reminiscences of a Short Life which appeared in The Sun in 1889. The article alleged that Wilde had a habit of passing off other people's witticisms as his own—especially Whistler's. Wilde considered Vivian's article to be a scurrilous betrayal, and it directly caused the broken friendship between Wilde and Whistler. The Reminiscences also caused great acrimony between Wilde and Vivian, Wilde accusing Vivian of "the inaccuracy of an eavesdropper with the method of a blackmailer" and banishing Vivian from his circle.

Shorter fiction

Wilde published The Happy Prince and Other Tales in 1888, and had been regularly writing fairy stories for magazines. In 1891 he published two more collections, Lord Arthur Savile's Crime and Other Stories, and in September A House of Pomegranates was dedicated "To Constance Mary Wilde". "The Portrait of Mr. W. H.", which Wilde had begun in 1887, was first published in Blackwood's Edinburgh Magazine in July 1889.It is a short story, which reports a conversation, in which the theory that Shakespeare's sonnets were written out of the poet's love of the boy actor "Willie Hughes", is advanced, retracted, and then propounded again. The only evidence for this is two supposed puns within the sonnets themselves.

The anonymous narrator is at first sceptical, then believing, finally flirtatious with the reader: he concludes that "there is really a great deal to be said of the Willie Hughes theory of Shakespeare's sonnets." By the end fact and fiction have melded together.Arthur Ransome wrote that Wilde "read something of himself into Shakespeare's sonnets" and became fascinated with the "Willie Hughes theory" despite the lack of biographical evidence for the historical William Hughes' existence. Instead of writing a short but serious essay on the question, Wilde tossed the theory amongst the three characters of the story, allowing it to unfold as background to the plot. The story thus is an early masterpiece of Wilde's combining many elements that interested him: conversation, literature and the idea that to shed oneself of an idea one must first convince another of its truth.Ransome concludes that Wilde succeeds precisely because the literary criticism is unveiled with such a deft touch.

Though containing nothing but "special pleading", it would not, he says "be possible to build an airier castle in Spain than this of the imaginary William Hughes" we continue listening nonetheless to be charmed by the telling. "You must believe in Willie Hughes," Wilde told an acquaintance, "I almost do, myself."

Essays and dialogues

Wilde, having tired of journalism, had been busy setting out his aesthetic ideas more fully in a series of longer prose pieces which were published in the major literary-intellectual journals of the day. In January 1889, The Decay of Lying: A Dialogue appeared in The Nineteenth Century, and Pen, Pencil and Poison, a satirical biography of Thomas Griffiths Wainewright, in The Fortnightly Review, edited by Wilde's friend Frank Harris. Two of Wilde's four writings on aesthetics are dialogues: though Wilde had evolved professionally from lecturer to writer, he retained an oral tradition of sorts. Having always excelled as a wit and raconteur, he often composed by assembling phrases, bons mots and witticisms into a longer, cohesive work.

Wilde was concerned about the effect of moralising on art; he believed in art's redemptive, developmental powers: "Art is individualism, and individualism is a disturbing and disintegrating force. There lies its immense value. For what it seeks is to disturb monotony of type, slavery of custom, tyranny of habit, and the reduction of man to the level of a machine." In his only political text, The Soul of Man Under Socialism, he argued political conditions should establish this primacy – private property should be abolished, and cooperation should be substituted for competition. At the same time, he stressed that the government most amenable to artists was no government at all. Wilde envisioned a society where mechanisation has freed human effort from the burden of necessity, effort which can instead be expended on artistic creation. George Orwell summarised, "In effect, the world will be populated by artists, each striving after perfection in the way that seems best to him."

This point of view did not align him with the Fabians, intellectual socialists who advocated using state apparatus to change social conditions, nor did it endear him to the monied classes whom he had previously entertained. Hesketh Pearson, introducing a collection of Wilde's essays in 1950, remarked how The Soul of Man Under Socialism had been an inspirational text for revolutionaries in Tsarist Russia but laments that in the Stalinist era "it is doubtful whether there are any uninspected places in which it could now be hidden".

Wilde considered including this pamphlet and The Portrait of Mr. W.H., his essay-story on Shakespeare's sonnets, in a new anthology in 1891, but eventually decided to limit it to purely aesthetic subjects. Intentions packaged revisions of four essays: The Decay of Lying, Pen, Pencil and Poison, The Truth of Masks (first published 1885), and The Critic as Artist in two parts. For Pearson the biographer, the essays and dialogues exhibit every aspect of Wilde's genius and character: wit, romancer, talker, lecturer, humanist and scholar and concludes that "no other productions of his have as varied an appeal". 1891 turned out to be Wilde's annus mirabilis; apart from his three collections he also produced his only novel.

The Picture of Dorian Gray

The first version of The Picture of Dorian Gray was published as the lead story in the July 1890 edition of Lippincott's Monthly Magazine, along with five others. The story begins with a man painting a picture of Gray. When Gray, who has a "face like ivory and rose leaves", sees his finished portrait, he breaks down. Distraught that his beauty will fade while the portrait stays beautiful, he inadvertently makes a Faustian bargain in which only the painted image grows old while he stays beautiful and young. For Wilde, the purpose of art would be to guide life as if beauty alone were its object. As Gray's portrait allows him to escape the corporeal ravages of his hedonism, Wilde sought to juxtapose the beauty he saw in art with daily life.

Reviewers immediately criticised the novel's decadence and homosexual allusions; The Daily Chronicle for example, called it "unclean", "poisonous", and "heavy with the mephitic odours of moral and spiritual putrefaction". Which he clarified his stance on ethics and aesthetics in art – "If a work of art is rich and vital and complete, those who have artistic instincts will see its beauty and those to whom ethics appeal more strongly will see its moral lesson." He nevertheless revised it extensively for book publication in 1891: six new chapters were added, some overtly decadent passages and homo-eroticism excised, and a preface was included consisting of twenty two epigrams, such as "Books are well written, or badly written. That is all."

Contemporary reviewers and modern critics have postulated numerous possible sources of the story, a search Jershua McCormack argues is futile because Wilde "has tapped a root of Western folklore so deep and ubiquitous that the story has escaped its origins and returned to the oral tradition." Wilde claimed the plot was "an idea that is as old as the history of literature but to which I have given a new form".Modern critic Robin McKie considered the novel to be technically mediocre, saying that the conceit of the plot had guaranteed its fame, but the device is never pushed to its full.On the other hand, Robert McCrum of The Guardian deemed it the 27th best novel ever written in English, calling it "an arresting, and slightly camp, exercise in late-Victorian gothic."

Theatrical career: 1892–95

Salomé

The 1891 census records the Wildes' residence at 16 Tite Street, where he lived with his wife Constance and two sons. Wilde though, not content with being better known than ever in London, returned to Paris in October 1891, this time as a respected writer. He was received at the salons littéraires, including the famous mardis of Stéphane Mallarmé, a renowned symbolist poet of the time. Wilde's two plays during the 1880s, Vera; or, The Nihilists and The Duchess of Padua, had not met with much success. He had continued his interest in the theatre and now, after finding his voice in prose, his thoughts turned again to the dramatic form as the biblical iconography of Salome filled his mind. One evening, after discussing depictions of Salome throughout history, he returned to his hotel and noticed a blank copybook lying on the desk, and it occurred to him to write in it what he had been saying. The result was a new play, Salomé, written rapidly and in French.

A tragedy, it tells the story of Salome, the stepdaughter of the tetrarch Herod Antipas, who, to her stepfather's dismay but mother's delight, requests the head of Jokanaan (John the Baptist) on a silver platter as a reward for dancing the Dance of the Seven Veils. When Wilde returned to London just before Christmas the Paris Echo referred to him as "le great event" of the season. Rehearsals of the play, starring Sarah Bernhardt, began but the play was refused a licence by the Lord Chamberlain, since it depicted biblical characters. Salome was published jointly in Paris and London in 1893, but was not performed until 1896 in Paris, during Wilde's later incarceration.

Comedies of society

Wilde, who had first set out to irritate Victorian society with his dress and talking points, then outrage it with Dorian Gray, his novel of vice hidden beneath art, finally found a way to critique society on its own terms. Lady Windermere's Fan was first performed on 20 February 1892 at St James's Theatre, packed with the cream of society. On the surface a witty comedy, there is subtle subversion underneath: "it concludes with collusive concealment rather than collective disclosure". The audience, like Lady Windermere, are forced to soften harsh social codes in favour of a more nuanced view. The play was enormously popular, touring the country for months, but largely trashed by conservative critics. It was followed by A Woman of No Importance in 1893, another Victorian comedy, revolving around the spectre of illegitimate births, mistaken identities and late revelations. Wilde was commissioned to write two more plays and An Ideal Husband, written in 1894, followed in January 1895.

Peter Raby said these essentially English plays were well-pitched, "Wilde, with one eye on the dramatic genius of Ibsen, and the other on the commercial competition in London's West End, targeted his audience with adroit precision".

Queensberry family

In mid-1891 Lionel Johnson introduced Wilde to Lord Alfred Douglas, Johnson's cousin and an undergraduate at Oxford at the time. Known to his family and friends as "Bosie", he was a handsome and spoilt young man. An intimate friendship sprang up between Wilde and Douglas and by 1893 Wilde was infatuated with Douglas and they consorted together regularly in a tempestuous affair. If Wilde was relatively indiscreet, even flamboyant, in the way he acted, Douglas was reckless in public. Wilde, who was earning up to £100 a week from his plays (his salary at The Woman's World had been £6), indulged Douglas's every whim: material, artistic or sexual.

Douglas soon initiated Wilde into the Victorian underground of gay prostitution and Wilde was introduced to a series of young working-class male prostitutes from 1892 onwards by Alfred Taylor. These infrequent rendezvous usually took the same form: Wilde would meet the boy, offer him gifts, dine him privately and then take him to a hotel room. Unlike Wilde's idealised relations with Ross, John Gray, and Douglas, all of whom remained part of his aesthetic circle, these consorts were uneducated and knew nothing of literature. Soon his public and private lives had become sharply divided; in De Profundis he wrote to Douglas that "It was like feasting with panthers; the danger was half the excitement... I did not know that when they were to strike at me it was to be at another's piping and at another's pay."

Douglas and some Oxford friends founded a journal, The Chameleon, to which Wilde "sent a page of paradoxes originally destined for the Saturday Review". "Phrases and Philosophies for the Use of the Young" was to come under attack six months later at Wilde's trial, where he was forced to defend the magazine to which he had sent his work.In any case, it became unique: The Chameleon was not published again.

Lord Alfred's father, the Marquess of Queensberry, was known for his outspoken atheism, brutish manner and creation of the modern rules of boxing. Queensberry, who feuded regularly with his son, confronted Wilde and Lord Alfred about the nature of their relationship several times, but Wilde was able to mollify him. In June 1894, he called on Wilde at 16 Tite Street, without an appointment, and clarified his stance: "I do not say that you are it, but you look it, and pose at it, which is just as bad. And if I catch you and my son again in any public restaurant I will thrash you" to which Wilde responded: "I don't know what the Queensberry rules are, but the Oscar Wilde rule is to shoot on sight".His account in De Profundis was less triumphant: "It was when, in my library at Tite Street, waving his small hands in the air in epileptic fury, your father... stood uttering every foul word his foul mind could think of, and screaming the loathsome threats he afterwards with such cunning carried out". Queensberry only described the scene once, saying Wilde had "shown him the white feather", meaning he had acted in a cowardly way. Though trying to remain calm, Wilde saw that he was becoming ensnared in a brutal family quarrel. He did not wish to bear Queensberry's insults, but he knew to confront him could lead to disaster were his liaisons disclosed publicly.

The Importance of Being Earnest

Wilde's final play again returns to the theme of switched identities: the play's two protagonists engage in "bunburying" (the maintenance of alternative personas in the town and country) which allows them to escape Victorian social mores.Earnest is even lighter in tone than Wilde's earlier comedies. While their characters often rise to serious themes in moments of crisis, Earnest lacks the by-now stock Wildean characters: there is no "woman with a past", the principals are neither villainous nor cunning, simply idle cultivés, and the idealistic young women are not that innocent. Mostly set in drawing rooms and almost completely lacking in action or violence, Earnest lacks the self-conscious decadence found in The Picture of Dorian Gray and Salome.

The play, now considered Wilde's masterpiece, was rapidly written in Wilde's artistic maturity in late 1894. It was first performed on 14 February 1895, at St James's Theatre in London, Wilde's second collaboration with George Alexander, the actor-manager. Both author and producer assiduously revised, prepared and rehearsed every line, scene and setting in the months before the premiere, creating a carefully constructed representation of late-Victorian society, yet simultaneously mocking it. During rehearsal Alexander requested that Wilde shorten the play from four acts to three, which the author did. Premieres at St James's seemed like "brilliant parties", and the opening of The Importance of Being Earnest was no exception. Allan Aynesworth (who played Algernon) recalled to Hesketh Pearson, "In my fifty-three years of acting, I never remember a greater triumph than [that] first night."Earnest's immediate reception as Wilde's best work to date finally crystallised his fame into a solid artistic reputation. The Importance of Being Earnest remains his most popular play.

Wilde's professional success was mirrored by an escalation in his feud with Queensberry. Queensberry had planned to insult Wilde publicly by throwing a bouquet of rotting vegetables onto the stage; Wilde was tipped off and had Queensberry barred from entering the theatre.Fifteen weeks later Wilde was in prison.

Trials

Wilde v. Queensberry

On 18 February 1895, the Marquess left his calling card at Wilde's club, the Albemarle, inscribed: "For Oscar Wilde, posing somdomite" Wilde, encouraged by Douglas and against the advice of his friends, initiated a private prosecution against Queensberry for libel, since the note amounted to a public accusation that Wilde had committed the crime of sodomy.

Queensberry was arrested for criminal libel; a charge carrying a possible sentence of up to two years in prison. Under the 1843 Libel Act, Queensberry could avoid conviction for libel only by demonstrating that his accusation was in fact true, and furthermore that there was some "public benefit" to having made the accusation openly. Queensberry's lawyers thus hired private detectives to find evidence of Wilde's homosexual liaisons.

Wilde's friends had advised him against the prosecution at a Saturday Review meeting at the Café Royal on 24 March 1895; Frank Harris warned him that "they are going to prove sodomy against you" and advised him to flee to France. Wilde and Douglas walked out in a huff, Wilde saying "it is at such moments as these that one sees who are one's true friends". The scene was witnessed by George Bernard Shaw who recalled it to Arthur Ransome a day or so before Ransome's trial for libelling Douglas in 1913. To Ransome it confirmed what he had said in his 1912 book on Wilde; that Douglas's rivalry for Wilde with Robbie Ross and his arguments with his father had resulted in Wilde's public disaster; as Wilde wrote in De Profundis. Douglas lost his case. Shaw included an account of the argument between Harris, Douglas and Wilde in the preface to his play The Dark Lady of the Sonnets.

The libel trial became a cause célèbre as salacious details of Wilde's private life with Taylor and Douglas began to appear in the press. A team of private detectives had directed Queensberry's lawyers, led by Edward Carson QC, to the world of the Victorian underground. Wilde's association with blackmailers and male prostitutes, cross-dressers and homosexual brothels was recorded, and various persons involved were interviewed, some being coerced to appear as witnesses since they too were accomplices to the crimes of which Wilde was accused.

The trial opened on 3 April 1895 before Justice Richard Henn Collins amid scenes of near hysteria both in the press and the public galleries. The extent of the evidence massed against Wilde forced him to declare meekly, "I am the prosecutor in this case" Wilde's lawyer, Sir Edward George Clarke, opened the case by pre-emptively asking Wilde about two suggestive letters Wilde had written to Douglas, which the defence had in its possession. He characterised the first as a "prose sonnet" and admitted that the "poetical language" might seem strange to the court but claimed its intent was innocent. Wilde stated that the letters had been obtained by blackmailers who had attempted to extort money from him, but he had refused, suggesting they should take the £60 (equal to £6,800 today) offered, "unusual for a prose piece of that length". He claimed to regard the letters as works of art rather than something of which to be ashamed.

Carson, a fellow Dubliner who had attended Trinity College, Dublin at the same time as Wilde, cross-examined Wilde on how he perceived the moral content of his works. Wilde replied with characteristic wit and flippancy, claiming that works of art are not capable of being moral or immoral but only well or poorly made, and that only "brutes and illiterates", whose views on art "are incalculably stupid", would make such judgements about art. Carson, a leading barrister, diverged from the normal practice of asking closed questions. Carson pressed Wilde on each topic from every angle, squeezing out nuances of meaning from Wilde's answers, removing them from their aesthetic context and portraying Wilde as evasive and decadent. While Wilde won the most laughs from the court, Carson scored the most legal points. To undermine Wilde's credibility, and to justify Queensberry's description of Wilde as a "posing somdomite", Carson drew from the witness an admission of his capacity for "posing", by demonstrating that he had lied about his age on oath. Playing on this, he returned to the topic throughout his cross-examination. Carson also tried to justify Queensberry's characterisation by quoting from Wilde's novel, The Picture of Dorian Gray, referring in particular to a scene in the second chapter, in which Lord Henry Wotton explains his decadent philosophy to Dorian, an "innocent young man", in Carson's words.

Carson then moved to the factual evidence and questioned Wilde about his friendships with younger, lower-class men. Wilde admitted being on a first-name basis and lavishing gifts upon them, but insisted that nothing untoward had occurred and that the men were merely good friends of his. Carson repeatedly pointed out the unusual nature of these relationships and insinuated that the men were prostitutes. Wilde replied that he did not believe in social barriers, and simply enjoyed the society of young men. Then Carson asked Wilde directly whether he had ever kissed a certain servant boy, Wilde responded, "Oh, dear no. He was a particularly plain boy – unfortunately ugly – I pitied him for it." Carson pressed him on the answer, repeatedly asking why the boy's ugliness was relevant. Wilde hesitated, then for the first time became flustered: "You sting me and insult me and try to unnerve me; and at times one says things flippantly when one ought to speak more seriously."

In his opening speech for the defence, Carson announced that he had located several male prostitutes who were to testify that they had had sex with Wilde. On the advice of his lawyers, Wilde dropped the prosecution. Queensberry was found not guilty, as the court declared that his accusation that Wilde was "posing as a Somdomite " was justified, "true in substance and in fact".Under the Libel Act 1843, Queensberry's acquittal rendered Wilde legally liable for the considerable expenses Queensberry had incurred in his defence, which left Wilde bankrupt.

Regina v. Wilde

After Wilde left the court, a warrant for his arrest was applied for on charges of sodomy and gross indecency. Robbie Ross found Wilde at the Cadogan Hotel, Pont Street, Knightsbridge, with Reginald Turner; both men advised Wilde to go at once to Dover and try to get a boat to France; his mother advised him to stay and fight. Wilde, lapsing into inaction, could only say, "The train has gone. It's too late."On 6 April 1895, Wilde was arrested for "gross indecency" under Section 11 of the Criminal Law Amendment Act 1885, a term meaning homosexual acts not amounting to buggery (an offence under a separate statute). At Wilde's instruction, Ross and Wilde's butler forced their way into the bedroom and library of 16 Tite Street, packing some personal effects, manuscripts, and letters. Wilde was then imprisoned on remand at Holloway, where he received daily visits from Douglas.

Events moved quickly and his prosecution opened on 26 April 1895, before Mr Justice Charles. Wilde pleaded not guilty. He had already begged Douglas to leave London for Paris, but Douglas complained bitterly, even wanting to give evidence; he was pressed to go and soon fled to the Hotel du Monde. Fearing persecution, Ross and many others also left the United Kingdom during this time. Under cross examination Wilde was at first hesitant, then spoke eloquently:

Charles Gill (prosecuting): What is "the love that dare not speak its name"?

Wilde: "The love that dare not speak its name" in this century is such a great affection of an elder for a younger man as there was between David and Jonathan, such as Plato made the very basis of his philosophy, and such as you find in the sonnets of Michelangelo and Shakespeare. It is that deep spiritual affection that is as pure as it is perfect. It dictates and pervades great works of art, like those of Shakespeare and Michelangelo, and those two letters of mine, such as they are. It is in this century misunderstood, so much misunderstood that it may be described as "the love that dare not speak its name", and on that account of it I am placed where I am now. It is beautiful, it is fine, it is the noblest form of affection. There is nothing unnatural about it. It is intellectual, and it repeatedly exists between an older and a younger man, when the older man has intellect, and the younger man has all the joy, hope and glamour of life before him. That it should be so, the world does not understand. The world mocks at it, and sometimes puts one in the pillory for it.

This response was counter-productive in a legal sense as it only served to reinforce the charges of homosexual behaviour.

The trial ended with the jury unable to reach a verdict. Wilde's counsel, Sir Edward Clarke, was finally able to get a magistrate to allow Wilde and his friends to post bail. The Reverend Stewart Headlam put up most of the £5,000 surety required by the court, having disagreed with Wilde's treatment by the press and the courts. Wilde was freed from Holloway and, shunning attention, went into hiding at the house of Ernest and Ada Leverson, two of his firm friends. Edward Carson approached Frank Lockwood QC, the Solicitor General and asked "Can we not let up on the fellow now?" Lockwood answered that he would like to do so, but feared that the case had become too politicised to be dropped.

The final trial was presided over by Mr Justice Wills. On 25 May 1895 Wilde and Alfred Taylor were convicted of gross indecency and sentenced to two years' hard labour. The judge described the sentence, the maximum allowed, as "totally inadequate for a case such as this", and that the case was "the worst case I have ever tried". Wilde's response "And I? May I say nothing, my Lord?" was drowned out in cries of "Shame" in the courtroom.

Imprisonment

When first I was put into prison some people advised me to try and forget who I was. It was ruinous advice. It is only by realising what I am that I have found comfort of any kind. Now I am advised by others to try on my release to forget that I have ever been in a prison at all. I know that would be equally fatal. It would mean that I would always be haunted by an intolerable sense of disgrace, and that those things that are meant for me as much as for anybody else – the beauty of the sun and moon, the pageant of the seasons, the music of daybreak and the silence of great nights, the rain falling through the leaves, or the dew creeping over the grass and making it silver – would all be tainted for me, and lose their healing power, and their power of communicating joy. To regret one's own experiences is to arrest one's own development. To deny one's own experiences is to put a lie into the lips of one's own life. It is no less than a denial of the soul.

De Profundis

Wilde was incarcerated from 25 May 1895 to 18 May 1897.

He first entered Newgate Prison in London for processing, then was moved to Pentonville Prison, where the "hard labour" to which he had been sentenced consisted of many hours of walking a treadmill and picking oakum (separating the fibres in scraps of old navy ropes), and where prisoners were allowed to read only the Bible and The Pilgrim's Progress.

A few months later he was moved to Wandsworth Prison in London. Inmates there also followed the regimen of "hard labour, hard fare and a hard bed", which wore harshly on Wilde's delicate health. In November he collapsed during chapel from illness and hunger. His right ear drum was ruptured in the fall, an injury that later contributed to his death. He spent two months in the infirmary.

Richard B. Haldane, the Liberal MP and reformer, visited Wilde and had him transferred in November to Reading Gaol, 30 miles (48 km) west of London on 23 November 1895. The transfer itself was the lowest point of his incarceration, as a crowd jeered and spat at him on the railway platform. He spent the remainder of his sentence there, addressed and identified only as "C33" – the occupant of the third cell on the third floor of C ward.

About five months after Wilde arrived at Reading Gaol, Charles Thomas Wooldridge, a trooper in the Royal Horse Guards, was brought to Reading to await his trial for murdering his wife on 29 March 1896; on 17 June Wooldridge was sentenced to death and returned to Reading for his execution, which took place on Tuesday, 7 July 1896 – the first hanging at Reading in 18 years. From Wooldridge's hanging, Wilde later wrote The Ballad of Reading Gaol.

Wilde was not, at first, even allowed paper and pen but Haldane eventually succeeded in allowing access to books and writing materials. Wilde requested, among others: the Bible in French; Italian and German grammars; some Ancient Greek texts, Dante's Divine Comedy, Joris-Karl Huysmans's new French novel about Christian redemption En route, and essays by St Augustine, Cardinal Newman and Walter Pater.

Between January and March 1897 Wilde wrote a 50,000-word letter to Douglas. He was not allowed to send it, but was permitted to take it with him when released from prison. In reflective mode, Wilde coldly examines his career to date, how he had been a colourful agent provocateur in Victorian society, his art, like his paradoxes, seeking to subvert as well as sparkle. His own estimation of himself was: one who "stood in symbolic relations to the art and culture of my age". It was from these heights that his life with Douglas began, and Wilde examines that particularly closely, repudiating him for what Wilde finally sees as his arrogance and vanity: he had not forgotten Douglas' remark, when he was ill, "When you are not on your pedestal you are not interesting." Wilde blamed himself, though, for the ethical degradation of character that he allowed Douglas to bring about in him and took responsibility for his own fall, "I am here for having tried to put your father in prison." The first half concludes with Wilde forgiving Douglas, for his own sake as much as Douglas's. The second half of the letter traces Wilde's spiritual journey of redemption and fulfilment through his prison reading. He realised that his ordeal had filled his soul with the fruit of experience, however bitter it tasted at the time.

> ... I wanted to eat of the fruit of all the trees in the garden of the world ... And so, indeed, I went out, and so I lived. My only mistake was that I confined myself so exclusively to the trees of what seemed to me the sun-lit side of the garden, and shunned the other side for its shadow and its gloom.

Wilde was released from prison on 19 May 1897 and sailed that evening for Dieppe, France. He never returned to the UK.

On his release, he gave the manuscript to Ross, who may or may not have carried out Wilde's instructions to send a copy to Douglas (who later denied having received it). The letter was partially published in 1905 as De Profundis; its complete and correct publication first occurred in 1962 in The Letters of Oscar Wilde.

Decline: 1897–1900

Exile

Though Wilde's health had suffered greatly from the harshness and diet of prison, he had a feeling of spiritual renewal. He immediately wrote to the Society of Jesus requesting a six-month Catholic retreat; when the request was denied, Wilde wept. "I intend to be received into the Catholic Church before long", Wilde told a journalist who asked about his religious intentions.

He spent his last three years impoverished and in exile. He took the name "Sebastian Melmoth", after Saint Sebastian and the titular character of Melmoth the Wanderer (a Gothic novel by Charles Maturin, Wilde's great-uncle).Wilde wrote two long letters to the editor of the Daily Chronicle, describing the brutal conditions of English prisons and advocating penal reform. His discussion of the dismissal of Warder Martin for giving biscuits to an anaemic child prisoner repeated the themes of the corruption and degeneration of punishment that he had earlier outlined in The Soul of Man under Socialism.

Wilde spent mid-1897 with Robert Ross in the seaside village of Berneval-le-Grand in northern France, where he wrote The Ballad of Reading Gaol, narrating the execution of Charles Thomas Wooldridge, who murdered his wife in a rage at her infidelity. It moves from an objective story-telling to symbolic identification with the prisoners. No attempt is made to assess the justice of the laws which convicted them but rather the poem highlights the brutalisation of the punishment that all convicts share. Wilde juxtaposes the executed man and himself with the line "Yet each man kills the thing he loves". He adopted the proletarian ballad form and the author was credited as "C33", Wilde's cell number in Reading Gaol. He suggested that it be published in Reynolds' Magazine, "because it circulates widely among the criminal classes – to which I now belong – for once I will be read by my peers – a new experience for me". It was an immediate roaring commercial success, going through seven editions in less than two years, only after which "[Oscar" was added to the title page, though many in literary circles had known Wilde to be the author. It brought him a small amount of money.

Although Douglas had been the cause of his misfortunes, he and Wilde were reunited in August 1897 at Rouen. This meeting was disapproved of by the friends and families of both men. Constance Wilde was already refusing to meet Wilde or allow him to see their sons, though she sent him money – three pounds a week. During the latter part of 1897, Wilde and Douglas lived together near Naples for a few months until they were separated by their families under the threat of cutting off all funds.

Wilde's final address was at the dingy Hôtel d'Alsace (now known as L'Hôtel), on rue des Beaux-Arts in Saint-Germain-des-Prés, Paris. "This poverty really breaks one's heart: it is so sale , so utterly depressing, so hopeless. Pray do what you can" he wrote to his publisher.He corrected and published An Ideal Husband and The Importance of Being Earnest, the proofs of which, according to Ellmann, show a man "very much in command of himself and of the play" but he refused to write anything else: "I can write, but have lost the joy of writing".

He wandered the boulevards alone and spent what little money he had on alcohol. A series of embarrassing chance encounters with hostile English visitors, or Frenchmen he had known in better days, drowned his spirit. Soon Wilde was sufficiently confined to his hotel to joke, on one of his final trips outside, "My wallpaper and I are fighting a duel to the death. One of us has got to go". On 12 October 1900 he sent a telegram to Ross: "Terribly weak. Please come". His moods fluctuated; Max Beerbohm relates how their mutual friend Reginald 'Reggie' Turner had found Wilde very depressed after a nightmare. "I dreamt that I had died, and was supping with the dead!" "I am sure", Turner replied, "that you must have been the life and soul of the party."Turner was one of the few of the old circle who remained with Wilde to the end and was at his bedside when he died.

Death

By 25 November 1900 Wilde had developed meningitis, then called "cerebral meningitis". Robbie Ross arrived on 29 November, sent for a priest, and Wilde was conditionally baptised into the Catholic Church by Fr Cuthbert Dunne, a Passionist priest from Dublin,Wilde having been baptised in the Church of Ireland and having moreover a recollection of Catholic baptism as a child, a fact later attested to by the minister of the sacrament, Fr Lawrence Fox.Fr Dunne recorded the baptism,

As the voiture rolled through the dark streets that wintry night, the sad story of Oscar Wilde was in part repeated to me... Robert Ross knelt by the bedside, assisting me as best he could while I administered conditional baptism, and afterwards answering the responses while I

367

gave Extreme Unction to the prostrate man and recited the prayers for the dying. As the man was in a semi-comatose condition, I did not venture to administer the Holy Viaticum; still I must add that he could be roused and was roused from this state in my presence. When roused, he gave signs of being inwardly conscious... Indeed I was fully satisfied that he understood me when told that I was about to receive him into the Catholic Church and gave him the Last Sacraments... And when I repeated close to his ear the Holy Names, the Acts of Contrition, Faith, Hope and Charity, with acts of humble resignation to the Will of God, he tried all through to say the words after me.

Wilde died of meningitis on 30 November 1900. Different opinions are given as to the cause of the disease: Richard Ellmann claimed it was syphilitic; Merlin Holland, Wilde's grandson, thought this to be a misconception, noting that Wilde's meningitis followed a surgical intervention, perhaps a mastoidectomy; Wilde's physicians, Dr Paul Cleiss and A'Court Tucker, reported that the condition stemmed from an old suppuration of the right ear (from the prison injury, see above) treated for several years (une ancienne suppuration de l'oreille droite d'ailleurs en traitement depuis plusieurs années) and made no allusion to syphilis.

Burial

Wilde was initially buried in the Cimetière de Bagneux outside Paris; in 1909 his remains were disinterred and transferred to Père Lachaise Cemetery, inside the city. His tomb there was designed by Sir Jacob Epstein. It was commissioned by Robert Ross, who asked for a small compartment to be made for his own ashes, which were duly transferred in 1950. The modernist angel depicted as a relief on the tomb was originally complete with male genitalia, which were initially censored by French Authorities with a golden leaf. The genitals have since been vandalised; their current whereabouts are unknown. In 2000, Leon Johnson, a multimedia artist, installed a silver prosthesis to replace them. In 2011, the tomb was cleaned of the many lipstick marks left there by admirers and a glass barrier was installed to prevent further marks or damage.

The epitaph is a verse from The Ballad of Reading Gaol,

And alien tears will fill for him

Pity's long-broken urn,

For his mourners will be outcast men,

And outcasts always mourn.

Posthumous pardon

In 2017, Wilde was among an estimated 50,000 men who were pardoned for homosexual acts that were no longer considered offences under the Policing and Crime Act 2017. The Act is known informally as the Alan Turing law.

Honours

In 2014 Wilde was one of the inaugural honorees in the Rainbow Honor Walk, a walk of fame in San Francisco's Castro neighbourhood noting LGBTQ people who have "made significant contributions in their fields."

Biographies

Wilde's life has been the subject of numerous biographies since his death. The earliest were memoirs by those who knew him: often they are personal or impressionistic accounts which can be good character sketches, but are sometimes factually unreliable. Frank Harris, his friend and editor, wrote a biography, Oscar Wilde: His Life and Confessions (1916); though prone to exaggeration and sometimes factually inaccurate, it offers a good literary portrait of Wilde. Lord Alfred Douglas wrote two books about his relationship with Wilde. Oscar Wilde and Myself (1914), largely ghost-written by T. W. H. Crosland, vindictively reacted to Douglas's discovery that De Profundis was addressed to him and defensively tried to distance him from Wilde's scandalous reputation. Both authors later regretted their work. Later, in Oscar Wilde: A Summing Up (1939) and his Autobiography he was more sympathetic to Wilde. Of Wilde's other close friends, Robert Sherard; Robert Ross, his literary executor; and Charles Ricketts variously published biographies, reminiscences or correspondence. The first more or less objective biography of Wilde came about when Hesketh Pearson wrote Oscar Wilde: His Life and Wit (1946). In 1954 Wilde's son Vyvyan Holland published his memoir Son of Oscar Wilde, which recounts the difficulties Wilde's wife and children faced after his imprisonment. It was revised and updated by Merlin Holland in 1989.

Oscar Wilde, a critical study by Arthur Ransome was published in 1912. The book only briefly mentioned Wilde's life, but subsequently Ransome (and The Times Book Club) were sued for libel by Lord Alfred Douglas. In April 1913 Douglas lost the libel action after a reading of De Profundis refuted his claims.

Richard Ellmann wrote his 1987 biography Oscar Wilde, for which he posthumously won a National (USA) Book Critics Circle Award in 1988and a Pulitzer Prize in 1989. The book was the basis for the 1997 film Wilde, directed by Brian Gilbert and starring Stephen Fry as the title character.

Neil McKenna's 2003 biography, The Secret Life of Oscar Wilde, offers an exploration of Wilde's sexuality. Often speculative in nature, it was widely criticised for its pure conjecture and lack of scholarly rigour. Thomas Wright's Oscar's Books (2008) explores Wilde's reading from his childhood in Dublin to his death in Paris. After tracking down many books that once belonged to Wilde's Tite Street library (dispersed at the time of his trials), Wright was the first to examine Wilde's marginalia.

> Later on, I think everyone will recognise his achievements; his plays and essays will endure. Of course, you may think with others that his personality and conversation were far more wonderful than anything he wrote, so that his written works give only a pale reflection of his power. Perhaps that is so, and of course, it will be impossible to reproduce what is gone forever.

Robert Ross, 23 December 1900

In 2018, Matthew Sturgis' "Oscar: A Life," was published in London. The book incorporates rediscovered letters and other documents and is the most extensively researched biography of Wilde to appear since 1988.

Parisian literati, also produced several biographies and monographs on him. André Gide wrote In Memoriam, Oscar Wilde and Wilde also features in his journals. Thomas Louis, who had earlier translated books on Wilde into French, produced his own L'esprit d'Oscar Wilde in 1920. Modern books include Philippe Jullian's Oscar Wilde, and L'affaire Oscar Wilde, ou, Du danger de laisser la justice mettre le nez dans nos draps (The Oscar Wilde Affair, or, On the Danger of Allowing Justice to put its Nose in our Sheets) by Odon Vallet, a French religious historian. (Source: Wikipedia)

NOTABLE WORKS

ESSAYS

"The Decay of Lying" First published in Nineteenth Century (1889), republished in Intentions (1891).

"Pen, Pencil and Poison" First published in the Fortnightly Review (1889), republished in Intentions (1891).

"The Soul of Man under Socialism" First published in the Fortnightly Review (1891), republished in The Soul of Man (1895), privately printed.

Intentions (1891) Wilde revised his dialogues on aesthetic subjects for publication in this volume, which comprises:

- "The Critic as Artist"

- "The Decay of Lying"

- "Pen, Pencil and Poison"

- "The Truth of Masks"

"Phrases and Philosophies for the Use of the Young" first published in the Oxford student magazine The Chameleon, December 1894)

"A Few Maxims For The Instruction Of The Over-Educated" First published, anonymously, in the 1894 November 17 issue of Saturday Review.

FICTION

Novel

The Picture of Dorian Gray (1890/1891). The first version of "The Picture of Dorian Gray" was published, in a form highly edited by the magazine, as the lead story in the July 1890 edition of Lippincott's Monthly Magazine. Wilde published the longer and revised version in book form in 1891, with an added preface.

Stories

"The Portrait of Mr. W. H." (1889)

The Happy Prince and Other Tales (1888, a collection of fairy tales) consisting of:

- "The Happy Prince"
- "The Nightingale and the Rose"
- "The Selfish Giant"
- "The Devoted Friend"
- "The Remarkable Rocket"

A House of Pomegranates (1891, fairy tales)

Lord Arthur Savile's Crime and Other Stories (1891) Including "The Canterville Ghost" first published in periodical form in 1887.

Complete Short Fiction. Penguin Classics, 2003. Edited with an Introduction and Notes by Ian Small. Contains all works listed above plus Poems in Prose (1894) and one very short 'Elder-tree' (fragment).

POEMS

Ravenna (1878) Winner of the Newdigate Prize.

Poems (1881) Wilde's collection of poetry and first publication.

The Sphinx (1894)

Poems in Prose (1894)

The Ballad of Reading Gaol (1898)

PLAYS

Vera; or, The Nihilists (1880)

The Duchess of Padua (1883)

Lady Windermere's Fan (1892)

A Woman of No Importance (1893)

Salomé (French version) (1893, first performed in Paris 1896)

Salomé: A Tragedy in One Act: Translated from the French of Oscar Wilde by Lord Alfred Douglas, illustrated by Aubrey Beardsley (1894)

An Ideal Husband (1895) (text)

The Importance of Being Earnest (1895) (text)

La Sainte Courtisane and A Florentine Tragedy Fragmentary. First published 1908 in Methuen's Collected Works

(Dates are dates of first performance, which approximate better to the probable date of composition than dates of publication.)

The Importance of Being Earnest and Other Plays. Penguin Classics, 2000. Edited with an Introduction, Commentaries and Notes by Richard Allen Cave. Contains all from above save the first two. Salome is in English.

As an appendix there is one excised scene from The Importance of Being Earnest.

POSTHUMOUS (PREVIOUSLY UNPUBLISHED)

De Profundis (Written 1895-97, in Reading Gaol). Expurgated edition published 1905; suppressed portions 1913, expanded version in The Letters of Oscar Wilde (1962).

The Rise of Historical Criticism (Written while at college) First published in 1905 (Sherwood Press, Hartford, CT) privately printed. Reprinted in Miscellanies, the last volume of the First Collected Edition (1908).

The First Collected Edition (Methuen & Co., 14 volumes) appeared in 1908 and contained many previously unpublished works.

The Second Collected Edition (Methuen & Co., 12 volumes) appeared in installments between 1909–11 and contained several other unpublished works.

The Letters of Oscar Wilde (Written 1868-1900) Published in 1962. Republished as The Complete Letters of Oscar Wilde (2000), with letters discovered since 1962, and new annotations by Merlin Holland.

The Women of Homer (Written 1876, while at college). First published in Oscar Wilde: The Women of Homer (2008) by The Oscar Wilde Society.

The Philosophy of Dress First published in The New-York Tribune (1885), published for the first time in book form in Oscar Wilde On Dress (2013).

MISATTRIBUTED

Teleny, or The Reverse of the Medal (Paris, 1893) has been attributed to Wilde, but its authorship is unclear. One theory is that it was a combined effort by several of Wilde's friends, which he may have edited.

Constance On September 14, 2011, Wilde's grandson Merlin Holland contested Wilde's claimed authorship of this play entitled Constance, scheduled to open that week in the King's Head Theatre. It was not, in fact, "Oscar Wilde's final play," as its producers were claiming. Holland said Wilde did sketch out the play's scenario in 1894, but "never wrote a word" of it, and that "it is dishonest to foist this on the public." The Artistic Director Adam Spreadbury-Maher of the King's Head Theatre and producer of Constance pointed out that Wilde's son, Vyvyan Holland, wrote in 1954, "a significant amount of the dialogue (of Constance) bears the authentic stamp of my father's hand". There is further proof that the developed scenario that Constance was reconstituted from was written by Wilde between 1897 and his death in 1900, rather than the 1894 George Alexander scenario which Merlin Holland quotes.